"What d[...]
Sophie's ne[...]

Cheeks burning, Sopl[...] to look at him, watching instead his large hands near the chessboard, how they clenched and the knuckles went white.

"I would say she hasn't changed all that much."

"How can you say that?" said Nathan's mother, who'd just entered the room and was setting a plate of cookies on the coffee table.

Sophie inwardly cringed. Of course. She'd known, hadn't she, that a new dress wouldn't alter the way Nathan viewed her.

"She hasn't changed," Nathan drawled softly in the gathering silence, "because she's always been beautiful, inside and out."

Startled, Sophie's gaze shot to his face. Surely she hadn't heard right? And yet there, in the softening of his mouth, the flicker of a smile, she witnessed appreciation and approval. A giddy sort of joy infused her insides, warming her from the inside out.

Indicating the board, where he had no legal moves left, he said, "Stalemate."

She stared. Very rarely did they call a draw. The game's outcome was clear, however. Neither one of them was a winner.

Books by Karen Kirst

Love Inspired Historical

*The Reluctant Outlaw
*The Bridal Swap
 The Gift of Family
    *"Smoky Mountain Christmas"
*His Mountain Miss
*The Husband Hunt

*Smoky Mountain Matches

KAREN KIRST

was born and raised in East Tennessee near the Great
Smoky Mountains. A lifelong lover of books, it wasn't
until after college that she had the grand idea to write
one herself. Now she divides her time between being
a wife, homeschooling mom and romance writer. Her
favorite pastimes are reading, visiting tearooms and
watching romantic comedies.

The Husband Hunt

KAREN KIRST

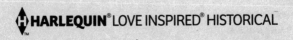

LOVE INSPIRED BOOKS

Recycling programs
for this product may
not exist in your area.

ISBN-13: 978-0-373-82990-3

THE HUSBAND HUNT

Copyright © 2013 by Karen Vyskocil

www.Harlequin.com

Printed in U.S.A.

"For my thoughts are not your thoughts, neither are your ways my ways," declares the Lord. "As the heavens are higher than the earth, so are my ways than your ways and my thoughts than your thoughts."
—*Isaiah* 55:8–9

For a beloved aunt, Linda McLemore, whose support and encouragement mean the world to me. Thanks for all the laughs and the prayers. I love you.

This dream would not be possible without my Lord and Savior Jesus Christ.

John 15:5: I am the vine, you are the branches. If you remain in me and I in you, you will bear much fruit; apart from me you can do nothing.

Chapter One

She was trapped. Stuck high above the ground in her place of refuge—a sugar maple with a trunk too wide to get her arms around and century-deep roots—cornered by a skunk, of all things. The varmint had sauntered up and planted itself at the tree's base and showed no intentions of leaving.

Gripping the branch above her head, Sophie leaned forward and commenced trying to reason with him. "Yoo-hoo! How about you move along? I'm sure there are tastier earthworms along the stream bank. You might even catch yourself a frog."

His frantic digging continued. How long was she going to have to wait?

"You're keeping me from my chores, you know." She blew a stray hair out of her eyes. "Will and Granddad will be wanting their supper soon." Beans, fried potatoes and corn bread *again*. Her specialty.

The snap of a twig brought her and the skunk's head up simultaneously.

Her gaze landed on a face as familiar to her as her own, clashing with silver eyes that seemed to perpetually taunt or condemn her. She swallowed a sigh. She'd long ago given up hoping for approval from Nathan O'Malley.

"Hello, Nathan."

One dusky eyebrow quirked. "I see you've made a new friend."

She peered down. The animal's focus had shifted to Nathan, and it was now stamping the ground in warning. "Yeah, well, my friend doesn't seem to like you very much."

He eyed the skunk with caution. Sunlight shifting through the trees glinted in his light brown hair, cut short so he wouldn't have to fool with it, and bathed his classic features in golden light. Features that were branded into her brain. A straight, proud nose flanked by prominent cheekbones. Square jaw. The crease beside his full lips that flashed every time he smiled.

And who could forget those quicksilver eyes? They dominated her daydreams, hovered at the edge of her consciousness as she drifted off to sleep at night. It was downright irritating.

"I really need to get down," she informed him, scooting closer to the trunk. That jittery feeling was back. If she didn't eat soon, she chanced tumbling out of this tree in a dead faint. Wouldn't that impress him.

"Could you try to lure him away?"

He tore his gaze from the irate skunk to stare up at her. "And how do you propose I do that?"

"I don't know." She cast around the forest floor for inspiration. When none came, she suggested, "If you move away, maybe he'll follow. Toss a stick in the direction of the stream. Maybe he'll get distracted and realize there's more to eat there."

"He's not a dog."

Frowning, he edged sideways. The skunk hissed. Followed.

"It's working!" Sophie swung her body around and stretched her foot down to the knotted branch below.

"Sophie, stop," Nathan ordered. "Wait until he's gone."

She chose to ignore his warning. Unfortunately, her boot slipped. Her grip on the trunk slackened. Scrambling for purchase, she whipped her head around in time to see Nathan surge forward as if to catch her.

The skunk reacted as expected. Tail aloft, he sprayed.

Sophie gasped. Nathan attempted to shield his face with his arms, to sidestep, but he was too slow. Because his focus was on rescuing *her*. Groaning, she shimmied down the trunk and hopped to the ground as the offended animal scampered in the opposite direction.

"Oh, Nathan, I'm so sorry!" She advanced toward him, only to halt in her tracks as noxious fumes assaulted her nose. He smelled like rotten eggs and garlic. Ugh. Wrinkling her nose, she covered the bottom half of her face with one hand. "Did it get in your eyes?"

His lids blinked open, revealing twin chips of forged steel. Uh-oh.

"No."

Wearing a disgusted expression, he carefully wiped the moisture from his face with his shirtsleeves. He looked down and grimaced. "These were my most comfortable trousers."

He didn't have to say it. Those trousers were headed for the burn pile.

Pivoting on his heel, his long strides quickly ate up the distance to the stream. Sophie followed at a reasonable distance, making a point to breathe through her mouth. Oh, this was terrible. Worse than terrible. He would never forgive her.

On the bank, he tugged off his brown leather work

boots, tossed them onto the grass and waded into the sluggish water. While the crystal-clear Smoky Mountain stream dissecting her property wasn't deep enough for diving, it was deep enough to submerge oneself in, and that's what he did. When he came up for air, he threaded his fingers through his hair to dislodge the moisture. His white shirt molded to thick, ropy shoulders, chiseled chest and flat stomach carved from countless hours milking cows, mucking out stalls and working the fields. A farmer's physique.

She forced her too-interested gaze elsewhere, forced herself to remember. *Nathan is my neighbor. My childhood friend. He probably doesn't even think of me as a girl.*

And why would he when she didn't have a clue how to act or dress like one?

Brushing bits of dirt from her earth-hued pants, she fiddled with her rolled-up sleeves and mentally shrugged. She may not dress all fancy like other girls her age, but at least her clothes were clean and pressed and, most importantly, comfortable. Farming was backbreaking, sweaty work. It didn't make sense to wear frilly skirts and fine silk blouses that would only get ruined.

Still…she couldn't help but wonder sometimes what it might be like to wear a dress, to have her hair done up in a sophisticated style. Would Nathan think her beautiful then?

Get your head out of the clouds, Soph.

"We've got canned tomatoes in the springhouse—" she pointed downstream "—I'll go and get them. Surely that will get the smell out."

"Forget it." Not sparing a glance her direction, he sloshed up and onto the bank. "I'll take a vinegar bath at home."

Twisting her hands together, she took halting steps forward. She wanted to go closer, but she was standing downwind and the odor was overpowering. "How long are you going to be mad at me?"

Pausing in tugging his boots on, he shot her a hard glance and retorted, "For as long as it takes the smell to wear off."

"But—"

"No." He cut her off with a jerk of his hand. "Honestly, Sophie, when are you going to learn to curb your impulses? Think before you act? One of these days you're going to land yourself in a real heap of trouble and I may not be around to help. Quite frankly, I'm getting kind of tired playing rescuer."

Nathan reached his parents' cabin and was climbing the back porch steps just as Caleb emerged. One whiff had his younger brother backing up and raising his arm to cover his nose.

"What happened to you?"

"Sophie Tanner happened, that's what," he muttered, still aggravated with the headstrong tomboy. If she'd only listened to him and stayed put a few more minutes, he wouldn't smell like a rotten bucket of pig scraps. He unbuttoned his shirt. "Do me a favor. Grab the vinegar from the cabinet. And ask Pa if he'll help you milk the cows. I doubt they'll let me near them reeking of polecat."

"What has Sophie done now?"

Explaining what happened as he undressed, he chucked his shirt, pants and socks into a heap to be burned later. Caleb's resulting laughter didn't bother Nathan. His brother laughed so rarely these days that he relished the sound of it, no matter that it was at his expense.

Clad in nothing but his knee-length cotton drawers, he prompted, "The sooner I get that vinegar, the better. Hurry up."

"I wish I could've seen your expression when that ole

polecat doused you. And Sophie…I imagine she was fit to be tied." Brown eyes full of mirth, he was still chuckling and shaking his head as he disappeared inside.

Half sitting on the porch rail, Nathan recalled Sophie's last expression all too clearly. Her eyes wide and beseeching, her face pale, even distraught, as he stomped off.

He pinched the bridge of his nose to dispel the blossoming ache behind his forehead.

You didn't handle that very well, did you, O'Malley?

Caleb reappeared, a black handkerchief concealing the lower half of his face. The wicked scar near his eye lent him a sinister air.

"You look like a bank robber."

"I won't say what you look like." Caleb held out the vinegar bottle. "Why the hangdog expression? Oh, wait. Let me guess. You gave Sophie a piece of your mind, and now you're feeling guilty."

Grabbing the bottle, Nathan pushed upright and descended the steps. The grass pricked the sensitive soles of his feet. "She's too impulsive."

Following a couple of paces behind, Caleb remarked, "She's been that way since we were kids. Remember that time she took a flying leap off Flinthead Falls and nearly drowned?"

"Don't remind me." His stomach hardened into a tight knot just thinking about it. She'd been fourteen to his nineteen, a beautiful wild thing oblivious to danger, bursting with life and optimism that infused the air around her with sparkling energy. He'd rescued her as he'd done many times before. Lectured her, too. Now eighteen, she'd settled down since then, but he knew that untamable streak yet lingered, poised to make an appearance at any moment.

Caleb waited outside while Nathan retrieved the copper tub from the toolshed.

"And remember that time you and Danny Mabry were

entrenched in a tug-of-war and Sophie distracted you? Hollered your name?" He chuckled. "You fell flat on your face in the mud."

Nathan pursed his lips. Talk about being embarrassed. A girl he'd fancied had been watching that tug-of-war and his goal had been to impress her with his strength and skill. She'd taken one look at his mud-caked face and shared a hearty laugh with her friends. That was before he'd decided females were too much trouble to fool with.

Lifting the other end of the tub, Caleb helped him carry it to the porch.

"Oh, and do you remember—"

"I have the same memories as you, Caleb." He cut him off, uninterested in rehashing all the scrapes and fixes Sophie Tanner had gotten herself—and him—into. "I just want to get this smell off."

"Fine." He helped maneuver the tub and straightened, yanking the handkerchief down around his neck, his uncharacteristic good humor gone. "Tell Pa I'm going to get a head start on the milking."

Watching him stalk across the yard, Nathan regretted his abrupt words. The accident that had scarred Caleb and nearly killed his best friend almost two years ago had transformed the lighthearted prankster into a surly loner. He hardly recognized his own brother and it had nothing to do with his altered face.

Please, God, heal his hidden hurts. Help us to love him unconditionally and to be patient. He missed the old Caleb. He wondered if he'd ever glimpse that man again.

Three days and several vinegar baths later, his family no longer cringed when he entered a room. Poor Kate hadn't come around since that first day. His brother Josh's wife was expecting their first child, and her delicate condition magnified her sense of smell, which meant simply breathing the air around him had made her nauseous.

They were seated around the table Thursday night enjoying Ma's pecan pie when a soft knock sounded on the kitchen door. Pa went to answer it. When Nathan heard Sophie's quiet voice, he gulped the remainder of his coffee and, excusing himself, went to greet her.

Hearing his approach, Pa bid her goodbye and returned to the table.

Sophie's gaze collided with his, remorse churning in the blue depths. The final pieces of irritation dissolved and he wished he had gone to see her before this.

"Hey, Soph." He gripped the smooth wooden door and rested his weight against it. "Ma made pecan pie for dessert. Care to join us?"

Not much of a cook herself, she usually took him up on such offers.

She hesitated, fingers toying with the end of her neatly woven braid, honey-blond hair gleaming like spun gold in the sunlight. Spun gold? Where had that fanciful thought come from? He was not a fanciful man. He was a sensible man. A practical man who dealt with day-to-day reality. He wasn't a reader like Josh or his cousins, so his mind wasn't filled with poetry and romance. Must be the effects of the skunk stench.

"No, thanks. Do you have a minute?"

"Sure." Joining her on the porch, he pulled the door closed behind him and went to lean against the railing, arms folded over his chest.

Sophie faced him squarely, hands tucked in her pants' pockets and shoulders back in a familiar stance that said she had something to prove. "I came to apologize for the other day."

The apology didn't come as a surprise. One thing about

his neighbor—she was quick to own up to mistakes. "Forget about it."

"I hope the smell didn't disrupt things too much."

Disrupt? As in having to steer clear of the barn while his brother and father assumed his share of the chores? As in having to take his meals on the front porch so as not to make everyone gag at the supper table?

"Nah, not really." He smiled to erase her lingering regret.

Bending at the waist, she sniffed the air around him. Shot him a hopeful smile. "You smell fine to me. Does this mean we can be friends again?"

He gave her braid a playful tug. "We'll always be friends. You know that."

But his words didn't have the desired effect. Her smile vanished as quickly as it had appeared, long lashes sweeping down. "I don't expect you to rescue me, you know."

Straightening, Nathan settled his hands on her shoulders. "Sophie, look at me." When she lifted her face to his, he said, "I shouldn't have said that. I was angry, and I spoke without thinking. You know you can always count on me, don't you?"

She slowly nodded. He was struck by her diminutive stature, her slender build and the delicacy so often overlooked because of her tomboyish appearance and the air of capability she exuded that had carried her through the many hardships life had thrown her way. But now, gazing into her face, he was reminded that she was no longer the rough-and-tumble little imp trailing behind him and his brothers, insistent on joining in their fun.

The muted light of the summer evening washed her fair skin with a pink tinge of health, her cheeks and bee-stung lips the color of delicate rosebuds. The collared button-down shirt she had on was blue like the sky overhead. The bright hue made her eyes glow like the blue sapphire ring

Emmett Clawson had taken in on trade a couple of weeks ago and that now occupied a premier spot in the jewelry case for everyone to admire.

With a start, he realized he was staring and Sophie was watching him with an uncharacteristic guardedness. He released her at once. *What's gotten into you, O'Malley?*

Clearing his clogged throat, he pivoted away to grip the railing, slowly and methodically cataloging the rows upon rows of cornstalks swaying in the breeze, the stately apple orchard marching along the fields in front of Josh and Kate's cabin and the forested mountains ringing the valley.

Okay, so Sophie was all grown up now. So what? That didn't mean he was free to think of her in terms other than neighbor and friend. Disaster lay down that path....

If, and that was a *big* if, he ever decided to marry, Sophia Lorraine Tanner would not be up for consideration. Not ever.

She was trouble, pure and simple. Too impulsive. Too headstrong. Too much. No, if he did decide to find himself a wife, he'd search for someone sensible, cautious and levelheaded. Someone like him.

Chapter Two

Sophie wrapped a hand around the wooden post for support and attempted to appear nonchalant about the effects of Nathan's touch. His nearness. It wasn't as if such touches were rare. They were friends, had been friends as far back as she could remember, and while her handsome neighbor had strict ideas about what constituted appropriate behavior, he was an affectionate man. Compassionate, too. Dependable and trustworthy.

Nathan was everything her wayward pa wasn't. He would never dream of doing something as despicable as abandoning his pregnant wife and child for another woman.

"How's Tobias?" he asked.

Sophie tracked a pair of dragonflies flitting on the wind, their iridescent wings a mix of blue and silvery green. The worry she'd battled since her granddad had taken ill three weeks ago eroded her peace of mind. "Still the same. Weak. The medicine Doc Owens gave him doesn't seem to be helping the cough. I try to encourage him to eat, but he doesn't have much of an appetite."

"I'll ask Ma to make him some of her chicken noodle soup."

Feeling his gaze on her, she turned her head and found strength and a promise of support in the silver depths. "Surely he won't be able to resist that." Her attempt at a smile fell flat. "He won't get well on my cooking alone."

Her heart stuttered in her chest. What if he didn't get better? What would she do without the only real father figure she'd ever had? Her grandfather had practically raised her and her little brother, Will, after her pa left and her ma passed away.

"I don't like that look on your face," he gently reproved. "Don't let your mind go there. We're all praying for Tobias's recovery." A grin transformed his serious face. "Besides, you know as well as I do what a tough old codger he is. Stubborn, too. Though not nearly as stubborn as his granddaughter."

That earned him a punch in the arm. "If anyone is stubborn around here, it's you, Nathan O'Malley."

Chuckling, he rubbed his arm as if it had really hurt. "I won't deny it." Jerking his head, he said, "Come on, I'll walk you home and look in on him. See if I can't convince him to eat something."

Following him down the worn steps and into the lush grass, she moved to walk beside him, keenly aware of his height, the restrained power in his hardened body and the self-assuredness with which he carried himself. He smelled of summer, of line-dried clothes and freshly cut hay. And maybe a little of pecans and corn syrup, which made her regret refusing a piece of Mary's pie.

As they passed the dairy barn, she noticed the cows weren't crowded around the entrance and all seemed quiet. "You already did the milking?"

"Supper was a tad late getting on the table, so I did it beforehand."

"On my way here, I spotted Caleb heading for the high

country." She tossed him a sideways glance. "How long is he going to be gone this time?"

Shrugging, he blew out a breath. "I suppose that depends on how long it takes him to snag a bear."

She dodged a fat bumblebee that zoomed into her path. "When are you going to stop coddling him, Nathan? He has a responsibility to you and the rest of your family."

"In his mind, he is fulfilling his responsibilities. By stocking the smokehouse with all the meat he brings home, he's helping to feed the family. Not to mention the trade value of the hides and furs."

Passing into the dense forest where the air was sweet and cool, the lowering sun's rays filtered through the towering oaks, maples and various other trees, casting sidelong lines of light that made odd patterns on their clothing.

"I understand the accident changed him…and not only on the outside." It had been a painful thing to witness the almost night-and-day change in his personality nearly two years ago. She missed the fun-loving, mischievous Caleb and feared her childhood playmate was gone for good. "I just don't think it's fair that he goes off whenever he feels like it and leaves you behind to do all the work."

"It's frustrating. And sometimes I get resentful." His gaze volleyed between the root-studded ground and her. "To be honest, I haven't a clue how to talk to my own brother."

The admission clearly hadn't come easily. Nathan wasn't a complainer. When Caleb had first started taking off for days at a time, Nathan had simply picked up the slack, milking all the cows himself twice a day, feeding and watering them, caring for the sick and expectant, mucking out their stalls, delivering the milk and cheese Mary made to the mercantile. And when he wasn't doing all that, he was working in the alfalfa, hay and cornfields. His older brother had pitched in to help, but now with his furniture business taking off and Kate expecting for the first time, Josh had little time to spare.

"Why not tell him the truth? That you need him here?"

When his brow creased in contemplation, she reached out and touched the bare forearm exposed by his rolled-up sleeve. The smooth, fine hairs covering the sun-kissed skin tickled her fingertips. She snatched her hand away.

"What?" He threw her a questioning glance.

Clearing her throat, she said almost defensively, "Nothing. Look, I'm concerned about you, that's all. You work too hard."

"I can say the same about you."

Their gazes met and clung. Sophie basked in the warmth of his rare and fleeting admiration. Then he grabbed her hand and tugged her sideways, saving her from smacking face-first into a tree. He chuckled low in his chest. Feeling foolish, she concentrated on the path beneath her heavy black boots.

In the branches far above their heads, birds twittered, hooted and warbled in a melodious tune that echoed through the understory. She loved this place, the vast forest both awe-inspiring and peaceful, expansive yet somehow intimate; a testament to God's power and creativity. A gift of both beauty and practicality.

She loved her home. Had no itch like some people her age to venture out of these East Tennessee mountains and experience city life. *Imagine the gawking stares a tomboy like you would get in the city!* The folks of Gatlinburg knew her and accepted her for what and who she was: a simple farm girl just trying to survive, to keep the farm afloat, to be both mother and father to her brother and caretaker of her beloved granddad. She had no grand dreams for her own future, no big expectations. Better to take each day as it came.

The trees thinned, allowing more light to spill into

the meadows as they neared her family's property. Much smaller than the O'Malley farm, the Tanner spread consisted of a single-pen cabin in the midst of a small clearing, a cantilever barn whose top-heavy structure resembled a wooden mushroom, a very tall, very skinny chicken coop and a springhouse straddling the cold, rushing waters of the stream winding through the trees. A small garden beside the cabin provided just enough vegetables for the three of them. Compared to Nathan's place, her farm looked worn around the edges, a bit forlorn, the buildings sagging and bare. Even if she had the resources to fix everything that needed attention, there wasn't enough time in the day. Still, she loved this land that she poured so much of her heart and soul into.

"Hey, Nathan!" Crouched in the water, Will let the large rock he was looking under resettle in the silt and hurried up the bank. He snatched up his pail and crossed the grass in his bare feet, unmindful of his mud-splashed overalls.

"Hey, buddy." Always patient with her ten-year-old brother, Nathan greeted him with a ready smile. "What you got there?"

"I caught five crawdads. Wanna see?" He held up the pail, enthusiasm shining in his blue eyes handed down from their mother, the same hue as her own. A streak of dirt was smeared across his forehead and flecks of it clung to his brown hair.

Nathan peered at the miniature lobsterlike creatures and made an approving grunt. "Looks like you got some big ones."

"Will, where are your shoes?" Sophie frowned. "What happens if you step on a bee or cut your foot on a rock?"

He rolled his eyes. "I won't."

"You don't know that."

"You worry too much." He laughed off her concern.

"I'm going to see if I can catch some more. See ya, Nathan."

The last year had wrought many changes in her brother and not all of them bad. He'd shot up two inches, his face had thinned out and he was *always* hungry. A bright kid in possession of a tender heart, his boyish enthusiasm had calmed and smiles had to be coaxed out of him. More and more it seemed as if he was pulling away from her in an effort to gain his independence. The brother she'd practically raised herself was growing up, and she didn't know how she felt about that.

"An ounce of prevention is worth a pound of cure," she called to his retreating back.

Nathan angled toward her and lifted a sardonic eyebrow. "Prevention, huh? I wonder if you thought about that right before you plunged off the falls? Or when you befriended that stray wolf that everyone warned you was probably rabid? Oh, and what about the time Jimmy Newman dared you to cross the fallen log high above Abram's Creek with your eyes closed?" He scowled. "Thought for sure my heart was going to give out that time."

Sophie resisted the urge to squirm. Why couldn't he conveniently forget her past shenanigans like a true gentleman? "If you'll remember, I made it across just fine." She brushed past him and headed for the cabin. "And that was a dog, not a wolf," she corrected, tossing the words over her shoulder.

"And what about the falls?" His challenging tone stopped her.

She turned around. "What about it?"

He prowled toward her, residual anger churning in his stormy eyes, reminding her of that long-ago summer day and the frothy, forceful water that had sucked her under, stealing her breath until she'd thought her lungs might burst. And then strong arms had wrapped around her waist, pulling her to safety. How well she recalled him frantically calling her name. His hands cradling her with a tenderness she hadn't known since she was a little girl, since before her mother died. How amazing…how sweetly wonderful it had felt to be held in his arms!

It was in that moment that she'd realized she was in love with Nathan O'Malley. And, as his concern had morphed into a familiar lecture, she had known he would never love her back.

His features were set in an obstinate expression. "You nearly died, Sophie."

"That was four years ago. Why are you so angry all of a sudden?"

"I'm not angry, exactly." He paused, a tiny crease between his brows as he mulled over his next words. "I just want you to take your own advice. Think before you act. Exercise caution."

In other words, think like he did. Frustration over her own shortcomings and the futility of trying to please him sharpened her voice. "Is this about the skunk? Because I'm not sure what else you expect me to say—"

"No, it's not that." He dropped his hands to his sides. "Let's just drop it, okay? I'm going inside."

This time, it was he who brushed past her. Why did she suddenly feel as if she'd been dismissed?

The inside of the Tanners' cabin looked much the same as it had when he was a young boy. Plain. Austere. The small glass windows were clean but bare. No pictures adorned the thick log walls. There was only one rug, faded and worn and situated close to the stone fireplace opposite the cast-iron stove. A simple square table with four chairs, a brown sofa that had obviously seen better days and two rocking chairs were the only furnishings. Tobias slept in the single bedroom beside the kitchen while Sophie and Will shared the loft space overhead.

What the place lacked was a feminine touch.

As he passed the fireplace, his gaze lit on a small tin-type of Sophie and Will's parents, Lester and Jeanine Tanner. He barely remembered Sophie's mother. Not surprising considering he'd been thirteen when she died giving birth to Will. A quiet woman, she'd hovered in the background like a shadow as if to blend in. Perhaps to avoid attracting her husband's attention?

Unfortunately, Nathan remembered Lester Tanner all too well. The man was hateful, lazy and in possession of an explosive temper that all the local kids feared and tried their best to avoid. The family was well rid of him.

He couldn't help but wonder if Sophie might have turned out differently had she had a mother's tender hand to guide her instead of being thrust into the role of caretaker at eight years old.

He tapped lightly on the door standing ajar. "Tobias?"

A breathy voice beckoned him in. He moved deeper into the shadows where a single kerosene lamp on the bedside table cast the elderly man's face in sharp relief. Nathan sucked in a startled breath, alarmed at Tobias's frailty and the changes wrought in the one week since he'd last seen his neighbor. Knowing Tobias wouldn't appreciate his pity, he carefully schooled his features.

Easing into the straight-backed chair beside the bed, he folded his hands in his lap. "How are you today?"

"Not so good." The cloudy blue eyes staring back at him were filled with resignation.

"I'm sorry to hear that. Your granddaughter tells me you don't have much of an appetite. How about I bring some soup tomorrow?"

Bringing one gnarled hand up to cover a cough, the gray-headed man shook his head, panted to catch his breath. "I appreciate the offer, son, but not even Mary's cooking sounds good these days."

Nathan swallowed against sudden sorrow. He sensed Sophie's grandfather had given up.

"I'm glad you're here. Need to talk to you about Sophie and Will." Sadness tugged at Tobias's craggy face. "I'm worried more about my granddaughter than I am about the boy. Can I count on you to watch out for her after I'm gone? She may act tough but inside she's as sensitive as her mother." His chest rattled as he pulled in more air. "She needs someone to take care of her for a change."

"My family and I will always be here for them. But you're strong, sir. I have faith you can beat this."

"No, son, I'm ready to meet my Lord and Savior face-to-face. And I long to see my sweet Anne and Jeanine again. It's time."

Throat working to contain the tide of emotion, Nathan surged to his feet and stepped over to the window. Beyond the warped glass, Sophie unpinned laundry from the line and placed it in the basket at her feet. The sight of her pensive expression made his heart weigh like a stone in his chest. Losing Tobias, the closest thing to a parent she'd ever known, would devastate her. How in the world was he supposed to help her deal with that?

Chapter Three

Sophie bolted upright in bed. What was that awful racket?

Her hens' hysterical squawking shattered the quiet. Her heart sank. At this time of night, it could only mean one thing—predator.

Blinking the sleep from her eyes, she shoved the quilt aside and sank her tired feet into her boots without bothering to lace them. In the bed opposite hers, only the top of Will's head was visible above his blanket. Thankful his slumber hadn't been disturbed, she made her way to the ladder in the inky darkness, rushed to light the lamp on the table below.

"Sophie?" Somehow her grandfather's breathless voice reached her above the din.

"I'm here." She wished he'd been able to sleep through this as easily as Will. He desperately needed his rest if he was going to recover. "I'm going outside to investigate."

"Watch yourself, ya hear?"

A grim frown touched her mouth at his labored effort to speak. "Don't worry, I'll be careful."

White cotton nightgown swishing around her ankles, she lifted her trusty Winchester from its place above the mantel and headed into the sticky night.

The barn loomed large in the semidarkness, the brittle structure and surrounding trees washed with weak moonlight. Adrenaline pumping, she rounded the corner of the cabin and stopped dead at the sight that greeted her. Her fingers went slack on the gun handle.

Her too-tall henhouse was no more. It had been tipped over and smashed into a hundred bits and pieces by an enormous black bear that was even now pawing one of her hens with the intent to devour it. Those who had managed to escape the beast's jaws were running around in endless circles.

"What have you done to my chickens?" Outrage choked any fear she might have had. They *needed* those birds and the precious eggs they produced.

Hefting the rifle up, she found the trigger and aimed for the air directly above his head. She should kill him. Considering his size, the meat would likely sustain them for a month or more. Not to mention the hide sure would make a nice rug for the living room.

But she wouldn't. Killing animals for food was a part of mountain life, and she had no issue with that—as long as the animal was a pig or chicken or fish. But bears, well, they fascinated her. Had ever since she was a little girl and she'd happened upon a mama and her three cubs fishing in a stream farther up in the mountains. The cubs had been so cute and playful, the mama tough yet tender and fiercely protective, that Sophie had hidden in the bushes and watched, barely breathing, until they'd moved on.

Focus, Sophie. Anchoring the butt against her shoulder, she fired off a single shot.

A limp hen caught between his teeth, the bear lifted his head and shifted his opaque black eyes to her. Her lungs strained for air. *Don't make me shoot you.* He took a step in her direction. Again, she aimed above his head. Fired a second time.

When the lumbering beast casually turned and disappeared into the forest, Sophie released the air in a relieved whoosh and lowered the gun, muscles as limp as soggy corn bread. She surveyed the damage, dreading the job that awaited her come daylight. Weariness settled deep in her bones. They couldn't afford to purchase lumber for a new henhouse. How was she supposed to find time to chop down trees, strip and saw them into planks when so many other chores awaited her?

Anxiety nipped at her heels as she coaxed the addled hens into the barn for the night. What she really wanted to do was park herself at Granddad's bedside until she was absolutely certain he was on the mend. A frisson of stark, cold despair worked its way through her body; the possibility of losing him looming like a menacing shadow. How sad that she simply couldn't spare the time. Not if the animals were to be fed, the vegetable garden tended, the laundry mended and washed, and food placed on the table.

Feeling sorry for yourself won't get you anywhere, Sophia Lorraine.

Traversing the tomblike yard, words of defeat slipped from her lips. "Lord Jesus, sometimes I just don't know how I can go on like this."

Sometimes she wondered what it might be like to have a strong man around to help shoulder the burdens. A partner. A helpmate. Someone like Nathan—strong and valiant and willing and able to meet any challenge. A man who could be both tough and tender. Sort of like that mama bear, she thought as she replaced the Winchester on its hooks.

But while her heart pined for him, in his eyes she was nothing more than an irritating brat. A down-on-her-luck neighbor he was forced to tolerate and occasionally rescue.

"Everything all right?" Tobias called.

Entering his room, she crossed to the narrow bed, straightened the quilts and took his hand between hers, tenderness welling in her chest at the feel of his feeble, knotted fingers.

"Everything's fine. You should go back to sleep."

"I worry about you." His eyes gleamed in the darkness. "This farm is too much for one young girl to manage."

She stroked his hand, determined to put his fears to rest. To ignore her own reservations. "I'm not a little girl anymore, you know," she gently reminded him. "I may not look like much but I can work as hard as any man."

"I'm not doubting your abilities, Sophie, but I want more for you and Will. I—" his chest expanded "—don't want you to struggle—" and deflated "—alone. Maybe it's time you settled down."

Her brows shot up, stunned at this first mention of marriage. "Why would I want to get hitched? Besides, I'm not alone. I've got you."

When he didn't respond, she leaned down and kissed his wrinkled forehead, smoothed his wispy gray hair. "I think we'll leave this conversation for when we're both rested and thinking straight. Good night."

"'Night." He sighed.

Pausing to grip the doorframe, she turned back, compelled to speak words rarely spoken between them. Not because they didn't care but because emotional expressions just wasn't their way. "I love you, Granddad."

"I love you, too." Pride and affection thrummed in his voice.

Once again in her bed, with no one around to witness her emotional display, she allowed the tears to fall, slipping silently onto her pillow. Fear, cold and black and relentless, threatened to crush her. The what-ifs, the endless responsibilities, nearly overwhelmed her.

Having a man around full-time would help. But was a husband really the answer? Her father's temper, his disdain for her mother and contempt for Sophie made her reluctant to hand over her life to just any man.

Their future was too important to gamble on.

Wiping the moisture from her forehead with her sleeve, Sophie tried once again to lift what used to be the henhouse's right sidewall. It refused to budge. A gloved hand appeared out of nowhere and covered her own. She jerked back and in the process scraped her palm on the jagged wood.

"Nathan!" She stared as he heaved the wall up as if it weighed nothing, shoulders and biceps straining his white-and-blue pin-striped shirt, and lowered it out of the way onto the grass. "What are you doing here?"

Pink and purple fingers of dawn gradually chased away black sky, lightening the wide expanse above to a pale blue. He should be at home milking his cows, not standing here in front of her with his hair damp and his cheeks smooth and touchable from a recent shave, his beautiful eyes gazing at her with resolute intentions.

"I ran into Will downstream and he mentioned what happened." His gaze swept the scattered feathers and eggshells, the bucket filled with carcasses and the splintered wood on the ground before zeroing in on her face. "Are you all right?"

"I'm fine." She shrugged off his concern. "I managed to scare him off with two shots."

"You could've killed him."

"You know how I feel about bears."

Stepping over the mess, he stopped in front of her, his chest filling her vision as he took the hand she'd been clutching against her midsection in his. He gently unfurled her fingers and lifted her palm up for a better view. Her stupid heart actually fluttered. Wouldn't he be amused if he knew how he affected her? Amused or horrified, one of the two.

His lips turned down. "This is a pretty bad scrape." Pulling a red handkerchief from his pants' pocket, he wound it around her palm and tucked the ends under. "Why aren't you wearing gloves?"

She wouldn't tell him that they were too far gone to provide any sort of protection and she didn't have the means to buy a new pair. Better he think her foolish than pity her.

She slipped her hand from his grasp. "You're right, I should have put them on."

A flicker of understanding warned her that he suspected the truth, but he didn't voice it. Instead he tugged off his own gloves and handed them to her.

"I can't take yours."

"Josh will be here soon. I have another pair in the wagon." He began to pick up the broken boards and pitch them in a pile.

"Why is Josh coming?" She gingerly pushed her fingers into the large deerskin gloves, the lingering heat from his hands a caress against her skin.

"He's bringing the lumber we need to rebuild your henhouse."

"He's *what*?"

Nathan tossed another board and arched a brow at her. "Now don't get all huffy on me. We have plenty to spare."

"You know I can't pay you."

"Don't expect payment." Shrugging, he turned his attention back to his task.

Torn, she fiddled with the end of her thick braid. "I don't want to sound ungrateful—"

"Then just say 'thank you' and let us help you." He was using his extra-patient voice, the one he used to coax her into seeing his side of things.

Frowning, she bent to gather crushed eggshells. For as

long as she could remember, the O'Malleys had been there for her family, stepping in to help whenever they had a problem or a need to be met. And while she was extremely thankful for their generosity, it was difficult to always be on the receiving end.

As the jingle of harnesses spilled across the meadows, they both straightened and turned toward the lane. "There he is now." Nathan dusted his hands on his pants and started forward to meet his brother.

Trailing behind him, she spotted Will perched on the seat beside Josh. As if sensing her unspoken question, Nathan tossed an explanation over his shoulder. "Will wanted to help load the wood. I didn't think you'd mind."

"No, of course not."

When the team halted, Will jumped down and joined Nathan at the back. Josh waved and smiled a greeting. "Hey, Sophie."

"Morning, Josh."

The eldest son of Sam and Mary O'Malley, Josh was a more laid-back, more outgoing version of Nathan. Only two years apart, they shared similar features. Both were tall, tanned and gorgeous. Josh's hair was a touch lighter than Nathan's, his eyes blue instead of silver and he sported a trim mustache and goatee that lent him a distinguished air.

He never looked at her with disapproval. But then, she'd never yearned for Josh's approval like she did Nathan's.

"How's Kate getting along?" she asked.

His smile widened, eyes shining with a deep contentment that made Sophie a little jealous. Okay, more than a little. What she wouldn't give to inspire such emotions in Nathan!

"She's feeling a lot better these days—as long as she steers clear of my brother." He shot Nathan a teasing look, laughing when he scowled in response.

Suppressing a grimace, she gestured toward the wagon. "You're a good neighbor."

"And here I thought we were friends." He winked.

"You know what I meant." She smirked, following him to the rear of the wagon.

When they had finished unloading the lumber, Josh turned to her. "Sorry I can't stay and help, but I've got to deliver a dining set before lunch."

"I understand you've got a lot to do. It's no problem."

He hooked a thumb toward the cabin. "Before I go, I'd like to say hello to Tobias if he's awake."

"Yes, please do," she said, smiling through her worry. "He'd like that."

As Josh let himself in the cabin, Nathan and Will joined her beneath the wide-limbed oak tree. Even though the sun had a long way yet to climb, the air was thick with humidity and the promise of scorching heat.

"I don't want beans again for supper," her brother informed her, sweat glistening on his face, "so I'm going fishing. Will you fry up my catch?"

While they could use his help with the henhouse, beans for the third night in a row didn't appeal to Sophie, either. Maybe fried fish would tempt Granddad to eat. "Sure thing." She squelched the urge to smooth his hair. A few years ago, he wouldn't have minded. Things were different now, though.

She watched as he ambled off to the barn to fetch his fishing pole.

"Are you ready to get started?" Nathan prompted.

She shifted her gaze to his face, shadowed by his Stetson's black brim. "Not yet."

"Uh-oh, I've seen that look before. What's on your mind?"

"If you want to help me, you have to allow me to give you something in return."

Something mysterious slipped through his eyes, some-thing she'd never seen before—a mini-explosion of heat and want immediately contained, hidden from view as if it had never been. Her heart thudded in her hollowed-out chest. What—

"Sausages," he blurted.

"Huh?"

His entire body stiff, he turned and walked away, jerk-ing up the ends of four long planks and dragging them to-ward the spot where they would rebuild.

"Everyone knows you make the best-tasting sausages around. If you insist on paying me, I'll take some of those."

Sophie stayed where she was, not a little confused by his reaction to a simple statement. "Okay. Sausages it is. If you're sure that's what you want."

He dropped the planks and shot her an enigmatic look. "I'm positive that's all I want from you."

She went to help him, certain she was missing something and feeling her mother's absence more keenly than ever.

Chapter Four

Three hours later, Nathan hammered the last nail into place on the new roof. Despite his fatigue, the thin film of sweat coating his skin and the hunger pangs in his belly, satisfaction brought a smile to his face. He stepped back to admire his and Sophie's handiwork.

This henhouse was shorter and wider than the original...and all but impossible to tip over. A small ladder led up to the hatch above the man-size door, allowing the chickens to come and go as they pleased during the day.

"What do you think, Soph?" He glanced over to where she was replacing her tools in the box.

She shot him a tired smile over her shoulder. "I think this one will outlast you and me both." When she stretched out her hand to snag her hammer lying in the grass, he noticed her fingers shaking.

Chucking his own hammer on the ground, he crossed to the elm tree and the basket of food he'd put there. "Can you help me with something?"

Straightening, she flipped her golden braid behind her shoulder and joined him without a word, taking the ends of the red, white and blue pinwheel quilt he held out to her and helping him spread it on the ground.

"Now what?" She looked to him for direction.

"Have a seat." He knelt on the quilt and withdrew the smoked ham and cheese sandwiches, jar of pickled beets and container of coleslaw.

Eyeing the bounty, she gestured behind her. "I should put my tools in the barn and go check on Granddad."

"You checked on him fifteen minutes ago." He lifted two mason jars full of sweet tea and propped them against the trunk. "How about you eat something first? I packed enough for both of us. Will, too. I'm sure he'll come 'round when he's hungry."

She wavered.

Nathan produced a cloth-covered plate. "Aren't you curious what's under here?" he teased.

When Sophie sank down on the quilt, the hunger finally showing on her face, he couldn't suppress a grin.

"Oatmeal cookies?" she asked hopefully.

"Nope."

Tapping her chin, she mused, "Peach turnovers?"

"Uh-uh."

She threw up her hands. "Tell me already."

He lifted the white cloth to reveal thick slices of apple crumb cake.

"Mind if I have my dessert first?" She grinned mischievously and swiped a slice, humming with pleasure as she sank her teeth into the spicy-sweet cake.

Nathan couldn't tear his gaze away. Her eyes were closed, and he noticed for the first time how her thick lashes lay like fans against her cheeks, how her neat brows arched with an intriguing, sassy tilt above her lids. A breeze stirred the wisps of hair framing her oval face.

She opened her eyes then, caught him staring and flushed. Shrugged self-consciously. "I forgot to eat breakfast."

He pointed to where stray crumbs clung to her lips. "You, ah, have some, ah…"

Averting her gaze, she brushed them away. He turned his attention to his sandwich, his thoughts flitting around like lightning bugs trapped in a jar. Why all of a sudden was he noticing these things about her? Why was he acutely aware of her appearance when he hadn't been before? Whatever had caused the change, he didn't like it. Not one bit. Not only was this preoccupation inconvenient, it had the potential to embarrass them both.

Halfway through his meal, he put two and two together. If Sophie went too long between meals she got jittery and light-headed. And it had been right around suppertime when he had come upon her and that skunk.

He lowered his sandwich to his lap. "Sophie?"

"What?"

"The other day when the skunk had you cornered, why didn't you tell me you were feeling puny?"

She swallowed her last bite of cake and looked at him in surprise. "You didn't give me a chance."

Of course he didn't. He'd been livid. "I'm sorry."

She hitched a shoulder. "I could've waited a little longer. Moved a little slower."

"No." He shook his head. "Your well-being comes first, no matter what."

Remembering how he'd scolded her, he grimaced, regret tightening his stomach.

It was a pattern, he realized. Back when they were kids and she'd first insisted on tagging along with him and his brothers, he alone had seemed to mind her presence. Josh had treated her with the same teasing affection as he did their cousins, and Caleb, impressed with her adventurous spirit, had been thrilled to have her around. Not Nathan. More often than not, the two of them had been at odds. While he was cautious and tended to think before he acted, she was impetuous and spontaneous and didn't always anticipate the consequences of her actions.

Which led to disagreements. And him lecturing her like an overbearing older brother.

She's not a little girl anymore, O'Malley. She's a mature young woman in charge of her own life and capable of making her own decisions. No doubt she doesn't appreciate your know-it-all behavior.

Perhaps it was time to step back and give her some space. This friendship of theirs was morphing into something unrecognizable, with strange new facets he wasn't quite comfortable with.

Sophie didn't know what to say. Or think. Nathan was an intelligent man. Perceptive, too. A quality that served him well in dealing with his five female cousins. That he'd noticed her need just now—the shakes had set in with a vengeance right about the time she'd begun sorting her tools—and understood that her haste the other day had stemmed from the same issue didn't surprise her.

Hasn't he always watched out for you? Even when he was tempted to throttle you.

It was true. Nathan's protective instincts were legendary. Not only had she heard the O'Malley girls complain about his overprotective ways, she herself had been on the receiving end of his lectures countless times—lengthy discourses about safety and the wisdom of taking proper precautions—and, she recalled with a shudder, his ire when he thought she'd acted recklessly. To give him credit, many times she *had* deserved his set-downs.

What she couldn't figure out was why he was acting strangely today. There was a distracted air about him, a confounded light in his eyes that aroused her curiosity.

As she finished her sandwich, the salty ham and cheese

between soft white bread chasing away her hunger pangs, he helped himself to the cake.

She dabbed her mouth with her napkin before broaching the subject that had been bothering her ever since she'd interrupted the conversation between him and her granddad last evening.

"What were you and Granddad talking about when I came into his room? The two of you looked awfully serious."

Nathan's bleak expression had troubled her long into the night.

Now he schooled his features into a careful blandness that scared her. If he was trying to avoid hurting her, then she was right to worry.

"Nothing special." His fingers tightened on the jar balanced on his thigh. "I tried to tempt him with Ma's cooking but he insisted he wasn't hungry. He doesn't seem to have much energy."

An understatement. "Doc Owens has been tight-lipped, as usual, but I can tell by his manner that he's concerned."

"When is he supposed to come and check on him again?"

"In a couple of days, unless he gets worse and I need him before then...." *Please, Lord, don't let that be the case.* "Are you sure that's all you talked about? He didn't say anything strange?"

Nathan lifted the jar to his mouth. "Like what?"

"Like asking you to marry me."

He choked. Sputtered. *"Marry you?"* His brows shot to his hairline, and he jammed his thumb into his chest. "Me? And you?"

Humiliation burned in her cheeks. Shoving to her feet, she glared down at him with clenched fists. "Is the prospect of marrying me so distasteful, then? You think no man in this town would want me?"

"No! That's not it!" He quickly stood, his eyes dark and searching. "You just shocked me is all. D-did Tobias suggest it to you?"

"No."

The relief skittering across his face pierced her heart. Sent her confidence tumbling. Unable to look at him, she observed a ladybug clinging to a swaying stalk at her feet. "He did suggest I start thinking of settling down. That I need a man around to take care of me," she scoffed. "Imagine!"

She'd been taking care of herself since she was eight. Why did Granddad think she needed help?

Weren't you thinking the same thing just last night? an unwelcome voice reminded.

"He's your grandfather. Of course he wants to see you settled and happy." Nathan looked particularly *un*settled, a line forming between his brows as he looked past her to the cabin.

"A husband can't guarantee me that." Her own mother's misery was proof.

He shifted his gaze back to hers. "Tobias wants to make certain your future is taken care of."

"You make it sound as if he's not going to be around for it," she accused.

"Sophie—" He moved to close the distance between them, but the sympathy wreathing his mouth sent her a step back, away from him.

"Don't." She held up a staying hand. She couldn't handle his compassion right this moment, couldn't bring herself to face what was happening to her grandfather. Not if she didn't want the tears welling up to spill over. Losing control of her emotions in front of this man wasn't something she was willing to do.

Will's whistling saved her.

Nathan twisted around, silent as her brother approached

with a proud smile, pail swinging from one hand and his pole in the other. "I caught four rainbow trout," he told them, lifting the pail for them to inspect.

"Nice catch," Nathan admitted, but his somber gaze was on Sophie.

"I'll take those inside for you," she quickly volunteered, taking the pail from his willing hand. Tilting her head to indicate the quilt spread out behind them, she said, "Nathan brought us lunch. Help yourself."

Will's eyes lit up. "Miss Mary's the best cook around." Setting his pole out of the way, he plopped down and began rifling through the basket.

Before Nathan could speak, she rushed ahead. "Thank you for everything today. I should go in and change. I have errands in town this afternoon."

He nodded slowly. "I have chores waiting, too. I'll keep Will company while he eats, then head out."

"See you later, then?"

"Later."

The promise in his deep baritone let her know not only would he be seeing her, but sooner or later they would finish this conversation.

The bell above the mercantile door jingled. Sophie didn't look up from the two thread spools she was trying to choose between. Because her brother spent much of his time on his knees in the creek, it seemed like every other week there was another tear for her to mend.

Light footfalls and feminine giggles drifted closer. She frowned. Recognizing the voices, she peered over her shoulder and spotted April Littleton and her two closest friends, sisters Lila and Norma Jean Oglesby. The same age as Sophie, the trio was extremely popular with Gatlinburg's single male population. And why shouldn't they be? Besides being beautiful and stylish in their pastel dresses and beribboned curls, they were accomplished flirts, able to monopolize a man's attention with very little effort.

Next to them, Sophie felt ordinary. Gauche.

April caught her staring. Brown eyes narrowing, she made no attempts to hide her disdain.

"Hello, Sophie." Her nose pinched as if the air around her suddenly reeked.

An only child born to her parents late in life, April had been coddled and adored from the moment of her birth, and the results were a spoiled, self-absorbed young woman. Her parents weren't well-off, just simple farm folk like many of the families in this mountain town, but they scrimped and saved to be able to outfit her as if she was a city debutante.

"Hi, Sophie." Lila offered her a tentative smile. The older sister, Norma Jean, remained silent. Both were slender, blonde and blue-eyed with fair skin.

"Hello." She quickly replaced one of the spools without making a conscious color choice. No reason to linger for what would prove to be an unpleasant encounter.

April's jealousy fueled her dislike of Sophie. Not of her appearance, of course. April didn't consider her competition. It was Sophie's friendship with Nathan that she envied. Even if Lila hadn't let that little nugget slip, it was obvious the dark beauty wanted him for herself, and it killed her that Sophie shared any sort of connection with him.

"We were discussing our outfits for the church social tomorrow night," April said with mock innocence. "What are you going to wear, Sophie?"

Clutching the thread, she pivoted to face them. Shrugged as if she didn't care. "I haven't given it much thought."

April raked her from head to toe and shot a knowing glance at Norma Jean. "Of course you haven't."

"Tell her about your new dress," Lila encouraged her friend, her round face devoid of malice. Sophie sometimes wondered why Lila would waste her time with a girl like April. The seventeen-year-old appeared to have a good heart.

April's eyes shone with confidence as she ran her hands over her glossy brown ringlets. "It's buttercup-yellow…"

She went on to describe the dress in excruciating detail. Sophie tuned her out, biding her time until she could escape. She had no interest in scalloped hems and pearl buttons.

The mention of Nathan's name snapped her out of her reverie.

"What was that about Nathan?"

"I'm making Nathan's favorite for the social. Apple pie."

Sophie bit her lip. That wasn't his favorite—it was rhubarb.

"What are you bringing?" Norma Jean smirked. "Sausages?"

The girls' laughter stirred her temper. For once, Sophie wanted to prove she was as capable as any other girl. "Actually, I'm baking a pie, too," she blurted.

The laughter died off as all three stared at her in amazement.

A delicate wrinkle formed between Lila's brows. "I didn't know you baked."

"Everyone knows she doesn't," Norma Jean muttered in a too-loud aside.

April, however, grinned in expectant pleasure. "Well, I, for one, am looking forward to tasting your pie. What kind is it?"

"Rhubarb."

"Oh, how…interesting. I'll look for it tomorrow night. Let's go, girls. I want to find just the right color hair ribbon to match my dress."

Sophie hesitated, watching as they gravitated toward

the fabrics whispering feverishly together, before hurrying to the counter to pay for her purchase.

Outside, walking along Main Street, she was oblivious to the sun's ruthless heat, the stench of horse manure and the nods of greeting aimed her way.

What had she gotten herself into?

She didn't know how to bake! After her ma passed, Granddad had taught her the basics: how to fry bacon and eggs, how to make flapjacks and corn bread. Stews and soups. Roast chicken. And, of course, beans. That was the extent of her kitchen skills. Not once had she attempted to bake a cake, let alone a pie.

What had she been thinking? Despite her trepidation, she couldn't back out. She refused to give April the satisfaction.

Determination lengthening her steps, she reached the cabin in less than the usual time. Sophie had found a collection of recipes in her ma's cedar chest a while back. Surely there was something in there she could use.

As she cut across the yard, her gaze went to the new henhouse. She stopped short. There, strutting around in the dirt, were approximately five new chickens. Dark Brahmas, a hearty breed revered for their gentle disposition. She pushed the door open and entered the dark interior of the cabin.

"Will?" She set her small package on the table. "Granddad?"

"In here."

"Hey, there." Sinking gently down on the edge of Tobias's bed, she held his hand. Propped against a mountain of pillows, his skin had a sallow cast. "Can I get you anything? Would you like for me to open the curtains? It's a bit stuffy in here." And dreary, she thought, compared to the bright summer day outside.

His dry, cracked lips shifted into a grimace as he shook his head.

"I noticed some unfamiliar chickens outside. Do you know anything about that?"

"Nathan," he wheezed. "He brought us two dozen eggs, too."

To replace the ones they'd lost. She squeezed her eyes tight, deeply touched by the gesture.

"You all right?"

She inhaled a fortifying breath and eased off the bed. "How does a cup of chamomile tea sound?"

"No need to trouble yourself—"

"It's no trouble at all. I'll make some for both of us. We'll sit together and drink our tea and visit." The endless farm demands could wait a little while longer.

In the kitchen, she filled the scuffed tin teakettle with water from the bucket and set it on the stovetop, then added kindling to the firebox. As she readied two mugs, her mind refused to budge from Nathan.

Why did he have to go out of his way to be thoughtful? It would make things easier if he were hateful. Or selfish. Maybe then she wouldn't yearn for his high regard. Maybe then she wouldn't entertain foolish, impossible dreams. Maybe, just maybe, she would see him as no one special, an ordinary guy who didn't matter to her at all.

Chapter Five

At one end of the dairy barn lit by kerosene lamps hanging from post hooks, Nathan stood in front of the waist-high wooden shelves replacing lids on the crocks of milk he'd just filled. In the stalls stretching out behind him on either side of the center aisle, his cows were happily munching hay.

In the corner where they kept a bin of clean water, he washed and dried his hands, the familiar scents of cowhide, hay and fresh milk filling his lungs. Satisfaction pulsed through him. He relished his work, the straightforward nature of it and the solitude. He liked that he could plant a seed of corn and watch it grow tall, witness a calf enter this world and help it thrive. Farming was in his blood, passed down from his father and grandfather and great-grandfather. If he could do this for the rest of his life, he'd be a happy man. No need for a wife or kids. Well, kids might be nice. A wife he wasn't so sure about.

Mentally rehashing that awful turn in his and Sophie's conversation yesterday, he grimaced. He hadn't meant to hurt her feelings. It was just that the notion of a union between the two of them was so absurd as to be laughable.

He and Sophie were like oil and water, dry forest and lightning. They just didn't mix. Not romantically, anyway.

The barn door creaked and he turned, expecting to see his pa. But there, framed in the predawn darkness, stood Sophie, a cloth-covered bucket in her arms.

"Hey. Is everything all right?" Laying the cloth on the shelf, he went to her, hoping against hope this early morning visit and the shadows beneath her eyes didn't mean what he thought it might.

One slender shoulder lifted. "I couldn't sleep, so I thought I might as well bring over the sausages I promised you."

Nathan exhaled. He accepted the bucket she held out, tucking it against his middle while he did a careful study of her. Aside from the troubled light in her eyes, she looked much the same as usual. Her long hair had been freshly brushed and plaited, the sleek, honeyed strands pulled back from her face, emphasizing her cheekbones and the gentle curve of her jaw.

"Thanks for these." He cocked his head. "Walk with me to the springhouse?"

"Yeah." Noticing the crocks, she walked over and slipped her hands around one. "How many are you storing?"

"Just two this time. I'm taking one to Ma and the rest will go to Clawson's. That's heavy," he said when she started to lift it. "Why don't you take the sausages and I'll get the milk?"

Before Tobias got sick, a suggestion like that would've gotten him an earful. Sophie didn't take kindly to insinuations that she was weak or incapable. The fact that she didn't protest was proof of her preoccupation.

Using the moon's light to guide them, they walked the dirt path to the stream and the stone springhouse that housed perishables. Trickling water intruded upon the hushed stillness of the fields and forest. Beside him, Sophie was silent.

I don't know what to say to ease her anxiety, God. I don't like seeing her like this. Please show me how to help her. How to reassure her.

Stooping beneath the low doorframe, he carefully placed the containers inside and pulled the door closed, letting the latch fall into place. When he straightened, he noticed her staring at the moonlight-kissed stones scattered in the streambed. Her lost expression tugged at his heart and made him want to wrap his arms around her and shelter her from heartache.

She'd been dealt too many blows in her life. If Tobias didn't make it, would she break? The idea terrified him. Sophie was one of the strongest people he knew. He couldn't imagine her any other way.

He stood close but didn't hug her. Instead he reached out to graze the back of her hand and somehow found his fingers threading through hers. Her head came up, blue eyes flashing to his, dark and questioning. She didn't pull away, though, and he decided it would be awkward to disengage now. Besides, her skin was cold, the bones fragile. Let his heat warm her.

Friends could hold hands and not have it mean anything, couldn't they?

"What you did yesterday…" she said, her voice muted. "The henhouse, the chickens and eggs… It means a lot to me. To all of us. Thank you."

"I did it because I wanted to, not because I felt I had to," he pointed out. "I like helping you."

As long as he was able, he'd eagerly meet any and all of the Tanners' needs. Growing up, he'd witnessed his parents' generosity toward others, giving selflessly of their time, energy and possessions. It was a lesson he'd taken to heart.

"I know."

She surprised him by laying a hand against his chest.

Her touch seared through the material, scorching his skin. His heart jerked.

"You're a good man, Nathan. The best." Then, as if deciding she'd said too much, she pulled free of his hold. "I should go."

"Wait." Sophie didn't often dole out praise, so it meant a lot coming from her. He just couldn't figure out why she'd sounded so resigned. So solemn. "Are you going to the social tonight?"

She grimaced. "I am. Mrs. Beecham cornered me last week and insisted on sitting with Granddad so that Will and I could go. There's no arguing with that woman."

"It'll be good for you to get out and socialize."

She looked dubious. "If you say so."

"Think of all the delicious food you'll have to choose from."

Her mouth lifted in a pretty, albeit fleeting, smile. "Since I don't dance, the food is the biggest draw for me, you know. And speaking of food, I have to get back before Granddad or Will wake to find me gone. They'll be wanting their breakfast. I need to get to it."

"See you later, then."

Nodding, she gave a little wave and walked away, head bent and long braid bouncing against her back. He watched until the trees swallowed her up, thinking it might not be a bad idea to find himself a date for tonight. Nothing serious. Just harmless fun.

Because whatever it was sensitizing him to Sophie— loneliness, although he didn't exactly *feel* lonely, the unrecognized need for female companionship, perhaps—had to be snuffed out before he did something stupid.

"You don't expect me to eat a slice of that pie, do you?" Will bounced on his toes, eager to make his escape.

Sophie slid it onto the dessert table in between a towering stack cake and a buttermilk pie. "It doesn't look half bad." She eyed her creation critically.

While the crust wasn't perfectly round and smooth, it did have an appealing golden hue like the other pies on the table. And the rhubarb filling had filled the cabin with a sweet, pleasant aroma. She'd followed her ma's recipe carefully. Surely it would be edible. Maybe even good.

"I don't understand why you decided to make one, anyway," Will said doubtfully. "You don't bake."

She couldn't understand it, either. Oh, yeah. April and her insults. And a desire to prove to those girls—and Nathan, too—that they were wrong about her. That she was more than just a rough-around-the-edges, act-before-she-thought-it-through tomboy.

"There's a first time for everything," she told him with false confidence.

"Hey, Will." Redheaded, freckled Charlie Layton halted midstride and motioned him over. "We're gettin' ready to race. Want to join us?"

"Sure thing!" With a muttered farewell, he ran to join Charlie. The two friends jogged off in the direction of the trees edging the church property where a group of about twenty boys their age had gathered.

The social was already in full swing, many of the men clustered alongside the white clapboard church, no doubt comparing farming techniques or debating quicker, more improved trade routes with the larger towns of Maryville and Sevierville, while the women relaxed on quilts, chatting and laughing and tending to fussy infants. Children darted in and out of the mix, chasing each other in friendly games of tag. Courting couples strolled arm in arm in the distance, keen on a little privacy.

At six o'clock, the heat of the day lingered despite the puffed cotton clouds suspended in the cerulean sky. Not even a hint of a breeze stirred the air. Sophie's neck was damp beneath her braid, and she pictured her ma's honey-blond hair arranged in a sleek, efficient bun, a throwback to her childhood in a strict Knoxville orphanage. If Jeanine had lived, would she have taught Sophie how to arrange her hair the same way? She'd tried her hand at it, of course, but with disastrous results.

"Sophie?"

Kenny Thacker weaved through the tables to reach her.

"Hi, Kenny." She smiled at the skinny, pleasant young man who, because of their last names and the teacher's penchant for alphabetical seating, had occupied the seat beside her throughout school.

"The guys are arm wrestling out at the old stump." He gestured behind the church. "They sent me to ask if you're up to joining us."

She really shouldn't. However, she did get a kick out of showing up guys like her pa who thought girls were weaker and dumber than them.

"I think Preston wants a rematch. He can't accept that he was beaten by a girl." He grinned broadly.

Sophie debated. She sure wouldn't mind besting that arrogant Preston Williams a second time.

"Well, I—"

"Oh, hey, Nathan." Kenny nodded in greeting.

Turning her head, her wide gaze landed on her too-handsome-for-words neighbor. Wearing a charcoal-gray shirt that molded to his corded shoulders and broad chest, the deep color made his silver eyes glow and shorn hair gleam a richer brown. Black trousers emphasized his long, lean legs, and he wore a sharp-looking pair of black leather lace-up boots. Quiet confidence radiated from his stance, his square shoulders and straight spine, his determined jaw and the unspoken message in his expression that he could handle any challenge that came his way.

Nathan wasn't the showy type. Nor was he a man who

liked to be the center of attention. His appeal was his complete unawareness of his attractiveness, his obliviousness to the single young ladies' admiring glances.

Sophie hadn't heard his approach, but apparently he'd been there long enough to hear Kenny's question because his cool gaze was watching her closely, waiting for her response.

What will it be? his eyes seemed to challenge. *Will you do the proper thing, or will you give in to impulse and act the hoyden?*

Because she knew that no matter what she did she could not ultimately win his approval, Sophie was tempted to do it simply to irk him.

"I'm ready now, Nathan." Pauline Johnson approached with a goofy grin and a buoyant light in her eyes. The tall, curvaceous blonde, stunning in teal, sidled close to Nathan. "Oh, hello, Sophie. Kenny."

Sophie opened her mouth but couldn't find her voice. Her heart beat out a dull tattoo. They were clearly here together. On a date. When was the last time Nathan had squired a girl around? He wasn't interested in pursuing a relationship. Wasn't that what he always said whenever his brothers gave him a hard time about being single?

Seeing Pauline curl her hand around his forearm, Sophie felt physically ill.

"Just a minute." He barely allowed the blonde a glance, still obviously intent on Sophie's response to Kenny's summons.

Sophie glanced once more at the pie. It mocked her now. The foolish piece of her heart that refused to listen to reason, that still clung to the hope that one day he'd see her as an accomplished and attractive young woman worthy of his regard, withered and died.

Jerking her chin up, she determined he would never guess how deeply he'd wounded her. "Hello, Pauline," she said, forcing a brightness to her voice. *Please let it ring true.* "You're looking lovely this evening."

Her grin widened, cobalt eyes shining with humble gratitude. "You're kind to say so." She gestured over her shoulder to where the O'Malleys were gathering. "Will you be joining us?"

Us. As in Pauline and Nathan and his family.

"I'm afraid not." Not now, anyway. Her throat thickened with despair. *Admit it, you're jealous.* Ugh! The kicker was that she actually liked Pauline. The same age as Nathan, Pauline was not only beautiful but considerate, friendly, and one of the best sopranos in Gatlinburg. Folks loved it when she sang specials at church.

Smart, sensible and accomplished. Unlike Sophie, Pauline was perfect for Nathan.

The knowledge cut deep.

"I actually have other plans." To Kenny, she said, "Tell Preston I accept his challenge."

His eyes lit up. "Nice."

"Sophie—" Nathan growled.

Holding up a hand, she shot a pointed glance in Pauline's direction. "You should tend to your guest. Enjoy the picnic, Pauline."

Head high, she pivoted on her heel and called out to Kenny, "Wait up. I'll walk with you."

She left him standing there, bristling with disapproval. But she refused to let it sway her decision. Worrying about Nathan O'Malley's opinion of her was a complete waste of time.

Nathan wanted nothing more than to go after her. The young lady at his side prevented that. *Probably just as well. You're not Sophie Tanner's keeper. Distance, remember?*

"Nathan?"

Ripping his gaze from the duo's retreating forms, he

plastered a placating smile on his face. "Let's go join my family, shall we? Or we can sit with yours, if you'd rather."

It would spare him Josh and Kate's curiosity. The happily wedded couple had recently started hinting it was time he think about settling down. And, since this was the first time in months—possibly years—he'd escorted a girl anywhere, they were right to have questions.

Maybe that's why Sophie had seemed so shocked to see him with Pauline. Her face had gone as white as the clouds above—

"I'd prefer to visit with your family." The pretty blonde beamed at him, fingers clutching his sleeve a little too possessively. *Just your imagination.*

A long-time acquaintance, he'd chosen Pauline Johnson because she wasn't the type of girl to read too much into a single outing. Nor was she so romantically minded she'd be miffed at his last-minute invitation.

Leading her past the long tables sagging beneath the weight of the food, he guided her to a prime spot on a gentle knoll beneath the protective branches of a sweet gum. Josh was propped up against the trunk, lazily observing the crowd. Keen interest sparked in his expression the moment he spotted them.

Ma elbowed Pa in the ribs, nodding and smiling as if he'd given her a surprise gift. Great. He had a sinking suspicion this wasn't going to be as fun as he'd imagined.

"Pauline, how nice to see you." Ma gestured to an empty patchwork quilt next to theirs. "Have a seat."

He waited until she was seated, her crisp skirts arranged around her, to lower himself a good twenty-four inches away. Not because he was afraid of his reaction to her— he'd established with immense relief that she didn't affect him in any way, good or bad—but because he wanted no illusions to form in her mind or anyone else's.

Her cloying perfume wafted from her sleek blond mane and tickled his nose. He sneezed.

"God bless you."

"Thanks," he muttered, inconveniently recalling Sophie's natural, pleasing scent.

"How is your sister and her new husband getting along?" Mary asked. "Do they like living in Sevierville?"

Pauline's mouth formed a moue. "Laura's homesick. Ma wishes they'd move back here, especially before they start a family." She relaxed back on her hands, extended so that her fingertips nearly grazed his thigh. Was that on purpose? He shifted slightly to the right.

A scowl curled his lips. Maybe this wasn't such a good idea. After all, Sophie still dominated his thoughts and hadn't that been the point of this exercise? Distraction?

Mary nodded. "I can understand. I feel so blessed Josh and Kate settled here. I'll get to spend a lot of time doting on my first grandchild."

The conversation turned to babies. Nathan tried to stay focused, he really did, but an irritating little voice demanded to be heard. What if Sophie got herself into a fix? Those guys could play rough sometimes. What if she got hurt?

A cloud of aggravation lodged in his chest, expanding until he couldn't ignore it a second longer. He jumped to his feet, earning him the attention of everyone present. "I, ah, have to check on something. I'll hurry back."

His date's look of confusion, his ma's barely hidden consternation and Josh's amusement stayed with him as he traversed the field. He was going to regret this. He just knew it.

Chapter Six

Adrenaline fueled by deep distress gave Sophie the upper edge. The sight of Nathan and Pauline looking cozy branded into her brain, she bested David Thomas. And John Beadle. And Preston Williams.

Granted, David was fifteen and spindly. And John was too much of a gentleman to put forth much effort into beating her. Cocky Preston, on the other hand, had been a true challenge. If not for her heated reaction to Nathan's surprise date, she very well could've lost.

Grumbling his displeasure, Preston shoved his way through the spectators.

"Who's next, fellas?" Sophie taunted, feeling dangerous. In this moment, she didn't care one whit about being a lady or what anyone else thought of her. Nor did she heed the burning sensation in her forearm and biceps. She needed an outlet for the restless energy thrumming through her, the weighty disappointment clamping down on her lungs.

"Don't you think you've proved your point?"

Nathan. Why was she surprised? The underlying steel in his cool voice warned her she was on shaky ground, but she wasn't in the mood to heed it. Spinning, she clasped her hands behind her back and arched a challenging brow. "What point would that be?"

Boots planted wide, hands fisted at his sides, a muscle twitched in his rock-hard jaw. "Do you really wanna discuss this here?"

All around them, young men ceased their talking to stare.

"You started it." She jutted her chin at a stubborn angle.

"And I'll finish it." His nostrils flared. "Just not in front of an audience."

Snickers and whistles spread through the small gathering.

When he reached for her arm, she jerked away, feeling slightly panicked. What if he got her alone and her true feelings spilled out? She didn't trust her mental muzzle right now. "Wait, don't you wanna give it a go? Or are you afraid you might lose to a girl?"

Though his eyes glittered silver fire, his tone was gentle. "I wouldn't want to ever hurt you, Sophie."

She caught her breath. *You already have. You just don't realize it.*

"Later, guys." Striding past him, she walked in the opposite direction of the crowd, stopping beside a grouping of young Bradford pears. "So tell me, what was so important you felt it necessary to abandon your date?"

Folding his arms across his substantial chest, he glared at her. "Would you believe I was actually worried about you?"

When he caught sight of her surprise, he laughed derisively. "I know. Silly, huh? After all, you know exactly what you're doing, right? You can take care of yourself."

"Of course. In case you've forgotten, I've been doing that since I was a kid. I don't need looking after, Nathan. I'm not one of your cousins, nor am I your little sister."

"Oh, believe me, I'm quite aware of that fact." He ran a frustrated hand through his short hair.

Nathan and sarcasm didn't normally go hand in hand. What had him so steamed? This wasn't the first time she'd engaged in behavior he deemed unfitting for a young lady.

Annoyance stiffened her shoulders. "Why do you have such a problem with me arm wrestling? Last I heard, it wasn't illegal."

His eyes narrowed. "Sophie—" Exasperation shifted quickly into resignation, and he gave a quick, hard shake of his head. "No. I told myself I wasn't going to lecture you anymore. You're an adult capable of making your own decisions."

"That's right, I am," she huffed. "And just because you don't happen to agree with my decisions doesn't mean they're wrong."

"While I agree we have different opinions about things, you can't argue the fact that you're flaunting clear-cut societal rules. Look around you—" he waved an impatient hand "—do you see any other young women arm wrestling? Engaging in spitting contests or tug-of-war games? *Wrestling* with grown men?"

Sophie lowered her gaze to the grass beneath her boot soles. She'd done all he'd said and more at one time or another. Not only did she enjoy a little friendly competition, she felt more comfortable around the guys. They didn't judge her based on her appearance. Nor did they expect her to discuss the latest fashions and recipes or know how to quilt and then make fun of her when she didn't.

"You don't understand. You never have."

"There you are." Josh rounded the tree closest to them, his astute gaze bouncing between them. "Nathan, Pauline is wondering what happened to her escort."

His expression shuttered. "I'm coming."

Kate appeared a couple of steps behind, stylish in a

forest-green outfit that made her skin appear dewy fresh. Today, her chocolate-brown mane had been tamed in a simple twist. "Sophie, how are you?"

"Just swell."

"Nathan let me sample one of your sausages at lunch," she said, her smile encompassing the two of them, "and it hit the spot. Your recipe is delicious. I have to have it."

"Only one?" Josh winked at his wife. "Are you sure about that?"

Her cheeks pinked. "Well, maybe two. Or three. I wasn't able to eat much breakfast, so I had to make up for the lack."

Of their own accord, Sophie's eyes slid to Kate's midsection. Was that a slight bump? The dark material made it difficult to tell. When the happy couple announced last month that they were expecting, Sophie had wondered for the first time what it might be like to have a baby of her own. The prospect simultaneously intrigued and frightened the daylights out of her.

"The bacon didn't sit well with her," Josh explained.

"Maybe the baby doesn't like bacon," Sophie ventured, then blushed furiously when Nathan returned his attention to her. *What an absurd thing to say. Muzzle, remember?*

But Kate just laughed in delight and linked her arm through Sophie's. "I think you may be right, dear Sophie. Why don't you come sit with us? There's ample space."

"I wouldn't want to intrude." Just what she'd envisioned for today—observing Nathan's courting efforts up close.

"Nonsense." Kate waved off her resistance "You're practically family."

With a sinking stomach, Sophie allowed herself to be led to where the O'Malleys had gathered. As Pauline watched their approach, a tiny crease appeared between her fine brows. Of course, she had a right to wonder what had taken Nathan from her side. Her greeting smile held a hint of bravery, however, and she pulled him into the conversation with his parents with ease.

Sophie held back. Where to sit?

Kate pointed to Nathan's blanket. "There's space there, Sophie. We've loaded up extra plates of food, so help yourself."

Reluctantly she lowered herself on his other side, as close to the edge as possible without actually sitting on the grass. Although he was concentrating on Pauline's words, tension bracketed his mouth. Unlike all the times before when she'd joined the O'Malleys, she now felt like an intruder. An interloper. Oh, this was a nightmare! But she couldn't very well be rude and abandon Kate after she'd gone out of her way to include her, could she?

Grabbing a plate without taking stock of its contents, she ate quickly, not really tasting any one flavor. It could have been liver and onions, for all she noticed. Conversation swirled around her. Nathan shot her a couple of furtive glances, but he didn't speak directly to her. As if she wasn't worth talking to. That hurt.

They were just finishing up their meal when a shadow fell across their legs. Sophie lifted her head and promptly dropped her fork.

April Littleton, looking sweetly feminine in the flowing yellow dress she'd described in the mercantile yesterday, bore a plate between her hands as if it held the Queen of England's crown. The spiteful gleam in her eyes put Sophie on guard.

"Hello, Sophie." Her smile smacked of gloating superiority. "Nathan." She completely ignored Pauline.

"Hi, April." Nathan set aside his empty plate. "How have you been?"

"I've been a busy woman of late, I must admit. I made this dress especially for tonight. What do you think?"

"I, ah…" Clearly not expecting such a question, he

scrounged for an appropriate response. Shot Sophie a help-me look, which she ignored. What could she do but wait April out? "It's very nice."

April batted her lashes, cherry-red lips widening into a wolf-in-sheep's-clothing smile. "Why, you're kind to say so. This isn't all I've been busy making, though. This here is a special family recipe—my great-grandmother Bertha's delicious cinnamon-apple pie. I heard apple was your favorite, so I brought you a slice."

She extended the plate toward him, which he accepted with a slight nod.

"That's thoughtful of you, April. Thank you."

Of course he would be polite. He wouldn't embarrass *her* by correcting her. It smarted that he had no such reservations when it came to Sophie.

She stared at the plate, feeling slightly queasy. The slice closest to her was the apple. But what was the other one? Was it too much to hope it wasn't what she suspected it was?

She craned her neck to get a glimpse.

"I also brought you a piece of Sophie's pie," April tacked on with an innocent air. "I haven't tried it yet, but I sure am eager to see what it tastes like, aren't you?"

Chapter Seven

Something told him this already dismal outing was about to get worse. Much worse.

Beside him, Sophie fidgeted with nerves, tugging on the sleeves of her brown shirt, fiddling with the collar. And April's too-cheerful demeanor rang false. By now, Pauline and his family were watching the exchange with interest.

Shooting Sophie a quizzical glance, he kept his voice low. "I didn't realize you'd made a pie."

"It was a spur-of-the-moment decision."

One she regretted, judging by the way she was gnawing on her bottom lip, dread stalking her eyes. The pulse at the base of her slender throat jumped.

"What are you waiting for?" April's silken voice prompted.

"Right."

Dreading this almost as much as Sophie, he sank his fork into the fluffy layers of crust and soft apples and lifted it to his mouth. April hadn't exaggerated. The blend of sweet fruit and spices melted on his tongue.

"I can understand why your family has held on to this recipe. It's wonderful."

Pauline leaned forward. "I like apple, too. I wish you'd brought me one, April."

A flicker of annoyance dimmed her gloating pleasure, and she shot the blonde a look that suggested she get her own. "Now the rhubarb."

Sophie inhaled sharply, but he didn't look at her. Couldn't.

Best to get this over with as quickly as possible. The pie didn't look half bad, he mused as he forked a bite. Maybe Sophie would surprise them all.

Then again, maybe not.

The crust tasted doughy as if undercooked, and the rhubarb filling was so tart it made his jaw ache. He fought a grimace as he forced himself to chew quickly and swallow the offensive bite, blinking at the tears smarting his eyes.

"Drink," he choked out.

Kate slapped her tea jar into his outstretched hand and he drank long and deep. He thanked her and she nodded, a line of concern between her brows.

"It doesn't appear you enjoyed that very much." Arms crossed, April wore a smug expression.

Without warning, Sophie leaned close and, snagging the fork from his hand, scooped up a piece for herself. He watched her chew once, her eyes growing big, lashes blinking furiously as she choked. Behind him, his ma made a commiserating sound.

"I don't understand." Sophie shook her head in consternation, her thick, shimmering braid sliding over her shoulder. "I followed Ma's recipe very carefully. I did exactly what it said—"

When she clapped her hand over her mouth, he prompted, "What?"

"There was a smudge." She spoke without removing her hand, muffling her words. "A water stain, actually, right where she'd written the amount of sugar. So I guessed."

April's lip curled. "Don't you know baking is a science? You can't guess at it or else you'll have a disaster on your hands." Whirling around in a swish of skirts, she marched in the direction of the dessert table, waving her hands to get the attention of those within hearing distance. "Do not eat Sophie Tanner's rhubarb pie, folks! Not if you want to avoid a terrible stomachache." Scanning the table, she located the pie and deposited it into the nearest waste bin. People stopped and stared. When Nathan caught the triumphant smirk she shot over her shoulder in their direction, his blood burned white-hot.

There was movement beside him, the air stirring and with it the familiar scent of Sophie—dandelions and sunshine and innocence. He pulled back from his anger long enough to see her hurrying away.

"I'll go talk to her." Kate started to get up.

"No, I'll do it." He waved her off before getting to his feet. "But first, I'm going to have a word with Miss Littleton."

"Nathan, wait." Josh pushed up from the tree and laid a hand on his shoulder. "What's it going to look like if you go marching over there and yell at her? Look around, brother. Everyone's watching. I think it would be best if you focus on Sophie right now."

"She didn't deserve to be humiliated like that," he grumbled.

"No, she didn't," Josh agreed, questions swirling in his blue eyes as he studied him. "It's not like you to lose it. What's going on?"

"Nothing."

At least, nothing he could confess. Josh was right. Of the three brothers, he was the calm, controlled one. The quiet one. Some would even say shy.

But for weeks now he'd been wrestling with confusing reactions to a girl he'd always viewed as a pal, an unexpected and unwelcome awareness of her that frustrated him to no end. And his ability to contain that frustration was becoming less and less sure.

Josh squeezed his shoulder. "Whatever it is, you know you can talk to me anytime."

"I know." Slowly, he unclenched his hands. Took a calming breath. "I'd better go find her."

He took a single step, then remembered. With an inward wince, he turned back. "I'm sorry, Pauline, but I have to—"

With a tentative smile, she waved him on. "Go. Your friend needs you right now."

"Thanks for being understanding."

Feeling slightly guilty for neglecting his date, he started off in search of Sophie, wondering why his life had suddenly become messy. He didn't do messy. He preferred things clear-cut. Straightforward. No surprises.

The problem was that Sophie was synonymous with unpredictability. She blurred his thinking. Knocked him off-kilter. He didn't like that.

He used to be able to ignore it or to simply brush her off, but…they weren't kids anymore. Things had changed without him wanting or expecting them to. And if he was going to reclaim any sense of normalcy, of balance, he was going to have to put some distance between them.

Right after he made certain she was okay.

He hadn't gone far when he spotted her boots swinging from a limb.

Of course she'd be up in a tree. It was her favorite place to go when she craved space. Too bad he wasn't going to give it to her. Not yet.

A fleeting glance was her only acknowledgment of his presence. Her features were tight as she stared straight ahead. No tears for Sophie.

Since they weren't within eyesight of the church, he grabbed hold of a low-slung branch and proceeded to climb up, settling on a thick limb opposite her. How long had it been since he'd done this? Years?

"I'm not in the mood for a lecture, Nathan. If that's why you're here, you can just climb back down and leave me in peace."

A green, leafy curtain blocked the outside world. His left boot wedged against the trunk and one hand balanced on the branch supporting him, he shook his head. "I'm not here to lecture you. I'm done with that."

Disbelief skittered across her face. He didn't blame her for doubting him. He'd made reprimanding her into a profession. "Besides, you didn't do anything wrong."

She frowned. "Didn't I? My pride is the reason I was just humiliated in front of the entire town. I let April's superior attitude get to me." A fuzzy black-and-orange caterpillar crawled over her hand, and she touched a gentle finger to it. "I was trying to prove a point. I proved one, all right."

Nathan hated the defeat in her voice. "It takes guts to try something new."

She was silent a long time, her attention on the caterpillar in her cupped hands. Her legs slowed their swinging. "Do you remember when we used to play in the treetops? You, me and Caleb?"

"How could I forget?" They'd made up all sorts of adventures for themselves.

Her lips twisted in a wistful sort of smile. "I liked playing pirates most of all. Caleb was the big, bad pirate, I was the damsel in distress and you…" Her eyes speared his as her words trailed off.

"I was always the hero, swooping in to rescue you," he finished for her, lost in her sapphire eyes full of memories and mystery.

"Yes." Lowering her gaze, she released the caterpillar onto the branch to go on his merry way. "Sometimes I miss those days."

Resisting the pull she had over him, he spoke gruffly. "Things change. *We've* changed. Don't you think it's time you stopped climbing trees, Sophie? Stop living in the past? Put our childhood behind us?"

For a split second he glimpsed the hurt his words—said and unsaid—inflicted. Then she jerked her chin up and glared at him.

"No, I don't. I like climbing trees, and I don't see any reason to stop. I'll probably still be doing it when I'm old and gray. With any luck, you won't be around to scold me."

And with that, she hurried down and stormed off. Left him there feeling like an idiot.

Today was a new day.

Sitting in a church pew with his family listening to the reverend's opening remarks, Nathan was confident he'd made the right decision. Lounging in that tree long after she'd gone, he'd determined that what he and Sophie needed was some space. As he'd reminded her last night, they weren't kids anymore. Maybe that was their error—assuming things could stay the same. He feared if they continued in this manner, one of them—more than likely *him*—was bound to say or to do something so damaging, so incredibly hurtful, their friendship wouldn't survive. He would hate that.

He had to be careful to make his distance seem natural, though. The very last thing he wanted was to hurt her. He would curtail his visits, and if she questioned him he could blame it on his heavy workload. She was busy, too. This would work.

No sooner had the thought firmed in his mind than the rear doors banged open. The reverend faltered, and the congregation turned as one to see who was behind the interruption. When he first saw her, disapproval pulsed through him. Not only was Sophie late, she'd made an entrance no one could ignore.

But then her panicked expression registered, and as she rushed to whisper in Doc's ear, Nathan grabbed his Bible and, pushing to his feet, hurried down the aisle toward her, his decision forgotten, uncaring what anyone else thought.

Something was wrong with Tobias.

As much as Nathan's immediate reaction of censure chafed, Sophie dismissed it. The disturbance couldn't be helped. Granddad was fading fast, and she didn't care if she had to interrupt the President of the United States himself if it meant getting help.

Gray hair flittering in the breeze, Doc ushered her outside and down the church steps. "Are you able to ride your horse or would you prefer to ride in my buggy?"

She knew she looked affright, her hair pulled back in a disheveled ponytail and her breathing coming in ragged puffs. "I'll take my horse."

With a curt nod, the middle-aged doctor settled his hat on his head and strode for his buggy parked near the church entrance.

"I'm coming with you."

Sophie jumped at the sound of Nathan's gravelly voice right behind her. She spun around, ready to tell him not to bother, only to falter at the disquiet darkening his silver eyes to gunmetal gray. He was offering her support. Something she desperately needed right now, even if she was irritated with him.

Admit it, you don't want to be alone if this truly is the end.

She cleared her throat, barely holding the tears at bay. "Fine."

Dropping his Stetson on his head, he strode to his horse

and, securing his Bible in the saddlebag, mounted up. They rode hard and fast through town and along the country lane leading to her place, arriving right behind the doctor. Will, who'd stayed behind, burst through the door, his small face pinched with fright.

Sliding to the ground, she dropped the reins and grasped his shoulders. "Will?"

"I'm scared, sis," he whispered, burrowing his face in her middle.

Her chest constricting, she wrapped her arms around his thin frame and held him close. The flimsy piece of string restraining her hair had broken free during the jolting ride and now her hair spilled over her shoulders, shielding her face. Good. Nathan wouldn't be able to see how close she was to losing it, the grief and fear surely written across her features.

He stood very close to them, almost touching, the strength emanating from his tall frame surrounding them like a tangible force. When she lifted her head, she risked a glance his direction, afraid he'd see through all her flimsy defenses and realize she wasn't as strong as she pretended to be. That she was, in fact, weak. Vulnerable. Fragile.

However, his eyes were closed and his lips moving. With a start, she realized he was praying. For her and Will and Granddad. While she knew Nathan's faith was solid and very important to him, he was a private man. She'd heard him pray a handful of times over a meal but this was personal. This was him petitioning God for her sake.

Her heart swelled, her love for this man burrowing so deep that she suspected she'd never be able to uproot it.

Movement in the doorway caught her attention.

"He's asking for you."

The finality in Doc's voice washed over her like a bucket of icy water and, despite the midmorning heat, goose bumps raced along her skin and she shuddered. With an arm around Will, she forced her feet to move, to lead them both inside.

Memories of another death slammed into her. It was as if she was eight again, fear and dread clawing in her chest as she walked into this very room to say goodbye to her ma. To place a kiss against her cool, colorless cheek. Granddad had been right there to hold her, to comfort her.

Why God? Why must I say goodbye? I'm not ready!

They hesitated in the entrance. Will trembled beneath her arm, and she hugged him closer, attempting to instill comfort with her touch.

Tobias's eyes fluttered open and he lifted a finger. "Come...closer, children."

Needing to be near him, Sophie eased down on the bed and took his withered hand in hers, clinging with as much pressure as she dared. Will stationed himself beside the bedside table, eyes huge in his face, hands clamped behind his back.

In the back of her mind, she registered Sam and Mary's voices mingling with those of Doc Owens and Nathan's in the living room.

"I love you both." Tobias dragged his gaze from Will's face to hers. His tired eyes exuded calm assurance. Acceptance. "And I'm proud of you."

"I love you, too, Granddad," Will murmured, sniffling.

Tears blurred her vision. Stroking his hand, she leaned down and kissed his sunken cheek. "You know how much I love you. How much I need you. Please, don't leave us." Her voice cracked.

God, help me. I can't do this.

"You'll be fine," he rasped, "just fine. The Lord's calling me home, Sophie." He was quiet a long moment, his lids sliding shut. "I wanna see my Anne."

Will stood solemnly staring down at him. Sophie held on to Tobias's hand, her fingers stroking back and forth.

The hushed voices in the other room filtered in but she couldn't make out the conversation. Tobias's jagged breathing sounded harsh in the stillness.

They remained that way for a long while. Half an hour, at least. Maybe longer. Sophie spent the time praying, her gaze trained on her granddad's face, memorizing the beloved features. Without warning, his chest stopped rising. His fingers went slack.

"Granddad?" She rested her head on his chest, but there was no heartbeat. "No. No!"

Tears coursed unchecked down her face. She couldn't breathe. The edge of her vision faded to black. Where was that heart-wrenching wailing coming from?

And then, suddenly, strong arms were lifting her up, cradling her. Murmuring softly, Nathan carried her away. She wasn't aware of where he was taking her. Eyes shut, she buried her face in his chest and let the tears flow. There was no hiding from him now. And right this minute, it no longer mattered.

Her granddad was gone, and she was all alone in the world.

Chapter Eight

Sophie gradually became aware of Nathan's slowed footsteps, of him lowering them both onto a fallen log out of the direct sunlight. The stream was nearby. She couldn't see it, but she heard the steady rush of water above her heart thwacking against her rib cage.

He held her securely, his arms looped around her waist and his chest solid and warm beneath her cheek.

"I'm sorry, Sophie," he whispered, his lips brushing the curve of her ear. "So sorry."

Sniffling, she lifted her head to gaze up at him, belatedly realizing her hands were still clasped behind his neck. She didn't remove them because she was caught by the sorrow mirrored in his eyes like dense fog cloaking the forest floor.

Granddad had been fond of Nathan, and she knew Nathan had reciprocated the feelings. He was hurting, too.

When a fresh wave of grief washed over her, she didn't try to mask her emotions. Here and now, in the shelter of his embrace, she felt free to be transparent. "What are Will and I going to do without him?" She sounded raw and broken. "We don't have anyone left."

His brows pulled together. Gently smoothing her hair

away from her face, he wiped the moisture from her cheeks with a tenderness that stunned her. "You have me. And my parents. My entire family." His gruff vow lent her an odd sense of comfort. "Whatever you need, we'll be here for you."

Watching Sophie's expressive features, Nathan floundered at the hopelessness brimming in her sad eyes. A fierce swell of protectiveness coursed through him and, more than anything, he wished he could shield her from this hurt.

He smoothed the long golden hair tumbling down her back, his fingers threading through the silken strands. Once again, the smell of dandelions filled his senses, and he had the insane urge to bury his face in the mass. With her hair unbound, her cheeks dewy and eyelashes damp from tears, she was purity and beauty and enticing vulnerability.

This was Sophie Tanner without her barriers, open and accessible to him. A rare and precious gift...a moment he'd cherish for the rest of his days, despite the fact their futures lay down different paths.

She must've seen the shift in his expression, the clanging shut of an emotional doorway, for she stiffened in his arms. Her gaze skittering away, she released his neck and popped up, turning her back on him. "I'm sorry for getting your shirt all wet."

Regret intertwined with relief. Had he so easily forgotten the decision he'd made to gain perspective where she was concerned?

He stood and dislodged the bits of dirt from his pant legs. "It'll dry soon enough."

"I should go back." She straightened her spine and pivoted back. Sunlight sifted through the leaves to make patterns on her navy shirt and set her hair to shimmering like a golden halo. "Will needs me."

"He's with my parents right now. Are you sure you don't want to stay here awhile longer?" He didn't think seeing Tobias again so soon would help. Better to wait until Doc prepared him for burial.

Her lower lip trembled even as a tiny flame of resolve flickered in her eyes. "I have to be strong for him, Nathan. I remember how I felt after Ma died, and I don't want him to worry about anything."

The reappearance of the I-can-do-it-all-by-myself Sophie sparked irrational anger low in his gut. When she made to walk past him, he sidestepped to block her path.

"And what about you?" he blurted, hating that once again she was left to bear the weight of responsibility. "Who's going to be strong for you?"

"Y-you've already offered to help," she stammered, "but if you've changed your mind…"

"I'm not talking about the farm, Sophie." He gentled his voice. "I'm asking who are you going to allow close enough to share your worries? Your fears? Your dreams? Who are *you* going to depend on?"

She looked as if he'd struck her. "Are you offering to be that person, Nathan?"

He froze. All the reasons why that would be an unwise choice, the risk such an undertaking would pose to their friendship, robbing him of coherent thought.

Her expression shuttered. "I didn't think so."

Pushing past him, she jogged along the bank. He watched her go, feeling like an unfeeling cad for upsetting her when all he'd really wanted was to lessen her pain.

The funeral passed in a blur. A sea of black-clad mourners shed quiet tears, conversed in hushed voices, faces drawn. Somehow Sophie made it through without breaking down as she was tempted to do, the entreaty "Help me, Lord Jesus" an unending refrain in her head. The knowledge that many of these people were praying for her and Will brought her a measure of peace. Still, the ache lodged in her chest refused to budge. Her gruff yet tenderhearted granddad was gone for good.

Try to keep it together a couple more hours, Sophia Lorraine. The folks mingling outside her cabin, eating the bounty Mary and a number of neighbor ladies had supplied, wouldn't stay forever.

Despite the crowd and their sincere sympathy, Sophie felt adrift. Alone. Not to mention strangely conspicuous in a frothy black concoction—Kate's thoughtfulness knew no bounds—that Sophie was certain made her resemble a harried crow. While the bodice and waist fit okay, the skirt was three inches too short and her clunky work boots peeked out from beneath the lace-trimmed hem. She wasn't sure if the furtive glances sent her way were on account of her loss or the unusual sight of her in a dress.

Pausing on the small square stoop, she searched for Will. Last night—their first without Granddad—had been rough. She'd held him as he'd cried himself to sleep long after his usual bedtime, soothing him when he woke calling for Granddad. She picked at the lacy wrist cuffs. How was he coping with all this?

Her gaze snagged on Nathan. Tall and dashing in an all-black suit that lent him city-flair, he stood with Josh and Kate, as well as barbershop owner Tom Leighton and Gatlinburg's sheriff, Shane Timmons. He'd hovered nearby ever since yesterday afternoon—she hadn't allowed herself to relive what had transpired between them—grim and withdrawn and looking like he'd lost his best friend.

Pauline was here, too, but it didn't appear as if they were together. Not if her frequent, pining glances in his direction were anything to go by. She really was quite beautiful. Her sleek blond hair shined bright and golden beneath the black veiled hat angled on her head, her black shirtwaist and skirt making her appear even taller and more statuesque than usual. Kindness, pure and unadulterated, radiated from her being.

Pauline Johnson wouldn't be caught dead arm wrestling with a bunch of rowdy men.

Sophie felt as if a dull knife had carved out her insides. This was the type of girl Nathan would admire, one he'd be willing to give up his bachelorhood for. One he deserved.

How long had Nathan harbored an interest in her? she wondered. Her midsection cramped. Was he— Had he decided to get married? And if so, how soon? How would she survive? It was one thing to accept he would never desire her, but to actually witness him pledging his life to another woman…to see them as husband and wife… starting a family…

Nathan shifted his weight and glanced her way, a ripple of regret crossing his face as his gaze intersected hers. Regret for what? Tobias? Their closeness yesterday? Their charged exchange?

The arrival of an unfamiliar carriage diverted her attention.

Nathan immediately separated himself from the group and strode over. "You expecting company?"

"No."

Conversation fell away as the driver halted the team, jumped down and, swinging open the door, assisted a fashionable lady down the carriage steps.

A well-cut plum ensemble fit her top-heavy figure like a glove and atop her brown curls a riot of black feathers bounced and bobbed with every tilt of her head. An uglier headpiece Sophie had never witnessed. As the newcomer peered haughtily around, the cucumber-thin nose, high cheekbones and pursed mouth nudged Sophie's memories and she gasped.

"Aunt Cordelia!"

"Your father's sister?"

"I had no idea she was coming." What had it been, four or five years since she'd visited?

Shaking herself out of her stupor, Sophie descended the steps and approached, aware that Nathan had stayed behind and foolishly wishing he had accompanied her. Cordelia was an intimidating woman. At least, she had seemed so to Sophie when she was younger.

Cordelia studied her with cool appraisal. "Sophia?"

"Hello, Aunt," she greeted cautiously, noting the fine lines radiating from her pinched upper lip and the streaks of silver webbed through her dark hair. "I didn't realize you were planning a visit. I'm afraid you've come—" *Too late.* Clearing her throat, she plunged ahead, "Granddad is gone. H-he passed away yesterday afternoon."

Cordelia's only response was a further compression of her lips, until they practically disappeared from her face. No surprise there. Sophie hadn't expected an overt display of emotion. After all, Cordelia had left Gatlinburg shortly after her eighteenth birthday and hadn't kept in close contact with her father or brother. Nor had she seemed to care about her orphaned niece and nephew. Sophie recalled her aunt's visit shortly after her ma's passing, how stern and forbidding she'd been, like a beady-eyed bat in her black mourning clothes. She hadn't held Will even once.

Where Sophie's pa had been all fiery temper, Cordelia was as cold as ice.

Twisting slightly, Cordelia addressed the driver awaiting her instructions beside the team. "Wait here for me. I won't be long." Returning her steel-blue gaze to Sophie, she stated, "You and I have some things to discuss. Shall we do it here in front of the entire town or in private?"

Things? What things? A sense of foreboding tightened her midsection. "We can go inside."

Ignoring folks' expressions of recognition, Cordelia

swept across the yard with single-minded purpose. Sophie followed a few paces behind, shaking her head at Nathan's uplifted brow asking, Do you want me to come with you? Since she didn't know what to expect, she'd rather he didn't witness this.

Thankfully, the handful of people in the living room cleared out as they entered.

"Would you care for a cup of coffee?" Sophie's quick retreat to the kitchen was hampered by her skirts. The stiff collar scratched the sensitive skin along her collarbone, and the bodice was given to twisting so that she was continually straightening it. What she wouldn't give for her comfortable pants right about now.

"I've reached my quota for the day. We stopped for lunch at the little café on Main Street before coming here. Not a horrible place," Cordelia allowed, lowering herself onto the worn sofa. Posture ramrod-straight, she let her sharp gaze roam over the cabin's interior, no doubt finding it lacking.

Too bad, Sophie thought. It was *her* home, and she liked it just fine.

Sophie went to sit on the opposite end of the sofa, hands folded in her lap.

"How was your trip?" She attempted politeness.

"Incredibly long." She sniffed. "Dusty and with enough bumps I no doubt will be covered in bruises by the morrow."

"That bad, huh?"

Cordelia angled toward her. "Where is Will?"

The question threw her. "I—I'm not exactly sure. He's probably with his friends down by the stream."

One pencil-thin brow lifted. "You should keep better tabs on the boy, Sophia. He should not be allowed to roam freely and do whatever he likes."

"He's ten," she said in defense. "Plenty old enough to be out of my sight."

"That may be the case here in the wilds, but not in civilized society."

The wilds where she herself grew up? Sophie bit off a retort.

"Will has a good head on his shoulders. I trust him not to make foolhardy decisions."

"You will understand why such a reassurance coming from you does not impress me. Do you think I'm unaware of your impulsive, unladylike behavior, Sophia Lorraine Tanner?" Her nostrils flared in distaste. "I may not reside here, but Father kept me abreast of all your exploits."

Her fingers curled into fists. Where was she going with this?

"Father wrote to me several weeks ago when he first became ill. He was concerned about your future. If something were to happen to him, he asked if I would be willing to do my duty by the two of you."

Sophie stilled. "What exactly does that mean?"

"I've come to take you and Will back to Knoxville to live with me," she stated with finality, as if they had no say in their future. She flicked a dismissive glance around. "From the looks of things, it shouldn't take long to pack."

"Will and I aren't going anywhere." Defiance laced with a tiny frisson of anxiety burned her throat. How dare she? "This is our home."

Just then, the door banged open and thudded off the log wall behind it. She and Cordelia quickly rose to their feet.

"It wasn't my fault, Sophie! Robbie pushed me first." A rumpled, sopping wet Will skidded to a stop in front of her, his mouth falling open when he spied their aunt.

Nathan entered behind him, wearing an apologetic expression. "I tried to stop him from interrupting your chat, but he slipped past me."

Why, oh why, did her brother have to pick today of all days to get into trouble? She braced her hands on her hips. "What happened?"

"We got into an argument. He said something bad about Pa." Gaze downcast, he scuffed the floor with his shoe. "It made me really mad, so I said something about his pa. He pushed me."

"They both ended up in the water." Hands on his hips, the sides of his suit jacket dislodged to show off his impressive physique, Nathan let his gaze slide between the two women.

"See what happens when you allow a child too much freedom?" Cordelia huffed. "Perhaps I was wrong in leaving Father to raise you. Things will have to change once we've returned to the city." She glared at Will. "Fighting will not be tolerated, young man. And you, Sophia, will learn to comport yourself like a lady. I daresay once we've smoothed out your rough edges, it won't take us long to find you a suitable husband."

Will tugged on Sophie's sleeve. "What is she talking about?"

Nathan dropped his hands and scowled. "What's going on, Sophie?"

She opened her mouth to speak, but Cordelia answered for her.

"Simple. Sophia and Will are moving to Knoxville."

Chapter Nine

"I won't go!" Will backed toward the door, a trail of water in his wake. "You can't make me!"

"Will—" Sophie reached out to him, but he dashed through the open door before she could utter another word. Aching for her brother, she rounded on the other woman. "How dare you waltz in here today of all days and upset him further? If you knew anything about raising children, you'd know not to dump news like that on an unsuspecting child." She didn't realize she was trembling until Nathan, standing behind her, settled comforting hands on her shoulders in silent support, lightly kneading her rigid muscles. "And let's get something straight right here and now—this is our home. We have no intention of ever leaving it. You've wasted your time."

A fine film of frost glossed Cordelia's blue eyes. "I disagree." She tilted her head at a condescending angle, the obnoxious black feathers bobbing above one brow. "This has given me an opportunity to see my father was right in contacting me. You've reached the age of maturity, which means I can't force you to come with me. However, Will has many more formative years ahead of him, and it's perfectly clear he needs discipline and guidance that you are either unwilling or unable to provide. Stay here if you wish, Sophia, but Will is coming with me."

"He's *my* brother!" Outrage pulsing through her veins, Sophie jammed a thumb against her chest. "I've been taking care of him since he was a baby. You can't take him away from me."

Cordelia didn't flinch in the face of her outburst. "Think about it. What judge is going to award guardianship to you instead of me? I'm comfortably settled in a fine house with the funds to see to his every need. He'll go to a well-appointed school with boys his own age where he'll learn proper manners as well as how to curb the cursed Tanner wild streak."

Sophie's stomach dropped to her toes. Cordelia was right. No judge would ever choose her—an eighteen-year-old struggling to make ends meet—over someone like her aunt. Cordelia's husband, Lawrence Jackson, had been a state representative and the two of them had been well-connected, well-liked fixtures in Knoxville society. Upon his death three years earlier, he'd left a small fortune to his wife.

Sophie couldn't compete with that.

Behind her, Nathan shifted, bringing his enveloping heat closer. His chest brushed against her back. His fingers stopped their kneading, but he didn't relinquish his hold on her. Sophie relished the sense of solidarity the connection gave her.

"Now is not the time for such a weighty discussion." He leveled his words at her aunt. "We're all attempting to deal with Tobias's death. Emotions are running high, and we're exhausted. I think it would be best if we postpone it until a later time."

"Who are you?" Cordelia looked stunned he would interfere.

"I'm Nathan O'Malley, Sophie's neighbor and good

friend." He leaned forward and extended one hand, which she reluctantly shook. "My family and I watch out for her and Will."

The older woman studied him, apparently heeding the undercurrent of warning in his voice.

"Fine. Since Gatlinburg still doesn't have a hotel to speak of, I'm going to let a room from the Lamberts. I will give you until tomorrow afternoon to think on what I've said, but I won't postpone my return much longer than that, so be prepared to give me your decision. You can come with us or remain here alone. It's up to you."

The door snapped shut and, for a moment, neither spoke. Then Sophie spun in his arms, clutched at his shirtfront. "Nathan, what am I going to do?" She stared up at him, willing him to make this nightmare disappear. "I can't lose him. I can't."

Losing Granddad had carved deep fissures in her lonely heart. Losing Will would break it clean in two. What kind of life could she have here without him?

He covered her hands with his own. "You're not going to lose him."

"How can you be so sure?"

"Will belongs with you." His noble features radiated a confidence she didn't share. "Once everyone's had a good rest and a chance to clear their heads, we'll talk to her. I'm certain we can make her see reason."

Panic spiraled upward. "And what if we can't? What if—"

"Sophie." He ducked down so that they were eye level, his gaze blazing into hers. "I'm not going to let her take Will, I promise."

There was a rap on the door. Josh poked his head in. "Most everyone is heading home."

Releasing her, Nathan swiveled to face his brother.

Josh walked in, nervously fingering his goatee, his gaze bouncing between them. "Is everything all right?"

"I don't mind if you tell him," she told Nathan, suddenly needing to find Will, to hold him tight. "I'm going to go talk to my brother."

She was on the stoop when Nathan called out, "It will be okay, Soph."

Glancing back over her shoulder at him, so grave with purpose, she nodded. But deep down, she wasn't sure she believed him.

Sophie found Will perched on a flat rock, chin resting on his knees pulled up to his chest, staring morosely at the water coursing past. His damp hair spilled onto his forehead, nearly obscuring his eyes. So sad. And lonely. Her heart twisted with regret.

God, why is this happening? Why did You take Granddad? We needed him, Father. And now Aunt Cordelia is threatening to tear us apart.

Jumping up at her approach, he jutted his chin in a familiar display of stubbornness. "I won't go with her. You can't make me. I'll run away if you try." Beneath the defiance lurked a desperation that matched her own.

Run away? "Will, I don't want you to go anywhere without me," she exclaimed. "No matter what happens, you and I will be together. I promise you that." A promise she would move heaven and earth to keep.

"But Aunt Cordelia said…" He faltered, clearly confused.

"We've agreed to table the discussion until later. She's tired from traveling and we…well, we've had a rough few days."

He dropped his arms to his sides. "I don't want to leave my friends or the O'Malleys. You're going to make sure we stay here, aren't you?"

Staying together? Definitely. Staying *here?* She wasn't so sure about that.

A seed of an idea sprouted in her mind.

"Sophie?"

She brushed the hair out of his eyes. "Leave everything to me, okay? You don't have to worry about a thing."

At the sight of his younger brother perched on a stool milking Bessie, Nathan stopped short and balanced a hand against the wooden stall post.

"When did you get home?"

Caleb hitched a shoulder without turning around or halting the rhythmic movement of his hands. "Not long ago. Where is everybody?"

"You'd know the answer to that if you stuck around any length of time," he snapped, not in the mood to coddle him. Sophie's problems weighed heavily on his mind. He'd waited around until everyone had left, thinking she'd return with Will. She hadn't. And with suppertime fast approaching, he'd had to come home to tend his cows.

Caleb shot a dark look over his shoulder.

Nathan huffed a weary breath. "Tobias passed away yesterday afternoon. The funeral was today."

Caleb's hands stilled. Shifting slightly, he pulled his lips into a frown. "How is Sophie?"

Nathan pushed off the post. "Again, something you'd know if you'd been around." Irate now, he stalked to the corner and washed his hands, filled a pail with clean water and settled himself in the stall opposite Caleb's. After washing Star's utters, he attempted to lose the tension cramping his back and shoulders. He didn't want it transferring to the cow.

"Nathan?" Caleb growled.

"How do you think she's doing? She just lost her grandfather." And to add insult to injury, she was dealing with a tyrannical aunt bent on wreaking havoc.

"What's gotten into you?" his brother demanded.

Jolting to his feet, he ignored the tipped stool and Star moving restlessly behind him. "I'm tired of shouldering your share of the weight around here. Of seeing Ma's disappointment when you don't show for yet another supper and Pa's unease when you don't come home for days on end. Josh and Kate are expecting a baby. You're going to be an uncle for the first time." He glared at Caleb, who was standing with boots braced apart in the straw, fists clenched and knuckles white. "What if something happened while you were gone and we had no way to reach you? How would you feel if you came home and discovered one of us had been hurt or worse?"

He blanched. "That's why I stay away," Caleb stormed. "To protect you all from my carelessness. To prevent any more accidents."

Nathan stared. Accidents. He was referring to the accident that had scarred him and nearly cost his best friend his life. And the more recent one last fall. The wagon he'd been driving had overturned during a thunderstorm, and their ma had suffered a broken leg. Apparently he still blamed himself.

"You honestly think you can protect us, keep us safe, by keeping your distance? You're not God, Caleb."

"*I* did this." He sneered, jabbing a finger to the jagged lines near his eye. "Because I was irresponsible and cocky. Adam almost died because of me."

"But he didn't. And you didn't. Because God deemed it so. He's the one who has the ultimate say in our lives."

He shook his head, his shaggy black hair scraping his shirt collar. "You don't get it."

Crossing the center aisle into the stall, he stuck his face near Caleb's. "No, *you* don't get it. Sophie needs me right now, and I aim to be there for her. In order to do that, I need for you to stick around and help out around here. Got it?"

His younger brother's heavy lids flared at this uncharacteristic display, the loss of control. "Fine. I'll stick close to home until things settle down."

It wasn't exactly the response he'd been looking for, but it was enough. For now.

"Good."

Shoving his hands through his hair, he returned to his stool and sat down hard.

Focus, O'Malley. Sophie and Will need you to be cool and levelheaded. Calm. Controlled. Acting rashly will not solve this mess.

He'd promised to make things right. Disappointing her was not an option.

As soon as the cows were milked, Nathan returned to Sophie's to check on her. He couldn't stop thinking about the moment Tobias died. Her gut-wrenching cries. The sorrow draining the light right out of her. He couldn't forget how he hadn't hesitated, hadn't even blinked before going to her, taking her in his arms and comforting her and the overwhelming protectiveness he'd felt. Still felt.

It was what was propelling him back there.

Sophie and Will were alone in that cabin, surrounded by painful reminders and facing an uncertain future. He owed it to her—as her friend and neighbor—to help in any way possible.

Dismounting Chance, he let the reins drop to the ground. The cabin door stood slightly ajar, and through the opening he witnessed a blur of movement. He placed a flat palm on the wood and eased it back.

"Sophie?"

Looking harried, she whirled from her spot in the

kitchen, her eyes a touch wild. Like a deer sensing a predator.

"Wh-what are you doing here?"

He took in the half-packed saddlebag open on the sofa and the dislodged dishes on the shelf above the stove. His gut clenched.

Removing his hat, he advanced into the room and lobbed it onto the scarred tabletop. Settling his hands on his hips, he surveyed her men's apparel. The odd-fitting black dress had been exchanged for her usual attire—dark pants, dark shirt and boots.

"Going somewhere?"

Hand trembling, she smoothed errant wisps away from her face.

Crooking his finger, he gently lifted her chin so that she had to look him in the eyes. "Hey, you can be straight with me."

She swallowed hard. "We're leaving town."

It was as he'd suspected. Frustrated with the situation and her utter lack of forethought, he let his hand fall to his side. "You're running away."

Her eyes pleaded with him to understand her point of view. "It's the only option. I won't let her take Will. And we're not going to Knoxville. Neither of us would be happy living with her."

He blew out a breath. *Be calm. Remember her loss, the panic that's clouding her thinking.* "Where will you go? Where will you live? It takes money to start over."

And they both knew she didn't have those kinds of resources.

Disquiet pulled her pale brows together. He pressed his case. "You don't want to end up lost in these mountains without shelter or food or protection. That wouldn't be doing what's best for Will."

She wrung her hands. "What do you expect me to do? Sit back and let her ruin our lives?"

"Of course not," he soothed, that protective instinct surging to the surface, obscuring the dawning horror the idea of her and her brother traipsing unprotected through the countryside spawned. Taking her shoulders, he guided her to sit in one of the hard-backed chairs situated around the table and then set the water to boil.

He sat across from her. "What we need is a solid plan of action. A practical solution that will allow you to stay while satisfying your aunt at the same time."

Doubt tugged her mouth into a frown. "Like what?"

He fisted his hands to prevent them from reaching over and covering hers, small and tight with tension. Gone was her usual confidence, the sparkle of determination in her big eyes. Tobias's death and her aunt's threats had stolen her inner fire. She appeared as fragile as fine china, easily breakable, with shadows beneath her eyes and her skin ashen.

"I don't know yet," he admitted. "But I'm certain if we take our time and examine the situation from all angles, we can come up with something foolproof."

"Staying here is risky."

"Riskier than running off?"

Although it didn't seem possible, she went paler.

Leaning forward, he gave in to the urge to touch her, taking her hands in his and stroking the petal-soft skin with his thumbs. "Give me some time to come up with a plan. At least until tomorrow morning."

"What happens if I don't like your plan? What then?"

"Then we'll come up with a new one. One you can live with."

She sagged in her seat, clearly unconvinced.

"I'm going to make you some tea," he said, going to the stove, "and then I'm going to go home and think this through." Kettle aloft, he turned and looked at her, tempted to camp out on her doorstep. "Can I trust you to stay here?"

Slowly, begrudgingly, she nodded. "I'll be here."

"Good."

He knew then he'd do just about anything to drive that stark fear from her eyes, to rekindle her inner flame, to make her smile again.

Chapter Ten

He'd failed her. All through the night, he'd tossed and turned, prayed and plotted and…nothing. Not one single good idea. No solid plan of action. Not even a hint of one. A situation that had him doubting himself and, if he were honest, just a little depressed. He was supposed to come through for her. He had the rescuer bit down pat, didn't he?

That he'd failed in this, her most desperate time of need, troubled him deep down in his soul.

He wasn't ready to wave the white flag of surrender, however. Hope yet lingered. What they needed was more time. Somehow he had to convince Cordelia to give them an extra day or two. Then he'd gather his family members and, together, they'd come up with an answer to Sophie's problem.

His knock was quickly answered by Will, who didn't grin or welcome him with his typical eagerness. "Hey, Nathan."

"Hey." Moving past him, he summoned a smile for the kid. "Catch any more crawdads recently?"

"Nope."

Nathan sought out Sophie, who was standing by the kitchen table appearing much more collected this morning, her hair neat and smooth and a hint of color in her cheeks. Her expression, however, was somber as she watched her brother. Picking up a plate laden with glazed round cakes, she offered, "How about you join us for some tea cakes and milk, Will? Mrs. Greene brought them from the café."

"Maybe later." He frowned and grabbed his hat off the wall hook. "I'll be in the barn for a while."

After he'd gone, Sophie lowered the plate. Sighing, she extended her hand to the chair opposite. "Have a seat. Can I get you milk? Coffee?"

"Coffee, please."

Lowering himself into the chair, he hooked his hat on the back and pushed a hand through his hair, watching as she filled the kettle and stoked the oven fire, her braid swinging side to side with each twist and turn. She really was a dainty thing. No doubt he could span her waist with his hands. She wasn't skinny, though. Sturdy and well-made with feminine curves in all the right places.

Stop right there, O'Malley.

Forcing his gaze elsewhere, he wondered why he couldn't be fascinated by Pauline's appearance. Or some other acceptable young lady. Why was his mind turning traitor of late? Such a waste of energy.

Sophie Tanner was his polar opposite. If he was what was considered a rule-follower, then she was a rule-bender. He saw the world in black and white; she, a riotous rainbow of color. He preferred the sidelines and she naturally attracted attention wherever she went. While he tended to proceed with caution, she rushed headlong into situations without thinking them through.

It was enough to drive him mad.

By the time she placed two steaming mugs of rich-bodied coffee on the table, he had his thoughts back on track. Sophie smoothed a white cloth napkin in her lap and offered him first pick of the tea cakes. "I hope that studied frown means you've come up with a plan."

He sipped the hot brew, wishing he didn't have to disappoint her. "Not exactly."

Her fingers worried the mug's handle. "What does that mean?"

"We need more time."

Storm clouds brewed in her eyes. "You don't have a plan, do you?"

With deep regret, he shook his head. Her reaction was what he'd expected. A growing sense of despondency twisted her features. Her posture dipped.

"What am I going to do?" she whispered through colorless lips.

"We'll think of something." *Lord, let it be so.*

"But what?" Pushing away from the table, she began to pace. "Cordelia doesn't exactly strike me as the patient type. What if she refuses to wait?"

"We'll involve the sheriff. She can't kidnap your brother. These things take time."

"She's wealthy, Nathan. Wealth equals power. I don't doubt she could take him anytime she likes and get away with it. Like she said, she holds all the cards. A lifetime of care is nothing compared to what she can give him."

"Do you think she's the type to forcibly remove him?"

"I honestly don't know."

The sorrow haunting her expression tore at him. "Come and sit down, Soph. Let's figure this out together."

Surprisingly, she sat without argument. Deflated. Defeated.

He pushed the plate toward her. "Eat. The sugar will do you good."

Again, she did as he suggested, nibbling on the round cake, seemingly a million miles away.

"Let's review the facts. Surely if we think this through

and look at all the angles, we'll come up with a solution. Two heads are better than one, right?"

"I suppose so."

"Your aunt's main concern is that Will isn't getting the guidance she thinks he needs. How can we convince her otherwise?"

"Discipline. You forgot discipline." Her eyes flashed defiantly.

"Okay. Guidance and discipline. Besides from a guardian, namely you, where would a ten-year-old boy get those things?"

"His schoolteacher?"

He nodded. "And the reverend."

"We could ask them to speak with her." She brightened, brushing crumbs from her lap. "They could assure her what a good kid he is."

"Will that be enough?"

"There's Mr. Moore, the mercantile owner. And your father."

All good suggestions. Would their assurances sway Cordelia's opinion?

"I think," he said slowly, finger tracing the indentions in the wood, "that having a permanent male influence in his life would be the best way to reassure her that Will was receiving steady, hands-on supervision."

He didn't mind accepting the responsibility. He and Will already spent a lot of time together. Though it would mean a tighter schedule, he could fit in at least an hour a day with the boy. Or perhaps Will could spend afternoons at his place, helping out around the farm, learning from Nathan, a stand-in father figure.

The more he thought about it, the better it sounded. They'd both benefit. He relaxed against the chair back. At last, a solution.

* * *

"You're brilliant!" Sophie suddenly exclaimed, an ecstatic smile chasing away her gloom like sunshine after a rainstorm.

His brows met over his nose. He hadn't shared his conclusions with her. "I am?"

"Why did I ever doubt you?" Shoving upright, she bounded around the table and planted a kiss right on his cheek. "A husband is exactly what I need!"

"A *what?*"

She playfully batted his shoulder. "Don't go acting all humble. You're right, if I marry, she won't have any objections to him staying with me. And even if she did pursue legal action, a judge would be far less likely to take Will away from two loving guardians. Oh, thank you, Nathan. I could kiss you right now!"

He absently rubbed his tingling cheek. "You already did."

"Oh, right." Soft pink color surged. She resumed her pacing, and he could practically see the wheels turning.

Her leap of logic left him reeling. Husband? For Sophie? That wasn't what he'd meant at all. The thought of her as someone's wife…well, he just couldn't fathom it.

"Ah, Sophie—"

"I'm not exactly marriage material, though. The men around here see me as a pal. A buddy, not a potential wife."

Sidetracked, bothered by this negative view of herself, he responded, "The only reason those men don't have romantic inclinations toward you is because of the way you dress. If you were to fix yourself up and maybe wear a dress once in a while, I guarantee they'd have their eyes opened real fast."

She chewed on her lower lip. "You really think so?" she murmured doubtfully.

He could've kicked himself. *You're supposed to be dis-*

couraging her from this ridiculous notion of marriage, not stoking the fire.

"I don't own any dresses, but your cousin Nicole is an excellent seamstress. Maybe she would agree to make some for me in exchange for my services. I could do her chores for a week or maybe she likes sausages?"

"Sophie, wait. I didn't mean—"

"I know!" She halted midstride. "We'll make a list of eligible bachelors. A list of decent, upstanding men whom I wouldn't mind marrying and who might not be averse to marrying me." Scanning the kitchen, she said, "Now where did I stash my pen and paper?" She snapped her fingers. "Right. Upstairs. I'll be right back."

Nathan's tongue stuck to the roof of his mouth. Nonplussed, he watched her disappear up the ladder. How could an innocent suggestion blow up in his face? His plan was so much easier. A mentor for Will. And yet here she was making a list—an actual list—of potential husbands.

Typical Sophie. Seize on an idea and run with it without giving it proper consideration. Woe to the unsuspecting males in this town!

When she sat across from him and began her list, he braced his forearms on the edge of the table and clasped his hands. "You misunderstood me."

His quiet yet forceful words brought her head up, forehead bunched in confusion.

"I wasn't suggesting you marry. I was actually thinking of taking Will under my wing. You know, spend more time with him here and at my place, teaching him things."

"Oh." Her lips puckered. "I thought… My mistake." Her gaze bounced around the room before finally zeroing in on him once more. Her chin came up. "A husband is a good idea, though. Better than your idea. Spending an extra hour or two with Will isn't going to be enough."

"That may be so, but are you certain this is the right

choice? This is a life-long commitment you're talking about. Marriage isn't something to be taken lightly."

"Don't look at me like that."

"Like what?"

"Like I'm an irrational child." Hurt flashed in her eyes. "I realize the seriousness of the situation. Otherwise, I wouldn't be considering hitching myself to some random man. But after Granddad... Let's just say I'm willing to do almost anything to keep my family intact."

"I don't want you to do something you'll regret. This is big, Soph. Huge. One of the most important decisions you'll ever make." He didn't want to cause her pain, but he had to make her see reason. "You don't want to end up like your ma, do you?"

She jerked as if slapped. "I will never end up like her. You want to know why?" Slamming her palm flat on the table, she leaned forward, sapphire eyes smoldering. "I'm not afraid to stick up for myself. And for my loved ones. I would never, ever, allow any man to treat me like my pa did her."

Sighing, he nodded. "I believe you." *But will you be happy?*

Frowning, not entirely satisfied, she returned to her list and began to tick off the candidates. A restless, unsettled feeling lodged in his chest. Every man she named was a man he knew, and it was strange to imagine Sophie with any one of them. He felt as if he was perched on the back of a bucking bull, moments away from being tossed to the ground and trampled.

"What about Tom Leighton?"

"My guess is he's not ready," he muttered. "He proposed to Megan last month, and she turned him down, remember?"

She didn't look up. "Right."

"I have to go." He finished off his coffee, unwilling to

help her with this wild scheme. While he may have inadvertently pointed her to this conclusion, he couldn't sit there and assist in a husband hunt.

That got her attention. "Now?"

Scooting his chair back, he smashed his hat onto his head. "I have to get out to the cornfields."

"Will you come back this afternoon? I'd feel better if you were here to help me explain this to Cordelia."

"Yeah. Sure."

"I have a good feeling about this plan." She smiled tentatively. "I know it isn't exactly what you'd envisioned, but I'm confident it will work."

Inexplicably cranky, he edged toward the door, eager for escape. "Right. I hope so."

"I'll be working on the list." She waved a hand over the paper. "Hopefully, I'll have it ready by the time you get back, and you can share your opinion on my choices."

"Fine. Bye."

Seizing the reins, he practically vaulted into the saddle, startling Chance. "Sorry about that, boy," he murmured, patting the horse's flank. "Let's get out of here before I lose my mind."

Looking refreshed and elegant in an ice-blue outfit, Cordelia sat stiffly in a rocking chair, hands curled around a matching reticule in her lap. She glanced from Sophie to Nathan, seated together on the sofa opposite. "You're getting married?" she repeated. "I hadn't realized the two of you were courting."

Nathan stiffened. The grave expression he'd arrived with darkened into something forbidding.

"You misunderstand, Mrs. Jackson. Sophie and I are friends. We don't see each other in a romantic light."

Hearing him voice his feelings in such a final, offhanded manner was like a dagger plunging deep into Sophie's heart. He didn't want her. Would never consider putting his name on her list.

When Cordelia's penetrating gaze rested on Sophie, she schooled her features. No one could know her secret.

"Who, then, are you planning to marry, young lady?"

Nathan answered for her. "There are many single, eligible men in this town. Sophie is considering her options."

Turning her head, Sophie studied his granitelike profile. Was that a hint of censure in his voice? His silver gaze flashed to hers and then away, but not before she glimpsed...what? Disappointment? In her?

"Let me get this straight." The grooves in Cordelia's forehead deepened. "You aren't currently being courted by anyone. Instead, you're compiling a list of men you'd like to marry?"

"A husband hunt," Nathan muttered with a slight shake of his head.

Sophie attempted to rein in her irritation. Whose side was he on, anyway?

Resisting the urge to toy with her braid, she pressed her hands together and addressed her aunt with what she hoped was calm assurance. "Will and I belong together. Here, in our home. I'm willing to do whatever it takes to make that happen. If that means I must find myself a husband, so be it."

Admiration flickered, but was quickly squelched. "I admit I don't know quite what to make of your scheme." Rising gracefully, crisp skirts rustling against the coffee table, Cordelia crossed to the window and stared out at the sun-washed yard.

Gaudy blue feathers spilling from her hat shivered over her forehead. What was she thinking? Did this place hold any good memories for her? Granddad had told Sophie that her pa, Lester, had taken pleasure in tormenting his younger sister.

"I believe the right male influence would do you both good," she said at last. Pivoting, she clasped her gloved hands at her waist. "However, the pool of potential husbands here must surely be limited to lonely, uneducated farmers or widowers with babies who want you for a substitute mother. In Knoxville, you can have your pick of men who would set you up in high style. Lawyers. Doctors. Business owners. With a good education, Will could go far in life. Why won't you at least consider it?"

Cordelia's frank curiosity, the absence of dictatorial attitude, caught her by surprise. For the first time since her aunt's arrival twenty-four hours ago, Sophie thought beyond her current predicament and wondered what was driving the other woman. Why would she bother with them? Was it simply to exercise her authority or something else altogether?

Twisting slightly in her seat, she met her aunt's steady appraisal. "I do appreciate your willingness to aid us, Aunt, but this is the only home we've ever known. We don't need prestigious schools or clothes or well-to-do friends to make us happy. Simple pleasures are enough for us. This is the life we want."

"I think you're being stubborn," she retorted, staring down her nose. "And foolish."

"I'm being honest."

Nathan unfolded his tall frame, his tanned hands curved at his sides and his turbulent gaze trained on her as he addressed her aunt. "Sophie doesn't have a shallow bone in her body. She knows what's truly important in life, things like family and friendship and a personal relationship with God. I've never met a more hardworking, tenderhearted person. Tobias was very proud of the young woman she's become. I know because he told me shortly before he died."

Sophie's breath caught in her chest, her heart melting like butter in a frying pan at the unexpected praise. She closed her eyes to ward off tears. *Oh, Granddad. I wish you were here. I wish I could hug you one more time. Tell you I love you.*

Cordelia's boots clicked against the floorboards.

Opening her eyes, Sophie saw the older woman motioning for Nathan to resume his seat. "Sit down, young man. There's no need to get feisty."

Her expression assessing, she studied them in a way that made Sophie uncomfortable. What was going on behind that eaglelike gaze?

When she had their attention once more, Cordelia said, "Have you given any thought to how long it will take to find a suitable husband? You should know I'm not willing to stay here indefinitely. We need a time limit. Three weeks should be plenty."

"Three weeks?" Sophie gaped.

"That's unreasonable." Nathan ran a weary hand down his face.

"I'll give you a month, no more. Though what I'm going to find to fill the time, I've no idea." Cordelia hefted a sigh and rolled her eyes.

"One month." She was expected to find a husband that quickly? Panic roiled through her stomach. What if none of the men on her list agreed to marry her?

"If you haven't managed to snag a husband by then, Sophia Tanner, your brother will be returning to Knoxville with me. Do you understand?"

"Unfortunately, I understand quite clearly."

She understood too well that she no longer had any control over her own life. A week ago, her biggest problems had been convincing Will to wear shoes outdoors and building a new henhouse. Now she was being forced to find a husband—not the husband she'd dared to let herself dream about but someone else altogether.

And while she could take another man's name and pledge to honor him the rest of her life, how in the world was she going to convince her heart to stop loving Nathan?

Chapter Eleven

Nathan didn't normally attend singles' shindigs. Without parental supervision, the girls were bolder than usual—a situation that didn't bother most guys in the slightest—and the games were silly. All too often the losers were expected to pay a forfeit. Something embarrassing such as reciting a poem or singing a solo. Not his style.

He wasn't in the market for a wife, nor was he the type to enjoy a shallow flirtation, so why bother coming? He'd have more fun camped out on his front porch whittling or playing checkers with his pa.

And yet here he was, stationed beside the fireplace in his cousin Megan's parlor sipping stout make-your-eyes-water lemonade and trying to avoid Amberly Catron's flirtatious gaze.

The moment he'd stepped through the door, she'd rushed up and invited him to walk the gardens with her; an invitation he'd declined with as much finesse as he could muster. A romantic, moonlit stroll through isolated gardens with a girl who had obvious designs on him would not be in his best interest, he was certain.

He shifted his stance to glance at Sophie, taking perverse pleasure in the way her lips pursed after a sip of lemonade. It was only fair she suffer along with him. "I can't believe I let you talk me into this."

She leaned in close, bringing with her the fresh, appealing scent that put him in mind of spring meadows in full bloom. "I need your input on my list of choices because you know these men better than I do. I trust your judgment."

Light from the chandelier candles above highlighted the golden streaks in her sleek blond hair. The memory of holding her in his arms resurfaced, reminding him of how wonderful it had felt to hold her. With her glorious hair framing her face, her delicate beauty had stunned him into speechlessness.

"After all—" her brow puckered "—I'll have to live with the man for the rest of my life."

Nathan tore his gaze from her to glare down at his boots. *Forget what happened. She was in need of comfort and you gave her that. You're here to help her choose a husband.*

Firming his resolve, he observed the game participants with her list in mind. Seated in front of a white sheet suspended from the ceiling, a man attempted to guess the identity of each person's shadow as they passed behind it. Landon Greene.

"Take Landon off the list." A hefty dose of charm and wit hid what Nathan knew to be a bullying, mean-spirited heart.

Sophie's curious gaze fell on the arrogant blond. "Why? He's well-liked. Funny. And from all accounts, a hard worker. His family's farm is productive and the animals are well cared for."

Reluctant to go into details, he speared her with a look. "I thought you said you trusted me."

Her brows lifted. "I do, but—"

"I'm here to help you, aren't I? How about Frank Walters?" He indicated the short, nondescript man trying to blend into the wallpaper. Although reserved, he was an intelligent, prudent man. And Nathan was confident he would treat Sophie well. If he was expected to play a part in this mad scheme, he would make certain she chose wisely.

She wrinkled her nose. "I don't know."

"You put him on the list, didn't you?"

Running a finger inside the collar of her forest-green shirt, she hedged, "Now that I think about it, I can't really picture myself with him. He's nice and all, but he's not exactly the type to inspire romantic notions."

Romantic notions? "Since when do you care about that?"

Sophie and romance didn't belong in the same sentence. She wasn't anything like his cousins, who fussed over their hair and clothes and sighed over popular romance heroes. His friend didn't concern herself with such things.

She averted her face to set her unfinished lemonade on a side table. Slipping her hands into her pants' pockets, she observed the room's occupants.

"You know what I mean," she remarked with studied carelessness. "There are some people you can see yourself with in a romantic relationship, while others simply don't appeal to you in that way."

"I suppose."

She angled toward him. "Does Pauline appeal to you in that way?"

The question stumped him, as did the husky note of vulnerability in her voice. "Pauline and I are friends," he grumbled with finality. He was not about to discuss this with her.

"Only friends? You don't have more serious intentions?" Her sapphire orbs glittered with an odd light. "Because as far as I can tell, she's perfect for you."

Why such a statement should irk him, he had no idea.

A dull throb set up behind his eyes. "We're here to focus on your love life, not mine."

The gathering erupted into high-pitched whistles and clapping. April emerged from behind the sheet looking like a cat with a bowl of cream. Landon, who must've finally guessed correctly, surged out of his seat and received a fair share of hearty claps on the back.

"What forfeit shall he pay?" someone demanded.

Wearing a smug smile, Landon raised his hands to curtail the suggestions. "Since I'm the one who made the right guess, I should name the forfeit." Holding out his arm, he wiggled his eyebrows. "How about a stroll in the gardens, Miss Littleton?"

"I'd love to." Eyelashes fluttering, she placed her hand on his arm and, together, the pair made their way to the exit amid suggestive laughter.

Nathan scowled. Surely Sophie didn't think Landon romantic?

Sophie tracked Landon and April's progress until they disappeared into the hallway, his blond-haired perfection set off by her dark hair and olive skin. They looked entirely too chummy for her peace of mind. Perhaps Nathan was right to ask—make that demand—that she remove the gentleman's name from her list. There was a self-important air about him, a look in his gorgeous eyes that led her to believe he was very aware of his attributes and how he affected women.

Still, it annoyed her that Nathan refused to explain himself, instead expected her to follow his directions without question.

Spying his identical twin cousins, Jessica and Jane, in the arched doorway, she decided to let it slide for the time being.

Nearly sixteen, the girls were lovely in both appearance and manner, their auburn hair similar to oldest sister Juliana's and blue eyes the same shape and hue as Megan's, the second eldest. Sophie and the girls were somewhat close in age, and the twins had occupied the seats in front of her and Kenny at school. They'd been unfailingly kind to her. Since completing her final term a year ago this past spring, she'd missed visiting with them. Oh, she saw them at church every weekend and occasionally at Nathan's place, but it wasn't the same.

Jessica, the more outgoing and spontaneous of the two, spotted them and waved, her heart-shaped face radiating her excitement. She nudged her sister and nodded in their direction. Jane's reaction was more reserved but no less sincere, her smile widening in genuine pleasure.

"The twins are here," she told Nathan, who was staring into his drink as if it held the answers to all his problems.

His brows lowered. "Aren't they a little young for this sort of thing?"

"Their birthday is in two weeks," she pointed out. "Besides, it appears your aunt Alice approved or they wouldn't have come."

As they made their way across the polished wood floor, their upswept curls shone coppery in the candlelight. Jessica wore a scoop-necked, sea-blue shirtwaist with cap sleeves and dainty silk bows adorning the skirt's hemline. Jane had chosen a more simple look—a holly-green, short-sleeved dress with a single row of pearl buttons on the bodice. The O'Malley girls were always dressed to impress due to middle sister Nicole's talent with a needle and thread.

Sophie became ultra-aware of her appearance, feeling drab and unattractive in her black pants and unadorned button-down shirt, the unsophisticated style of her hair and her lack of polish. How could she hope to snag any man's attention? Even if she was able to choose an acceptable candidate, what was the likelihood the man in question would be interested? Serious doubts wormed their way into her mind, doubts that she could pull this off, that she could keep Will with her.

She must have made some sort of noise, because Nathan's warm fingers grazed her elbow. "Soph?" His intent gaze probed hers.

"I'm fine." She drummed up a smile for her friends. "Hey, girls, I wasn't expecting to see you here."

Jessica gave her a quick hug. "We convinced Mama to let us come with Nicole." She motioned over her shoulder to their raven-haired sister staring moodily around, elegant in all black and easily the most beautiful girl in attendance. Her sourpuss attitude marred her features, however.

Jane took Sophie's hands in hers, expressive eyes brimming with compassion. "How are you holding up?"

Sophie fought the sorrow that reared up, the empty hole her granddad's passing had created threatening to swallow her whole. "I'm okay." That wasn't the case, of course, but she wasn't about to risk a meltdown here in front of everyone.

Nathan frowned.

She looked away, unable to bear his concern.

"Have you heard from Megan recently?" Sophie's voice was thick as she sought to change the subject. "How are she and Lucian enjoying their wedding trip?"

"We received a letter just the other day," Jane said, smiling gently, "and she wrote that they are enjoying their time in New Orleans so much that they are extending their stay another week."

"I'm glad. It's generous of them to allow us to use their house while they're away."

The stately yellow Victorian had belonged to Lucian Beaumont's late grandfather, Charles Newman, who, along with Megan, had opened it up for the community's use. Every Friday afternoon, Megan hosted story time for the local children. And once a month people met here for poetry night, musical recitals and plays. Fred and Madge Calhoun were in charge of the property until the couple returned home.

"Time for Blind Man's Bluff." Tanner Norton waved a bunch of white strips above his head. "Who's in?"

"I thought only one person played the role of the blind man," Jessica commented.

Sophie rolled her eyes. "Tanner is forever changing up the rules. Says it makes things more interesting."

As he passed out the blindfolds, the twins voiced their interest. "Let's play."

While Sophie didn't normally mind joining in the games—they were harmless fun—tonight she had an agenda. "I don't think so."

Jessica linked her arm through Sophie's. "You have to play! This is our first time at a single's party and we want to have fun."

Oh, what harm could one game do? "All right."

"Wonderful. Tanner, over here!" Extending her hand, Jessica caught his attention and snagged three strips, handing one to her sister and one to Sophie.

Jane looked at Nathan. "You're playing, too, right?"

Leaning against the wall, arms folded across his chest, corded forearms visible beneath the rolled-up sleeves, he surveyed the proceedings with indifference. "No, thanks," he drawled. "You girls go ahead. I'll watch."

"You aren't intimidated by an innocent little game, are you?" Sophie couldn't help prodding him, irritated when he refused to loosen up and try new things.

He turned those intense silver eyes on her and she felt their searing heat to the tips of her toes. Boy, was he in a mood tonight. A mood that had started, if she recalled correctly, the day she'd come up with the marriage idea. What she wouldn't give to get inside that complicated brain of his to see for herself what he was thinking!

"Intimidated? No. Bored out of my mind is more like it."

Tanner stood in the center of the room and made a slow circle. "Everyone split up and put on your blindfolds."

The twins moved away to stand beside the refreshment table before putting theirs on. With a shrug, Sophie tied the cloth around her eyes. Folded into layers, the material completely masked her vision.

"You all know the drill," Tanner said. "When you bump into someone, try to guess their identity. The first one to guess correctly gets to remove their blindfold. The other person must move on and continue playing. The last person left wearing their blindfold is the loser.

"Ready? Hold up. Nathan, I'm the only one who gets to be without a blindfold as I'm the overseer. You either play the game or leave the room."

Quiet filled the space. Then Sophie felt the air stirring as he passed her, his spicy aftershave teasing her nose. His boots thudded on the hardwood floor as he left. Disappointment rattled through her. Why couldn't he at least give it a try? He deserved a little fun now and then. A little laughter.

Tanner gave the signal to start and immediately the quiet gave way to muted laughter. Putting her hands out in front of her, she trudged along so that she wouldn't trip and crash into someone or something.

The first person she encountered was definitely a female, one who smelled of vanilla and cinnamon and whose hair was coarse and straight. But who was it? As she moved around the room, she realized she was at a disadvantage because of her braided hair.

The chuckles and conversation increased in volume as more and more people unmasked. Sophie got the sinking feeling that she was the last one in the game. Then male hands curved around her upper arms and her mind went blank.

Unlike the other guys who'd guessed her identity, this one's touch was confident and sure. She got a sense of his towering height, the muscular bulk of his torso blocking the light and the slow-burning heat his body emitted. Slowly, his hands moved upward, lightly skimming her shoulders until they encountered her neck. The slide of his work-roughened fingers against her sensitive skin discharged sparks along her nerve endings from shoulders to fingertips. Her ears tingled. Her stomach flip-flopped.

Only one man's nearness had ever affected her this way.

She whipped off her mask without a word, forcing his hands to drop. "I thought you weren't playing," she accused.

The sight of Nathan in the blindfold, his lean face partially obscured and the muscle jumping in his square jaw screaming his discomfiture, squeezed her heart. He looked miserable. And...vulnerable. He really did hate to be the center of attention.

Glancing around, she noticed everyone else had their blindfolds off. They were all staring. At them.

"Uh, Nathan, you can take it off now."

He did. And then he noticed their audience. Dull red crept up his neck.

Tanner pointed. "Nathan's the loser. What forfeit shall he pay, folks?"

Nathan stood stone-still, fingers curled into fists, waiting for the verdict like a man condemned.

Sophie hurt for her friend. She'd been wrong. This wasn't his idea of fun. She didn't mind the attention; she was used to it. But Nathan *despised* it. *Please don't let it be a poem. Or worse, a song.*

"A kiss!"

"Yeah, make him kiss Sophie!"

Horror filled her as Nathan jerked as if slapped. He kept his gaze glued to the floor, refusing to look at her.

"Good call," Tanner agreed with a laugh. "You heard them, O'Malley. Get to it."

Finally he lifted his head and looked at her. His eyes blazing an apology, his mouth pulled into a grimace as he stepped close. He looked ill.

No, no, no. This couldn't be happening. As many times as she'd dreamed about this moment, she'd give anything if she could rewind time and insist on sitting this one out. Nathan didn't want to kiss her. He *dreaded* it.

She stood immobile, afraid to blink, afraid to breathe as he dipped his head. What would it be like? His sculpted, generous mouth neared hers. The crowd faded to the edge of her vision, the furniture faded to black and it was just her and Nathan, breaths mingling, her heartbeat loud in her ears.

At the last second his mouth veered away and landed on her cheek. Warm and fleeting, like the brush of a butterfly's wings. And then gone.

Someone gasped.

"I don't blame him," she heard an unidentified male mutter. "I wouldn't wanna kiss a tomboy like her, either."

You're not gonna cry. You can't. Not here, not now. Not in front of him. He can't know....

She blinked rapidly. Struggled to drag air into her lungs. To remain upright. Humiliation rushed through her like a raging river, crashing over her again and again until she thought she might drown in it. All the taunts, the dismissive glances and the gossip couldn't compare to what Nathan had just done.

Chapter Twelve

What had he done?

The devastation darkening her eyes to storm-tossed blue kicked him in the sternum. He'd embarrassed her. Hurt her. All because he didn't trust his ability to hold himself aloof.

Admit it, you're scared you might actually like *kissing Sophie. What then?*

Amused titters pierced his self-recrimination. Anger pounded at his temples, anger at the insensitive clods who dared laugh and make unkind remarks in her presence and at himself for inciting their reactions in the first place.

So do something about it.

Soaking in Sophie's pallor, the trembling of her lower lip and the moisture clinging to her eyelashes, he made the decision. There was only one way to make this right.

Reaching up, he framed her face with his hands. Hmm. He'd been up close and personal with her countless times—usually in the heat of an argument—but it had never occurred to him that her skin would have the texture of a rose petal.

Her gaze shot to his. Confusion furrowed her forehead. Her bee-stung lips parted in surprise, snagging his attention.

As the reality of what he was about to do sank in, his heart bucked in anticipation.

He tipped his head. Settled his mouth against hers. He felt a shudder course through her, vaguely registering when she gripped his waist for balance. The room spun. He felt dizzy and out of control, yet somehow grounded at the same time, Sophie acting as his magnet, preventing him from flying apart. Her softness, her sweet sigh of surrender awakened unfamiliar emotions. The need to protect her was nothing new, but there was something else here he didn't recognize, something needy and wishful, something he was too much of a coward to analyze.

This is Sophie, remember? Too young and too headstrong. All wrong for you.

With great reluctance, he lifted his head and dropped his hands. For the first time in his life, he was grateful to be the center of attention. Because if not for their audience, he would have taken the embrace to a whole new level and that would have been a mistake. One of massive proportions.

He watched as Sophie touched her fingers to her mouth, wonder and longing mingling on her face. Then hot color surged in her cheeks. "I—I have to go." Pivoting on her heel, she rushed from the room. The front door slammed. Conversation erupted....

Nathan stood rooted to the spot, attempting to process her reaction. The twins appeared in front of him, mirror images of wide-eyed concern.

Jessica touched his arm. "Nathan, what was that? You and Sophie looked—"

"Don't say it," he warned. He didn't want to know. He could pretty well imagine, and it was as much of a shock to him as it must be to those who knew him. Knew *them*.

"She seemed really upset." Jane gave him a steady stare. "Aren't you going to go after her?"

He jerked a nod. "Don't be out too late, okay?"

Ignoring the stares as he passed by, he grabbed his hat from the entrance hallway table and let himself out, all the while scouring his brain for something to say that wouldn't make him sound like an idiot. But what? "I'm sorry I was such a jerk?" or "That kiss knocked me for a loop. Can we try it again?"

He groaned. "You're an adult, O'Malley," he muttered to himself, "how about you act like one instead of a hormonal teen?"

Main Street was deserted at this time of night, the shops were closed and a single light was shining in the jail's window. As he neared the Little Pigeon River, the balmy air stirred with the scent of churning water, the sound as familiar to his ears as his cows bawling or the hush of a scythe cutting through tall grass.

When his boot contacted with the wide wooden bridge spanning the river, a shadowed form poised near the railing turned. Smothered a gasp. A flash of pale hair as she took off divulged her identity.

"Sophie, wait!"

She wasn't running from him, exactly, but going fast enough to spike his heart rate. He caught up to her in the lane. With endless forest on either side, it was impossible to make out her expression. Neither of them had thought to bring a lamp, but then, they knew these parts like the backs of their hands.

"Soph, stop." He seized her wrist. "We need to talk."

"What do you want?" The distress roughening her voice gave him pause.

"Look, I'm sorry about what happened back there. It wasn't my intention to embarrass you." Not being able to see her, to read her body language, frustrated him. She was a formless outline, as insubstantial as the shadows cloaking them.

She jerked out of his grasp. "What did you think would happen after that pity kiss?"

"What?"

"Don't tell me you would've kissed Pauline Johnson on the cheek! Or April Littleton. Or any of those other girls!"

He closed his eyes. "I was trying to be a gentleman."

"No, Nathan. You're forgetting I saw your face right before—" The defeat in her voice had him imagining he could see the fight drain out of her. "You were rushing to my rescue yet again. That kiss was designed to silence the barbs. I'm just sorry doing your perceived duty was so abhorrent to you."

Abhorrent, ha! If she only knew. "Hold on a second." He moved in, his boots bumping hers. "Why does it matter so much *why* I kissed you?"

She inhaled sharply. "Y-you're right, it doesn't matter." Her boots shuffled in the dirt, her braid whacking his chest as she turned to go. "This conversation is over."

"We're not finished here, Soph."

"Oh, yes, we are."

She stalked off. There was nothing he could do to stop her—short of physically restraining her—and while he was tempted, it would only make her madder and less inclined to talk. It went against the grain to leave things unresolved, but at this point he didn't have a choice. Better to give her a chance to calm down.

Once they'd both regained proper perspective, they could put this event behind them and go back to the way things used to be.

Somehow Sophie summoned the wherewithal to smile and pretend all was right in her world in front of Sam and Mary O'Malley. While she waited for her brother to gather his things, she answered their questions about the party with surprising equanimity. If they noticed her fidgeting or her frequent glances out the window, they didn't let on.

The older couple were dear, special people, including her in their family gatherings as if she were one of them, going out of their way to lend a hand whenever she had a need. Leaving them behind would rip a hole in her heart similar to the one her granddad's passing had carved. It would hurt Will, too.

Which is why you have to put Nathan out of your mind and concentrate on finding yourself a husband.

She managed to hustle Will out of there before Nathan arrived, listening with half an ear during their walk home as he told her about his evening.

Only when absolutely certain he was asleep did she allow her composure to slip. Sinking onto the couch, she curled up on her side, yanked the quilt over her face and let the hot tears of self-recrimination fall.

You are a first-class fool, Sophia Lorraine. He will never want you for more than a friend. He will never love you.

The memory of his kiss taunted her. The anger he'd clearly felt at being forced into that position had melded into awful resolve, those unusual eyes of his glittering and hard as he bent his head to hers. So his careful handling of her had come as a complete shock. The gentleness in his hands, the soft pressure of his mouth… Sophie's world had gone topsy-turvy and she'd had to grab on to him to keep from falling.

Oh, Father, how am I supposed to marry another man when Nathan possesses my heart?

Helplessness and frustration swamped her. *Why are You allowing all this to happen, God? Why did You take Grand-dad away? Why aren't You doing something to stop Cordelia? It's in Your power to intervene…. Why don't You?*

She lay there until there were no more tears left to cry,

until she was too spent and weak to get up and change into her nightclothes. Lids heavy, head aching, she closed her eyes and had nearly drifted off to sleep when a verse from *Proverbs* she'd memorized as a child came to mind.

Trust in the Lord with all your heart, and lean not on your own understanding; in all your ways acknowledge Him, and He will make your paths straight.

Sophie understood that God was in control, and that He had a plan for her life. Sometimes, though, it was hard to trust. Hard not to try to take matters into her own hands. Hard to wait.

Help me, Father. I don't know what to do or which way to turn.

Slipping into a fitful sleep, she tossed and turned until the wee hours of the morning before finally settling down. Persistent knocking some time later jolted her upright. Shoving her mussed hair out of her eyes, she gasped when she noticed midmorning sunlight streaming through the window.

Will sat calmly at the kitchen table, eating his breakfast.

Throwing off the covers, she demanded, "Why didn't you wake me? And what are you eating?" She'd fixed his breakfast every morning since the day he was born. The boy didn't know how to cook.

Sipping his milk, he held up a cinnamon roll. "Miss Mary sent these home with me last night." His chin rose. "And I'm not a little kid anymore. I can get my own breakfast."

She quickly folded the quilt into a neat square. "But the chores—"

"I already fed the chickens and gathered the eggs. I can help out around here, Sophie. Together, we can keep the farm going."

This from her ten-year-old brother? "I know you're worried—"

Another rap on the door startled her. "Please don't let that be Aunt Cordelia," she muttered. Finding Sophie still abed at this hour and Will fending for himself would underscore Cordelia's concern. Give her ammunition to use if this went to court.

"Just a minute!" she called, smoothing her hair and straightening her wrinkled shirt as best she could before opening the door.

"Nicole?" Nathan's eighteen-year-old cousin rarely darkened her doorstep. Anxiety sharpened her voice. "Is something wrong?"

Assessing violet eyes scanned Sophie from head to toe, bow-shaped mouth pulling into a grimace at the sight of her disheveled state. "There's no emergency, if that's what you mean. I'm here to offer my services."

Still groggy, Sophie was having trouble connecting her thoughts. "I, uh—" She moved aside. "Why don't you come inside? I was about to fix myself some coffee. Would you like some?"

Giving a quick shake of her head, the movement setting her raven ringlets to quivering, Nicole entered the cabin. "No, thanks. I don't drink coffee or tea. It stains your teeth."

"Oh." Come to think of it, Nicole's teeth *were* white enough to blind a person. "How about some milk?"

"I'm not thirsty." Her gaze landing on Will, she nodded uncertainly. "Good morning."

"Mornin', Miss Nicole," he said, wiping his mouth on his sleeve. Hopping up from the table, he told Sophie, "I'm going to muck out the stalls now."

Sophie stopped him with a hand on his shoulder. "What did I tell you about using your napkin? And I'll clean out the stalls."

Shrugging off her hand, he backed away, his features earnest. "I want to help."

She slid a glance at their guest, who was busy inspecting the cabin. Now wasn't the time to have this conversation. "Okay."

Grinning as if she'd given him a gift, he lifted his faded tan hat off the hook and slipped outside.

Sophie tossed kindling in the firebox and prodded the pile with a short poker, praying her brother wasn't bound for disappointment. He cherished this place as much as she did, and if she couldn't find a way for them to stay...

With the kettle on to boil, she went to join Nicole. "Please, have a seat."

"I can't stay long. I promised Ma I'd make this visit quick. Today is laundry day." She sighed long-sufferingly.

Even dressed in casual clothes—a deep purple paisley skirt and coordinating blouse—she managed to look sophisticated. Maybe it was the elaborate hairstyle; some sort of fancy ponytail with shiny curls cascading down. More likely, it was the innate confidence oozing from her pores. Nicole was a natural beauty, and graceful to boot.

Sophie had been a little in awe of the other girl since childhood. It wasn't that Nicole had ever been hateful or unkind—she hadn't joined in with the other girls' taunts—but she'd never gone out of her way to befriend Sophie, either. Seemed to her, Nicole held herself apart from everyone else.

"So what can I do for you?"

"Actually, it's what *I* can do for *you*. You see, I overheard my cousins talking last night about your predicament. I can help you."

"My predicament?"

Her black brows winged up. "Your plan to snag a husband?"

Sophie's breath left her lungs in a whoosh. How could

Nathan do that to her? It wasn't his place to tell anyone. The last thing she wanted was for the whole town to know that poor Sophie Tanner was desperate for a husband.

"That's not something I'd like to get out."

Swinging her reticule from her wrist, she began to walk a circle around Sophie. "Oh, don't worry. My lips are sealed."

Sophie's brows collided. What in the world? "Um, Nicole?"

Her gaze carefully scanning as she completed the circle, she frowned and tut-tutted and sighed. "Let's be frank, shall we? You're going to need a complete overhaul. Luckily for you, I'm gifted in that area. I can supply you with a new wardrobe. Show you how to dress, how to style your hair." Excitement lightened her eyes. "I have a nearly completed dress that I believe will fit you. I just need to take your measurements."

Sophie watched, nonplussed, as Nicole pulled open her reticule and retrieved a cloth tape measure.

"I don't understand. Why would you want to help me? I can't possibly afford to pay you for your labor or the materials. Unless you want me to do chores for you?" Even if she agreed to this, how would she find the time?

Tape measure held aloft, Nicole smiled widely, transforming her countenance into something almost...sweet.

"All I want in return is credit for your transformation. Showing up for Sunday morning services together should do the trick, I think. If I'm ever going to achieve my dream of owning a boutique in the city, I'll need more revenue. When people see the new you, my hope is that the dress orders will come pouring in." Tugging Sophie's braid, she confided, "Besides, I've wanted to get my hands on you for years!"

"But the cost of the materials—"

"You're forgetting I have a wealthy new brother-in-law. One who is very generous to his poor relations."

As Nicole took her measurements and hastily scribbled them on a scrap of paper, all the while chatting about color palettes and accessories and hairstyles, Sophie's mind whirled with the implications. What would she look like when Nicole was finished? What would people think? If she were honest with herself, the only person's opinion that truly mattered was Nathan's, and at this point, she didn't think changing her hair and wearing a skirt would impact him in the slightest.

Chapter Thirteen

Sitting on a hard pew waiting for Reverend Munroe to take his place in the pulpit, Nathan resolved not to think of *the incident* for at least the next twenty-four hours. What had happened at that party had haunted him nearly every minute since. Waking or sleeping, the memory of their embrace refused to leave him be.

Help me focus on the goal here, Lord. To find Sophie a suitable husband and appease her aunt.

Across the aisle, Landon Greene slanted him a smirk; a silent reference to the very thing Nathan was trying to avoid thinking about. Although Landon had been escorting April through the gardens at the time, he'd certainly heard about it. Juicy gossip like that didn't stay contained for very long in this small town.

Beside him, Caleb's uneasiness was showing. Bent forward, elbows resting on his knees, he glared at the knotty pine floorboards as if they were responsible for him being there. He'd surprised them all when he'd arrived at the breakfast table dressed for services. Nathan couldn't recall the last time his younger brother had bothered to come. On the other end of the pew, their ma wore an expression of pure pleasure. Pa just looked anxious.

The rear doors opened and Nathan heard footsteps as late arrivals passed through the alcove and rounded the corner into the high-ceilinged space where the congregation gathered. Then a gasp echoed off the walls, unrest reverberating through the gathering.

Caleb twisted around, then elbowed him in the ribs, his hooded gaze entreating. *You have to see this.*

Nathan complied. At first his mind didn't register what his eyes were seeing. He recognized Nicole, of course, and the smug set of her features. But the lovely, elegant young woman beside her? It took a minute to place her. And when the truth finally penetrated, his jaw hit the floor.

She was… She was… He floundered for a fitting description. *Every man's dream.*

His lungs tightened. His childhood friend, the rumpled and at times downright dowdy tomboy, had transformed into a sweet, beautiful, poised lady. The cute caterpillar into a graceful butterfly.

Sophie was downright stunning. Mouth-drying, eye-popping, toes-curling-in-his-boots stunning.

Gone were the dark colors, the ill-fitting shirts and pants and clunky boots. In their place, a luxurious two-toned creation that hugged her slender frame and showcased her feminine curves, trim waist and the slight flare of her hips. The golden flower-print jacket with high, stiff collar and triangular opening at the throat spilled over her waist in gentle folds, and beneath it peeked a ruffled matte-rose skirt that skimmed the tops of cream-colored kid boots.

Running his gaze back up, he zeroed in on her honeyed hair, which had been swept to the side and smoothed into a sophisticated bun at the base of her neck, tendrils caressing delicate ears adorned with earbobs—earbobs!—and sleeker-looking cheekbones. Shimmering hair framing her face softened her features, made her sapphire eyes appear even larger, her pink mouth lush and beckoning.

This vision couldn't be his friend. Surely not.

The single men in the crowd wore matching expressions of awe.

Nathan snapped his mouth shut. Did he look as conked-on-the-head as they did?

The logical part of his brain assured him this was a good thing. She wanted a husband, didn't she? She'd worried she wouldn't be able to secure a gentleman's interest, hadn't she? Well, looking like this, all elegant and poised and like a brightly wrapped package, there would be no shortage of eager candidates.

Regardless of his reservations, Sophie was determined to pursue her current path. And there wasn't a doubt in his mind she'd be successful.

Sophie resisted the urge to flee.

Nicole had insisted on arriving right before services to achieve maximum effect. Judging from the seamstress's smug pleasure and the congregation's reaction, they'd achieved it.

Being the singular focus of a crowd this size proved unnerving.

This is what you wanted, though. A chance to change others' perception of you. Remember Nicole's instructions—shoulders back, head up, no reaching for the braid that is no longer there. Exude confidence.

Easier said than done.

Starting down the aisle—Nicole had insisted in that irritating way of hers that Sophie join her and her sisters in the second row—she mentally cataloged the varying expressions.

Many of the young women smiled encouragingly, obviously pleased for her, while others appeared jealous. Jealous. Of *her*. She could hardly fathom it.

Seated between her parents, April Littleton's initial slack-jawed disbelief changed to thin-lipped fuming. Sophie bit the inside of her cheek to stop a satisfied smile from forming. *Pride goes before destruction,* she scolded herself. *A haughty spirit before a fall.*

Kenny Thacker's reaction had her smothering a giggle. He and Preston Williams and all the other guys who viewed her as a buddy gaped as if she'd grown a set of horns. Landon, on the other hand, eyed her with awe-tinged appreciation. And a hefty dose of speculation. He wasn't the only one, either.

She sobered. Did this mean her husband hunt might be successful, after all?

They were nearing the O'Malley sisters' row when her gaze encountered Nathan's. At the curious mix of emotions on his face—wonder, admiration, wariness, regret—she faltered. Why regret?

Nicole linked her arm with Sophie's and unobtrusively guided her forward to sit, unfortunately, directly in front of Nathan and his brother.

It was a long, excruciating service.

Sophie sensed the attention directed toward her from the general congregation, but it was Nathan's gaze burning into her scalp that made her want to squirm. Aware of his every shift in the pew, every scuff of his boots against the floorboards, every huff and sigh, the reverend's words flew in one ear and out the other. *Forgive me, Lord, I simply cannot concentrate today.*

When Reverend Munroe at long last uttered the closing prayer, she'd barely made it into the aisle when the people descended to exclaim over her dress and her hair, much to Nicole's delight. The compliments boosted Sophie's confidence. For the first time in her life, she felt beautiful. Accepted. It was…nice.

Pauline's sincere compliments and quick hug sparked feelings of guilt. The woman was unfailingly kind. She didn't deserve Sophie's jealousy. It wasn't Pauline's fault she represented everything Sophie could never be, everything Nathan admired.

As the ladies dispersed and the men crowded around, she watched the tall blonde smile uncertainly at Nathan and utter a brief greeting before proceeding up the aisle.

He stood slightly apart, his expression stony, clearly uncomfortable and on edge, alert to possible danger. Ever her protector.

Cordelia parted the men with a single, superior arched brow. Her inscrutable demeanor made it difficult to ascertain whether or not she approved of Sophie's new look.

"I have to admit I'm surprised, Sophia. You look the part of the proper young lady. Was this your plan all along? To stun the men into offering for your hand?"

Sophie stiffened. Embarrassment rooted her to the spot.

Beside her, Kenny acted scandalized. "First you've gone and changed your looks, and now you're angling for a husband? I thought you weren't like the other girls. What will I do without my fishing buddy?"

Smirking, Preston bunched his biceps. "At least now we know who's the local arm wrestling champ." The guys chuckled.

"I can still beat you, Preston Williams, dress or no dress," she retorted.

Cordelia frowned at that.

Landon Greene chose that moment to insert himself between Kenny and Preston. Taking Sophie's hand, his lips grazed her knuckles.

Her aunt's frown deepened.

"I had no idea that beneath the tomboy exterior existed

a beauty more lovely than the rose, more stunning than the sunset, brighter than the biggest star," he breathed, blue eyes twinkling with mischief, earning good-natured groans and plenty of eye-rolls.

Sophie didn't have a chance to respond, because Nathan was suddenly there, his lean body hovering close. Staking his claim? But no. That was ridiculous.

"I think it's time to leave, gentlemen." His tone brooked no argument. "The lady's dinner is long overdue."

"As is mine," the reverend, who was always the last to leave, chimed in good-naturedly from the back of the church.

Eyes narrowing at Nathan, Landon reluctantly let her go. He dipped his head in her direction. "I'll see you soon, sweet Sophie."

Nathan opened his mouth to speak, but was cut off by the twins, who flanked her on either side. "Come with us to Aunt Mary's. We want to hear all the details."

Sophie found herself swept along by her eager friends, leaving Nathan to wallow in his self-imposed temper.

"Did you see the crowd that descended on Sophie after the service?" Seated on one end of Sam and Mary's sofa, Nicole looked up from the swath of material in her lap, needle hovering midair. "The men hovered like hungry bees. If not for Nathan's interference, I doubt they would've let us leave." Satisfaction brightened her expression.

Beside the massive stone fireplace, chessboard spread out between Nathan and herself, Sophie risked a glance at him. Perched on the chair across from her, elbows on his knees, he pondered his next move. Chess was their game. They were both good…and competitive, which meant the games would sometimes last for hours. As far as who was a better chess player, that hadn't been determined yet. She and Nathan were equally matched.

He must have sensed her regard, for his enigmatic gaze lifted, zeroed in on her. That intense focus heated the surface of her skin, brought every nerve to prickly awareness, on edge and yearning for his touch. What was he thinking?

All the way home, all through dinner, he hadn't uttered a word about her appearance. Not a single one. If she were honest, she'd admit his lack of reaction stung.

"I would say her transformation is a complete success." Nicole practically purred.

"You outdid yourself with that dress, Nicole." Kate lowered her copy of the *New York Times* sent to her by her parents. She smiled at her cousin-in-law. "The detail work is exquisite, the material choice inspired. Sophie, you look as if you stepped off the pages of *Harper's Bazaar*."

An heiress born and raised in the highest society circles in New York City, Kate knew fashion. Sophie shrugged. "Nicole is very talented."

"True," Kate agreed, "but it is you modeling her creation. You've never looked more beautiful."

"I agree." Josh sat very close to his wife, an arm slung casually around her shoulders. He crossed his legs at the ankles. "What do you think, Nathan?"

Cheeks burning, Sophie couldn't bring herself to look at him, watching instead his large hands, how they clenched and the knuckles went white. "I would say she hasn't changed all that much."

"Excuse me?" Nicole glared at him.

"How can you say that?" Mary, who'd just entered the room and was setting a plate of cookies on the coffee table, sounded personally affronted.

Sophie inwardly cringed. Of course. She'd known, hadn't she, that a new look wouldn't alter the way he viewed her.

Caleb surged up from his crouched position near the

fireplace. "Time to get your eyes checked, brother," he muttered on his way out of the room.

"She hasn't changed," Nathan drawled softly in the gathering silence, "because she's always been beautiful, inside and out."

Startled, Sophie's gaze shot to his face. Surely she hadn't heard right? And yet there, in the softening of his mouth, the flicker of a smile, she witnessed appreciation and approval. A giddy sort of joy infused her insides, warming her from the inside out.

Indicating the board, where he had no legal moves left, he said, "Stalemate."

She stared. Very rarely did they call a draw. The game's outcome was clear, however. Neither one of them was a clear winner.

Excusing himself, he left without another word.

"That was downright poetic." Josh winked at Sophie.

"I thought it was sweet." Kate sighed dreamily.

When Mary eyed Sophie with open speculation, she tried not to squirm.

Josh hopped up and assumed the seat his brother had vacated. "Finally, I get a chance to play Sophie."

Smiling gratefully, she replaced the carved wooden pieces. It appeared rescuing females was an O'Malley family trait. The game with Josh didn't last all that long. He didn't play often, so his skills were rusty, and she quickly bested him.

He grinned, long fingers stroking his goatee. "I see I need some more practice if I'm ever going to beat you."

"Thanks for the game, Josh." Standing, she glanced out the windows. Will had been there earlier, romping in the grass with the family's new puppy. "And thanks for the meal, Mary. Will and I need to be getting home."

"Anytime, dear."

Bidding everyone a good afternoon, she went outside.

Will was nowhere in sight. After scanning the fields and outbuildings, she decided to check the barn. Sometimes he played in there if kittens were in residence.

Skirts lifted several inches off the ground, she entered the dusky interior and peered down the center aisle. "Will? Are you in here?"

A dark form separated itself from the shadows, feeble light from the entrance falling on a familiar charcoal-gray shirt. "He's not here."

So this is where Nathan had disappeared to. She advanced down the aisle, her pulse picking up speed. This was their first moment alone since that awful row in the lane. "Have you seen him? My aunt is paying us a visit later this afternoon. She expects him to be there."

"No." He met her halfway. Folding his arms across his chest, he studied her with hooded eyes. His short brown hair was rumpled from one too many finger-combings. "Your aunt seemed to approve of your new look."

"Yes, well, I wish she hadn't mentioned the marriage thing."

His dark gaze roaming down the length of her felt like a caress. "How does it feel? Being all gussied up?"

Suppressing a shiver of want, she pressed a hand to the exposed flesh at the base of her neck. "Strange. Stiff. However, unlike the dress Kate lent me for the funeral, this one fits me like a glove. Nicole knows what she's doing. I daresay I'll get used to dressing like this eventually."

"So no more braids?"

She smiled at the teasing hint in his husky voice. "Did I mention she came after me with scissors?"

His arms fell to his sides. "She *cut* your hair?"

Sophie smoothed a light hand over the side-sweep. Of all the changes his cousin had wrought, she liked her hair the best. The moment she'd spied her image in the looking glass, she'd been transported back in time to when her ma had still been alive. With her hair arranged like this, she resembled her.

"She whacked a good six inches off. I don't mind, though." She shrugged. "It's easier to take care of."

"Six inches," he repeated, frowning.

Why was he acting as if it was a crime? As if her personal decisions affected him?

"You'll be happy to know I took your advice." She forced a brightness into her attitude she didn't feel. Side-stepping him, she moved to the stall where his horse, Chance, stood observing them with soft brown eyes.

"Oh, yeah? What advice is that?"

She stroked her fingers along his powerful neck, addressing the animal instead of the man. "I accepted an invitation from Frank Walters. He's taking Will and me on a picnic tomorrow afternoon."

Silence.

Sophie twisted around, wincing as her skirts caught on the wooden slats near her feet. She was going to have to be more careful. More aware of her movements if she didn't want to destroy Nicole's handiwork. "Aren't you going to say something?"

Heaving a sigh, he kneaded his neck with impatient fingers. "I'm not so sure you should've listened to me. Frank's a good man, but he's a bit passive for the likes of you."

"Are you insinuating I'm pushy?" She bristled. She wouldn't mention the outing hadn't been Frank's idea. When they had happened upon him outside the church that morning, Nicole had cunningly maneuvered him into it.

"You're a woman who knows her own mind." He joined her at the stall, his arm brushing her shoulder. His body heat radiated outward, tugging at her. He was too handsome for words; his generous mouth wielding tempting memories. His gaze probed hers. "What you need, Soph, is a strong man. A partner, not a pushover."

Are you volunteering? she almost blurted. Sliding her gaze away, she murmured, "I don't have time to be choosy."

"I don't like this."

"And you think I do?" she challenged.

"Can a man like Frank truly make you happy?"

No. No one except you will ever do.

She buried her fingers in Chance's black mane. "If it weren't for Cordelia's meddling, I wouldn't be contemplating marriage at all. I hate being forced into this, but I'll do anything to keep Will with me. That will have to be enough."

"I hope for both your sakes that it is."

Frank Walters was a nice guy. Shy, but nice.

A year older than Nathan, he was six years her senior. And while they'd grown up in the same small town, they hadn't exchanged more than a dozen words. Sharing a meal with him was proving to be an awkward experience.

"This pie is delicious," she told him between bites.

"My mother is an accomplished cook," he said soberly. "I sampled your rhubarb pie before April discarded it. Mother would be happy to teach you how—" He broke off abruptly, looking pained. "I didn't mean... That is, if you wanted her to."

She set her empty plate beside the picnic basket. "That might be nice." Inwardly, she grimaced. Bonnie Walters wore a perpetual expression of disdain. Nothing seemed to please her. Poor Frank. Perhaps he was searching for a reason to leave the home he shared with her?

Perspiration dampened the hair at her temples. The overhead shade did little to dispel the stifling August heat. Sophie adjusted her full peach skirt to make sure it covered her ankles, still finding it awkward to move and sit like a lady. When Frank had arrived at the cabin, he'd complimented her, saying the pastel hue made her skin luminous. Then his face had burned scarlet. Poor Frank.

He wasn't one of those men who stood out in a crowd. Of average height, he had a pleasant face and wiry build, brown hair that tended to curl if he went too long between haircuts and warm brown eyes. He dressed like every other farmer in Gatlinburg, his clothes neat and pressed.

So he's a decent guy. What will it be like to live with him? To prepare his meals and mend his clothes? To have children with him?

Sophie sucked in a sharp breath. For the first time since she hit upon the marriage idea, it hit her full-force what she was getting herself into. She looked at Frank. *Really* looked at him. At his mouth that would kiss hers, his hands that would hold hers. As his wife, she'd be expected to show him affection.

Sweat beaded her upper lip. The buttermilk pie churned in her stomach. She squeezed her eyes tight and focused on pulling grass-scented air into her nostrils.

Impulsive. Irrational. As usual, she'd seized on the solution to her problem without thinking it through. She'd been desperate for one. No doubt if Nathan had suggested joining the traveling circus, she would've packed their bags and hit the trail.

I can't do this—

"Watch out!"

A ball bounced precariously close to their log cabin–patterned quilt and the food and drinks spread out across it. Will, face streaked with sweat and grass stains on his pant knees, darted over. "Sorry about that."

Frank retrieved the ball from where it had rolled to a stop and tossed it to her brother. "No problem."

As Will returned to the clover-dusted field rolling into the distance, Sophie reminded herself why she was here. *You* can *do this. You have to. For Will's sake.*

First order of business? Get to know him.

"So, Frank, what do you like to do in your spare time?"

"Not much of that, as you know." He frowned, running his thumbs along his suspenders. "The farm takes up most of my time and energy."

"Yes, but surely there're moments when you're not working," she persisted. "What do you do then?"

He thought for a moment. "Normally at the end of the day, I read the newspaper while Mother knits."

Sounded...boring. Or restful, depending on which way you looked at it. *Look for the positive, Soph.*

"Do you like music?"

At the barn dances held throughout the community during spring and summer months, Frank mingled with the older men. He didn't dance. Sophie didn't, either, and not because she didn't enjoy music. She did. But instead of risking being abandoned on the sidelines—who'd want to dance with the resident tomboy, anyway?—she insisted she was too self-conscious to dance.

"I learned how to play the banjo as a boy, but Mother doesn't like noise."

Irritation swelled at Bonnie Walters's selfishness. It was Frank's house, too. "Couldn't you practice in the barn?" She smiled her encouragement. "I'm sure the animals wouldn't mind."

Frank looked at her in surprise. "The thought hadn't occurred to me." He scratched his head. "I suppose I could do that. My pa was the one who taught me. He was a fine banjo player." The note of wistfulness in his voice touched a chord deep inside.

He must miss his pa like she missed her ma and granddad.

Roy Walters died many years ago when they were still kids. From what she remembered, he'd been as jolly as his wife was taciturn. Poor Frank. Was there any lightheartedness, any fun, in his life anymore? Or had Bonnie snuffed it all out?

"I have an idea. Why don't you come over for supper one night this week and bring your banjo? You can play for us."

His brows shot up. "You're serious?"

"Yes, of course." His barely suppressed excitement softened her heart to the consistency of warm molasses. Such a simple thing, this request, and yet it brought him to life like never before. "Please say you'll come."

A rare smile brightened his features. "I'd like that very much. Thank you, Sophie."

Suddenly unable to speak, she nodded her reply. The way he was looking at her, as if she personally had a hand in hanging the moon and stars…well, no one had ever looked at her like that before. And it felt…wonderful.

If only Nathan—

No. Sophie resolutely shoved thoughts of him aside. She was going to have to come to terms with the fact that Nathan wouldn't be playing a starring role in her life. Someone else would fill that role. Someone like Frank Walters.

Chapter Fourteen

The following morning Sophie was on her hands and knees in the dirt, tugging weeds from between her pepper plants, when Philip Dennison rode onto her property. Strange. While she considered him a friend, he didn't make a habit of coming 'round.

Standing, she dislodged the dirt from her pants and, wiping the sweat from her brow, strolled to the end of the row. When the red-haired young man dismounted, he tucked his thumbs in his waistband and openly inspected the cabin and surrounding land.

"Mornin', Philip. Want to come inside for some lemonade?"

Finally his gaze got around to her. "No, thanks. I just came by to ask if you and Will wanna have lunch at our place on Sunday."

This was a first. Philip's parents didn't approve of her. They assumed she took after her pa. That she'd inherited his wild streak and one day she'd inevitably follow in his footsteps. "Uh, sure, I suppose we could do that."

"Great." His hazel eyes took in her appearance, and his lips compressed. "You're planning on wearing a dress, right? I mean, you aren't going to go back to dressing like a boy, are you?"

"I plan on wearing dresses to church—" she jutted her chin "—but that doesn't mean I'm going to get all fancied up just to dig in the dirt."

His face reddened, masking the smattering of freckles on his fair skin. "Don't get mad, Sophie. You know my ma. The only reason she asked was because she thinks you've turned over a new leaf."

"So this was her idea, not yours?"

"Actually, it was Pa's." Twisting his upper body, he again surveyed the outbuildings and fields. "You've done a remarkable job keeping up the farm."

Sophie gritted her teeth as annoyance flared. She was beginning to put two and two together and she didn't like the emerging picture. Still, she'd already accepted.

"Thanks." Jerking a thumb over her shoulder, she said, "I guess I should get back to work. Lots to do."

"I'll leave you to it, then." Tugging on the brim of his hat, he mounted up and waved. "See ya Sunday."

She stood at the edge of her small vegetable garden and watched him ride away, a disturbing thought weaving through her mind. Now that Tobias was gone, how many farmers viewed her land as up for grabs? And how many of them were willing to use her to get it?

"What's got you so distracted you didn't hear me coming?"

At the deep rumble of Nathan's voice near her ear, she yelped. Spun around, a hand to her chest. "You frightened me!"

"Sorry." He kicked up a shoulder, one brow quirked. "What were you thinking about?"

"Philip Dennison stopped by to invite me to Sunday lunch."

The good humor in his eyes evaporated like mist. His

expression closed, shutting her out. "Is that so? I guess Nicole worked her magic, huh?"

She jammed her hands on her hips, disguising her hurt with anger. "Why is it so difficult for you to believe a man might be interested in me?"

His mask slipped, exposing sincere contrition. "I didn't mean it that way." Burying his fingers in his choppy hair, he took out his frustration on a stick, kicking it away with his boot. "I wish we could go back to how things used to be. Before this crazy husband-catching scheme."

"I didn't ask for any of this, you know," she snapped. "Perhaps you should take up your objections with Cordelia."

The pounding hooves of an approaching rider deepened his scowl. "What is *he* doing here?"

Pivoting, Sophie recognized the horse first. "Why is Landon paying me a visit?"

"That's what I'd like to know."

Nathan positioned himself in front of her as if to intercept her visitor. What was with him? There weren't too many people in this town he couldn't tolerate, so what had Landon done to get himself on that short list?

Moving to stand beside him, she nudged his shoulder. His sharp-edged gaze slid to her.

"You don't really think I need protection from him, do you?"

"He's not for you, Soph," he said cryptically.

"Why—" But she was interrupted by Landon's cheerful greeting as his boots hit the ground.

"Sweet Sophie. How are you this fine day?" His grin was known to have a devastating effect on the general female population of Gatlinburg. And, she had to admit, the man was a looker. Blond hair, blue eyes, golden skin. Tall and strong as an ox. Charm oozing from his pores.

His gaze, when it flicked to Nathan, didn't alter one way or another. If anything, his grin grew wider. "O'Malley."

"What do you want, Greene?"

Landon's brows lifted. "I came to speak with Sophie, if that's all right with you," he drawled.

Sophie studied the two men. Nathan's dislike radiated off him in waves. Landon, on the other hand, attempted to conceal his. It was there beneath the surface, though.

"What can I do for you?" Reaching for the end of her braid out of habit, her fingers instead met the loose strands of her ponytail.

He tipped the brim of his caramel-colored hat up. "I came to ask if you'd accompany me to the singing this Saturday night."

Nathan's sharp inhale told her exactly what he thought of the invitation. He didn't want her to accept. Except, Landon was on her list. He was an upstanding member of the town, came from a good family who, unlike the Dennisons, treated her with respect. He wasn't known to indulge in alcohol. He was a faithful church attender. And even if he did possess a flirtatious nature, she couldn't afford to say no.

"I'd like that."

His eyes lit up. With triumph? Rubbing his hands together, he nodded. "That's great."

"She can't go with you."

Sophie's jaw dropped. Anger licked along her veins. Swiping her ponytail behind her shoulder, she demanded, "Nathan, what—"

"Have you forgotten you agreed to go with me?" he challenged, his expression warning her to play along.

Of all the high-handed— "Yes, I believe I have. I'm racking my brain, and I simply can't remember you asking me."

Landon spoke up, intruding on their silent battle of

wills. "That's a shame. I'd hoped to walk in with you on my arm and make all the other guys jealous."

That diverted her attention. She stared at him, absolutely certain no man had ever entertained a similar notion about her before.

"Since you've disappointed my hopes," he went on in light recrimination, "will you agree to go on a horseback ride with me Sunday afternoon?"

"Yes," she rushed to say before Nathan claimed to have plans with her then, too. "I'm having lunch with the Dennisons, but I'm sure that won't take long. How about we say two o'clock?"

"I'm looking forward to it."

An inexplicable gleam in the blue depths niggled at her, but she attributed it to her imagination. Landon Greene may be a bit of a rogue, but he was in no way dangerous.

When he'd left, she rounded on Nathan. "How dare you interfere!" She threw up her hands. "Have you forgotten that if I don't find a husband, my aunt is going to take Will away from me?" She'd already lost her beloved granddad. She couldn't lose her brother, too. Fear bubbling over, she shoved him, surprise forcing him back a step. "I don't have time for games."

Seizing her hands, he held them flush against his chest, ducking his head down so they were on eye level. Secrets swirled in the silver depths. "This isn't a game. You need to steer clear of him."

Being this close to him, his touch warm and sure, transported Sophie back to the party and the earth-shaking kiss. A kiss he wouldn't be repeating. She steeled herself against the yearnings coursing through her.

"Again the dire warning without explanation? I'm just supposed to trust you, is that it?"

His gaze slipped to her mouth. Snapped back up. "Yes."

"That's funny, because I seriously doubt you'd take my word about anything. You'd demand to know my reasons."

A muscle jerked in his rigid jaw. "You're right, I would. But in this situation, I can't go into details."

"Can't? Or won't?"

He released her then, and she fought a sense of abandonment.

Putting space between them, he rested his hands on lean hips, squinting in the bright sunlight. "You don't have to go with me if you don't want to. Just don't go with him. And please, cancel that ride."

"I'm not going with you on principle." Oh, how it hurt to refuse such an opportunity. *Better a little hurt now than a heaping helping later.*

"Who will you go with then?"

"Who says I have to have an escort? Men will be more apt to approach me if I'm alone, anyway."

"Right." Frowning, he tugged his hat down, casting his features in shadow. "I've got to go."

Not knowing what to say, Sophie watched him leave. It wasn't until he'd disappeared into the forest that she realized she didn't know why he'd come in the first place.

Ascending the stairs of the grand Victorian home Saturday evening, Sophie felt her heart quiver like a frightened rabbit's. She would rather be anywhere else but here, alone and dressed to impress, where everyone would watch and know her purpose. Thanks to her aunt's slip, the news of her quest would be buzzing around town.

In the entryway, she peeked in the oval mirror above the slim mahogany table and smoothed an errant strand to the side. Still wasn't easy to achieve this hairstyle, but she was getting the hang of it.

Guests milled around in the green-and-blue parlor on her left. The program was set to begin in an hour. Sixty minutes to scope out the place, and perhaps engage an eligible gentleman in conversation. She stuck out her tongue at her reflection. Had she really been reduced to this? A desperate female on the prowl?

Navigating the wallpapered hallways to the spacious dining room, she offered a harried-looking Madge Calhoun her assistance.

The plump, gray-headed lady waved her off. "No, child. Help yourself to a glass of ginger water and a cake. Enjoy yourself."

Choosing a pink-tinted glass, she wandered over to the wall of windows and soaked in the beauty of the flower gardens.

"Sweet Sophie." Landon appeared out of nowhere, his footsteps masked by the plush rugs. "You are especially lovely tonight." His blue eyes, warm with appreciation, scanned her outfit.

Sipping the tangy liquid, she returned his smile. "Thank you. So are you." She touched the yellow daisy tucked in his button hole. "That's a nice look."

Waggling his eyebrows, he leaned forward conspiratorially. "Makes me appear more sensitive in the ladies' eyes. Romantic."

"Ah." Well, at least he was honest.

Glancing over his shoulder, he said, "Where is your escort?"

Her smile faltered. "Nathan and I— That is, I told him I would rather come alone."

A peculiar gleam lit his eyes. "That's good news." Cocking his head, he held his arm aloft. "Would you care to accompany me to the gardens?"

It wasn't the best idea. While he was charming and handsome, something about the man set her on edge.

"I don't know—"

At the edge of her vision, she caught movement. Nathan stepped across the threshold, irresistible in a gray-and-white pin-striped shirt and black trousers, rich brown hair shiny in the candlelight. Tan and fit and lean.

But what was he doing here? He didn't attend these functions any more than she did. At least she had a reason. What was his?

Beside her, Landon stiffened. Nathan's slow survey of the room's occupants eventually jarred to a halt with them. Shock followed quickly by annoyance showed on his face. His lips pursed. He was going to come over here. Of course he was.

Feeling weak and susceptible where he was concerned, Sophie seized Landon's hand. "On second thought, I think a stroll is exactly what I need right now."

Surprise flashed. "As you wish, my lady." His satisfied near-sneer didn't bother her as much as it should have.

Hustling her out the door, Landon guided her down the back porch steps and along the winding stone path. Before long, they were deep in the lush gardens, hidden from view of the yellow two-story. Disconcerted and breathless from their hasty retreat, Sophie inhaled the fragrant, slightly sweet scent emitted by the rainbow of pastel blooms. The water fountain trickled in the distance.

That was a close call. Nathan had stayed away for days; an unwelcome reprieve albeit a necessary one. When he'd held her captive the other day, her hands imprisoned against him, his dear face hovering near, she'd been tempted to throw caution to the wind and kiss him, her irritation a minor thing compared to her need for him. The man of her heart.

Sinking onto a wide stone bench beneath a rose arbor, she arranged her skirts and clasped her hands in her lap. The setting sun warmed her skin as she observed two black-and-orange butterflies flitting above the blossoms.

You have to move past this, Sophie.

Her companion sat beside her, his thigh brushing hers; a bit too close for comfort. But there wasn't room on the bench to scoot away. Nathan's insinuations came to the forefront of her mind.

"That night you lost the shadow game, what exactly did you and April do out here?"

He tilted his head back and laughed heartily, the strong column of his throat a golden brown above his black suit coat. His blond hair, so light a color it was difficult to describe, glowed in the waning light. He smelled clean and soapy.

Setting an arm around her shoulders, he said, "Such candor! You are a refreshing female, Sophie Tanner." When he leaned in close as if to kiss her, she pushed hard on his chest and jumped up.

"I asked you to tell me what you did, not show me!"

Tugging on his sleeves, his mouth tightened in displeasure for a fraction of a second, so fast she wasn't sure she'd seen it at all. When he lifted his head, he once again wore a relaxed, unaffected grin. "No need to get riled, sweet Sophie. It was an innocent mistake."

"You and I aren't courting. I don't know about you, but I don't give affection freely."

He unfolded his tall frame. Approached. Quirked an insolent brow. "You kissed Nathan."

She stiffened, unhappy with the reminder. "That was a game." Studying him, she said, "Why don't you and Nathan like each other?"

"That's not an interesting topic. You, on the other hand, intrigue me." He crowded her, touched a finger to her earbob. "Pretty."

Stomach tightening, she backed up a step. "I'm ready to return to the house now."

Tipping his head, he offered her his arm. "As you wish, my lady."

She would not be sitting with Landon Greene tonight. Time to move on to the next available contender.

Nathan paced the wide porch wrapping around the house, debating whether or not to go after her. Most of the guests were already seated in the parlor, awaiting the recital set to start in fifteen minutes.

He scanned the trees and shrubs and flower beds. Surely Landon wouldn't try anything at such a public event.

Remember the last time you attempted to rescue her? She was fine. Perfectly capable of handling herself.

Still, his lungs deflated with relief when he caught sight of her and her escort emerging from the verdant vista. He studied her expressive face. No fear there. Irritation, maybe.

Goodness, but she was a sight. He couldn't help this stunned reaction every time he saw her looking more like a wealthy socialite than his childhood playmate. Her fitted jacket of aquamarine was trimmed in chocolate brown and caramel, the same hue as her voluminous skirts, and atop her coiled locks perched a petite, round, flower-bedecked straw hat. Stylish and breezily beautiful, she put the radiant blooms spread out around her to shame.

Landon spotted him first. The corners of his eyes tightened, his mouth turned down in dislike. Nathan challenged him with a glare and a silent threat—*hurt Sophie, deal with me.*

She didn't notice his presence until they had reached the top of the stairs. Lashes flaring, color bloomed in her apple cheeks. She surreptitiously edged closer to him and away from Landon. What exactly did that mean?

"I enjoyed our time together." Landon half bowed to her. Ignoring Nathan, he went inside.

"Your aunt sent me to find you," he told her, offering his

arm. "I'm to take you to her as soon as possible." Cordelia had phrased it exactly that way, too.

"I'm pretty sure I can find my own way."

"You would cause me to suffer her wrath?" he lightly challenged.

"Oh, all right." Blowing out a breath, she adjusted her jacket hem and fussed with her skirts, smoothed her hair and fumbled with her earbobs. If he didn't know any better, he'd think she was avoiding physical contact with him. That wasn't Sophie's way. It didn't used to be, anyway. Things were changing with breakneck speed. Who knew what was normal anymore?

When she at last tucked her gloved hand in the crook of his elbow, the pressure against his arm was faint, barely detectable, and yet her touch made him feel strong and capable and willing to protect her at all cost.

Was this how Josh felt about Kate? Eager to go to battle for her?

The notion was most unsettling.

Sophie didn't need him to do battle for her. What she couldn't handle on her own, her future husband would take care of.

Holding the door for her, he asked, "How was your outing with Frank?"

"Wonderful." She kept her gaze straight ahead.

"Truly?"

Lifting luminous eyes to him, she adopted an earnest air. "He may be shy, but Frank's a good-hearted man. Decent. Too hardworking, perhaps. He deserves a little fun in his life."

And what of her? What did she deserve?

"I'm certain you can give him that."

She looked surprised, which in turn surprised him. Wasn't she aware of all she had to offer?

He knew then what Sophie deserved. Love. She'd given

so much of herself to everyone around her. She'd sacrificed her childhood to care for Will. She'd bestowed her heart and compassion upon Tobias, had poured time, attention and hard labor into the family farm. She deserved to be taken care of, to be pampered, even.

As her friend, it was his duty to make certain the man she chose would treat her accordingly.

Chapter Fifteen

Much to Sophie's dismay, Nathan not only delivered her to her aunt's side, he joined them. Sandwiched between the two of them, she couldn't concentrate on the beautiful music or the words being sung. Could only focus on the keen awareness of his person so close to hers—his strong, tanned hands holding the program listing the evening's performers, neatly clipped fingernails, light blue veins beneath tanned skin, a stray nick on his knuckles. Occasionally, his black-clad knee bumped hers and she didn't mind it at all. That she would be so affected by her lifelong friend and neighbor was beyond fathoming.

Why did she have to feel this way for him? The one man who would never return those feelings?

The program dragged on interminably in her mind, stuck in a mad place between pleasure and pain. Afterward, her attempts at escape were thwarted. Cordelia commanded them to wait on her on the rear porch, giving no reason for her wishes.

"What was your favorite song?" he asked now, his back supported by a white column, his hip nestled against the railing that wrapped around the back of the house. Moonlight washed the gardens in pastel glory, the faint tinkling of the water fountain blending with cicadas' familiar hum. Distant laughter rippled through the night.

The air caressed her skin, teased the hair brushing her nape. "'Rose of Killarney' because of its haunting melody. What about you?"

"My favorite, 'What a Friend We Have in Jesus.'"

His smile burned itself into her consciousness. He didn't smile enough, she thought suddenly. Who would bring fun to Nathan's life? In her opinion, he needed a little shake-up.

"I like that one, too. Mr. Hostettler has a nice voice."

"If you're satisfied with this performance," a commanding voice intruded, "you should hear my church choir. Now there's real talent."

Nathan straightened and Sophie pushed away from the railing as Cordelia strolled into the pale light spilling through the windows, gray-threaded hair piled high and topped with yet another feathered concoction passing as a hat. Adorned in head-to-toe black, she wore her usual expression—mouth pinched in perpetual criticism, astute gaze missing nothing.

"I thought the singers were remarkable." Sophie met her aunt's stare with one of her own. The more time she spent in the older woman's company, the less intimidated she became.

"Hmm." She regarded them with narrowed eyes. "I will concede the cook—Mrs. Calhoun, I believe her name was—did a passable job with the hors d'oeuvres."

"It's Madge Calhoun. She and her husband, Fred, manage the property for Charles Newman's grandson, Lucian. Surely you remember them, Aunt? They've lived here many years."

Hands clasped behind her back, Cordelia glared imperiously down her nose. "When I left, I did my utmost to forget everything about this town, including the residents."

Sophie glanced at Nathan, whose classic features were

arranged in thoughtful consideration. Was he wondering—as she was—what life must have been like for her aunt? Based on her own experience, Sophie could only guess how the townspeople had treated the sister of Lester Tanner.

She touched her aunt's arm. "They must've been very cruel for you to want to do that."

Shock softened Cordelia's features. Then she snapped her mouth shut and reassumed control, sniffing as if such a sentiment was far-fetched. "I don't know what you're talking about, Sophia Tanner."

"It couldn't have been easy," she continued quietly. "Pa wasn't exactly well-liked, was he? I saw how horribly he treated my mother. And—" her heart squeezed with regret "—I also saw how he controlled and manipulated Granddad. If Granddad didn't stand up for Ma, I'm guessing he didn't do that for you, either." She loved Tobias with all her heart, but that didn't mean she was blind to his faults. "Lester must have made your life miserable."

Cordelia blinked fast. In the dim light, Sophie could see tears glistening. Her heart softened. She didn't really know her aunt at all, did she?

Cordelia addressed Nathan. "Would you mind giving us a moment alone?"

"I'll be inside." He shot Sophie a meaningful glance. He'd be nearby in case she needed him. Typical.

When they were alone, her aunt joined her at the railing, all business once again. The faint scent of verbena wafted over, the delicate perfume an unexpected choice for the tough-as-nails lady. "How is your hunt for a husband going?"

A sigh escaped. "Slow."

"You mustn't dillydally, Sophia. You need to use the momentum created by your transformation to snag one before the men's interest wanes."

"This decision will affect the rest of our lives. I won't

rush it." Sophie sucked in a calming breath. "Surely you want what's best for us?"

"You don't have to marry at all." Cordelia watched her closely. "You can come and live with me. Will would receive a good education, and you can get involved with the many social organizations available to young women. When you're ready to marry, you can have your pick of suitable men."

Sophie stilled at the note of entreaty in her voice. What had happened to her simply doing her duty? Could it be possible Cordelia *wanted* them there with her? If that were so, why would she be pushing Sophie to marry?

"We're happy here. We don't want to leave."

"In the city, you won't have to toil from dawn to dusk each and every day. We have indoor plumbing. The shops offer all sorts of merchandise. Why, we can get you a whole new wardrobe. My cook was once employed by a ritzy French couple, and she turns out the most delectable dishes you've ever tasted. How can you turn that down?"

"It does sound wonderful," Sophie admitted with a slight smile, "especially the indoor plumbing. But those things aren't important to me. You're right, life here can be difficult and demanding. But this is our home. Our heritage. While we appreciate your offer, this is where we want to be."

Compressing her lips, Cordelia turned her attention to the gardens, illuminated with flickering gas lamps. Hand in hand, a couple slowly wound their way along the stone path, heads close together as they swapped secrets. Her aunt's solitary station in life was impressed upon her then. Cordelia lived alone. Ate the majority of her meals alone. Sophie could picture her in an enormous dining room, seated at the head of a ridiculously long dining table, the chairs all empty. How depressing.

"Do you have a lot of friends, Aunt?" she blurted.

"Of course I do," she retorted sharply, glowering. "Why would you ask such a question?"

"No reason." Prickly, wasn't she?

"Speaking of friends, I'm certain they're becoming concerned over my prolonged absence. In case you haven't noticed, I've put my entire life on hold for you. The clock is ticking, Sophia. You have three weeks remaining. I won't wait a minute longer."

Engaged in a predictable conversation about farming, Nathan excused himself when he spotted Cordelia in the entryway preparing to leave. He beat her hand to the doorknob, earning an imperious look when he held the door for her. And when he followed her outside, she turned before descending the steps.

"You wished to speak with me?" she demanded.

"I'd like to talk to you about Sophie." *Lord, help me keep a cool head.* "What you're doing to her is wrong and unnecessary. It's unfair to them both."

"I'm not surprised you feel that way. You didn't have to utter a word for me to ascertain your opinion on the subject." She cocked her head, her forceful gaze reminding him of a certain intimidating schoolteacher he'd had as a boy. He held his ground. "Why unnecessary? Surely you admit a farm is too much for a young girl to handle on her own."

"It is." At her satisfied expression, he held up a hand. "But Sophie doesn't have to do it on her own. She's part of the family, and we take care of our own."

"You're very passionate about my niece's well-being. Why don't you marry her if you're so concerned?"

"Sophie and I would make each other miserable, believe me," he scoffed. "We're friends. That's all we'll ever be."

She looked thoughtful. "Are you so sure about that? Sometimes the best marriages start out as friendships."

"It's not going to happen."

"Well, then, I suppose you have two choices. Help her choose wisely or convince her to leave Gatlinburg."

Tipping her head, she bid him good-night. Left him there to stew over her parting advice, neither choice an appealing one. Either way, he would lose his friend.

"I enjoyed our ride, Sophie."

Strolling beside her in the shaded lane, Landon flashed a satisfied smile. He'd removed his hat and hooked it on the saddle horn, unaware the rumpled look lent him a boyish appeal, his short blond hair slightly damp at the temples and sticking up in spots.

Their horses plodding behind them, she said with some surprise, "I did, too."

After those few, awkward moments with him last evening, she'd been slightly apprehensive about spending the afternoon with him. As if to make up for his slipups, he'd turned on the charm, soothing the agitation aroused by her uncomfortable lunch at the Dennisons' home.

Philip was getting scratched off her list. He was nice and all, but she wasn't about to subject herself or Will to his parents' barely concealed dislike.

"Come out to the farm one day this week. Let me show you around for a bit and then you can have supper with us."

Another awkward family meal? Landon's parents were nice people. Perhaps it wouldn't be too bad. Besides, if she was seriously considering him, she'd have to spend time with them. Test the waters.

"Hey." He snagged her hand a little too forcefully, compelling her and her horse to come up short. She opened her mouth to protest, stalling when he lifted a finger and smoothed the line between her brows. "It's not a marriage proposal." He chuckled. "Just a simple dinner invitation. No need to fret over it."

She tugged her hand free and backed up a step. "I accept."

"Good."

"Soph? You all right?"

Spinning on her heel, she realized they were at the turn-off to her cabin. Nathan, a string of fish dangling from the pole balanced on his shoulder, stood watching them with narrowed eyes and a scowl shouting his displeasure.

"Of course she is." Landon stiffened, his good humor slipping away. "Are you insinuating I'm not a gentleman, O'Malley?"

Nathan's gaze never wavered from hers. "Soph?"

What was with these two? "I'm perfectly capable of taking care of myself."

Nathan thought the top of his head was going to blow off.

Her perturbed tone warned him to back off. Fat chance. The instant Landon touched her, fury had licked through his veins like flames in a pile of dry leaves, threatening to burn up every last shred of self-control. If the brute so much as left a finger imprint on her skin—

"Nathan."

Her cool fingers wrapped around his wrist, applying slight pressure. Glancing down, he attempted to blink away the red haze.

"He's leaving," she said, dark gaze shooting daggers.

Retreating horses' hooves finally registered. Sophie was safe for the time being, but men like Landon Greene didn't reveal their true natures in the beginning. No, they bided their time, lowering your guard until you were caught in their web of deception. Nathan knew from experience. He and Landon had been friends once, a long time ago.

Releasing him, she lifted a hand to flip her braid behind her shoulder only to realize there was no braid. She huffed in frustration. "Why are you here?"

"I'm spending time with your brother." He shifted the pole higher on his shoulder. "Do you have a problem with that?"

"You know I don't."

"Then why the attitude? Oh, wait, I know." He snapped his fingers. "You're irritated because I caught you in a lie."

She gasped. "What lie? I never said I would cancel my ride with him!"

"You let me assume. Same thing."

"That's not true." But her gaze slid sideways and she bit her lip, sure signs she wasn't being entirely forthcoming. He stamped out the urge to shake some sense into her.

"I thought you agreed to trust me on this. Behind the slick smiles, Landon Greene is a brute and a bully. His ultimate goal is to gain control over you."

"Why are you saying this? Are you jealous of him or something?"

A snort of derisive laughter escaped. "You're joking, right?"

"There have to be reasons for your allegations." She jutted her chin. "I'd like to know what they are."

He didn't blame her. What did he expect from the headstrong miss, anyway? To simply take him at his word? That wasn't her nature. His either, truth be told. Still, he couldn't bring himself to talk about the past. Too humiliating.

"I know what he's really like, Sophie. You only see what he wants you to see. He's doing his best to impress you. To gain your trust." When she continued to look at him with disbelief, he gritted his teeth. "If you set everything I've said aside and focus on his behavior toward women, would you agree he's a flirt?"

"I will give you that, yes."

"What do you think he and April were doing in Lucian's garden? Naming constellations?"

Her cheeks pinked. "I said I agreed, didn't I?"

"And you don't have a problem with that?"

Brushing past him, she shot him a look over her shoulder. "He's not married, nor is he in a committed relationship. Being a flirt doesn't make him an adulterer."

Fingers digging into the rough-hewn pole, he strode after her. "I would think after what your pa did that you'd want a man you could trust wholeheartedly. No reservations."

Sophie stopped so suddenly he nearly plowed into her. "What—"

"Don't do that." She spoke quietly. "I know you don't like Landon, but don't bring Lester into this."

He'd spoken without thinking. Knew how sensitive she was about the subject. "Soph—" He gently squeezed her upper arm. She flinched. Retreated again.

"Wait." Hurrying ahead, he cut her off, disregarding her withering glare. "I'm sorry. I didn't mean to bring up painful memories. What do you say we call a truce for one night?" He summoned a smile. "I've got these fish that need frying and a little friend who's probably wondering where I am."

Shifting her gaze to the forest and the descending dusk, she nodded. "And who's probably hungry, too." With a sigh, she thrust out her hand. "Fine. Truce."

Nathan wrapped his free hand around hers, unable to resist stroking the soft skin with his thumb. "Fine," he rasped, struck by an impossible yearning to ease her closer, to caress her nape, her face.

What would it be like to kiss her without an audience? an irrational voice prompted. *Enough.*

This was nothing but age-old physical attraction. He wasn't blind to the changes in his friend. Of course he would notice and be appreciative. That didn't mean he could give in to it.

With reluctance, he released her. Cleared his throat. "One more thing. You know how you feel about discussing Lester? That's how I feel about divulging my history with Landon. Can you understand that?"

Her brows pulled together, her blue eyes churning with speculation. "Something happened between you two. Something bad."

An understatement. "Yes."

"Okay."

"Okay?" She wasn't going to press him?

Her stomach rumbled, and she grinned. Surprised him by linking her arm with his and tugging. "Will's not the only one who's starving around here. Let's get going."

Lecturing himself all the way, he allowed her to lead him to her cabin.

Will did not attempt to hide his enthusiasm. He whooped and hollered and did a quick jig.

Chuckling, Nathan ruffled the boy's hair. Will was bright, sensitive at times, eager to please. As they crouched side by side at the stream, skinning and gutting the fish, it struck him that Sophie's marriage would change things. He and Will wouldn't have as much time to spend together. Her new husband would take the boy fishing and hunting, teach him the ways of farming.

He frowned. He didn't even know if they'd stick around. Maybe they'd go live on her husband's homestead.

Preoccupied, his knife slipped, slicing deep into his finger. He smothered an oath. Dropping the knife, he jerked his hand back before the blood dripped all over the fish.

"I'll get Sophie!" Will bolted toward the cabin before he could stop him.

Fumbling for the handkerchief in his pocket, he covered the wound and yanked the material taut. He hoped it wasn't deep enough to warrant stitches. Needles were for fabric, not human skin. He shivered.

What's the matter? a voice from the past taunted. *Not tough enough to handle the sight of blood?*

Forehead growing damp, he shoved away the memories. He heard the door slam open, and then Sophie was skidding to a stop in front of him, face white but otherwise calm. Will tripped along behind her.

"What happened?"

"It's nothing. A small cut, is all."

She focused on his hand, held steady against his belly. "Let me see."

As she peeled back the material, he trained his gaze on her hair. No need to risk making himself sick.

"It's still bleeding," she said matter-of-factly, replacing the blood-soaked handkerchief. "You're going to need stitches. Do you want me to do it or would you rather I take you into town to see Doc Owens?"

"Neither."

She pressed a hand against his lower back. "Come on, big guy," she cajoled. "Let's go get this over with. I'm known for my speed and precision. You won't even have a scar."

When she had him seated at her table, she flitted around the room gathering supplies. He watched her to keep his mind off the throbbing pain and the looming prospect of more.

"It's better if you don't watch," she warned as she gently cleansed the site.

"I wasn't planning on it," he drawled, closing his eyes and homing in on her delicate scent, the whisper of her skirts and the slight pressure of her leg against his thigh as she worked.

When she inserted the needle, a rogue groan escaped.

He locked his jaw and held his breath. To her credit, Sophie didn't pause. She worked quickly and efficiently and had him sewed up in a flash.

His finger ached something fierce, but at least the worst part was over. But then he made the mistake of looking at it, the misshapen, angry-looking flesh. Images from long ago rose up to taunt him. And his stomach revolted. Lunging for the door, he made it to the side yard before casting up his accounts.

Walking back inside, he felt shaky and weak. And foolish.

Sophie watched him with large, compassion-filled eyes. "Are you okay?"

Sinking onto the sofa, he grimaced. "You'd think I'd be able to handle a little blood. I am a farmer, after all. For some weird reason, I can handle animal blood a sight better than human."

She brought him a peppermint stick. When she smoothed his hair with a tender hand, Nathan's heart kicked against his ribs. With that simple touch, she was letting him know she cared, that she was worried and hated to see him in pain. Gratitude and longing flooded his chest, confusing him. This wasn't longing for her specifically... was it?

Were Josh and his sister-in-law right? Was it time he settled down, found himself a wife? Someone suitable. Someone like Pauline?

"Everybody has different tolerance levels. Just because you're a tad squeamish doesn't make you weak." Easing down beside him, affection shone brightly in the sapphire depths of her eyes.

He swallowed hard. Battled against a sudden, crazy need to hold her. "I hope I didn't ruin supper."

Cocking her head, she said, "Why don't I make fish stew instead? That might be easier on your stomach. I've already got the potatoes peeled, and it won't take any time at all to chop up an onion and carrot."

"That sounds good." He broke the candy into two sections and popped one in his mouth.

She held up her hands. "I'm not making any promises."

His stomach slowly settling, he chuckled. "As long as you don't try to feed me any pie."

A grin transformed her mouth. "Don't worry, my pie-making days are behind me."

Nathan was amazed at her calm demeanor, her take-charge attitude in the face of calamity and the tenderness in her treatment of him. He'd underestimated her, focused always on the things that drove him crazy instead of her strengths—her nurturing nature, her courage and indomitable strength, her loyalty and capacity for love.

Without thinking, he leaned close and cupped her jaw. She stilled, her gaze twining with his, sweet breath fanning across his mouth.

"You're going to make some lucky man a fine wife, Sophie Tanner," he murmured, his heart a jumble of confused emotions. Then, because it was all he would allow himself, he pressed his lips to her cheek. "My prayer is that you choose one worthy of you."

Chapter Sixteen

Weddings were the pits. Not only did Nathan have to wear a suit—a three-piece getup that hemmed him in and made his neck stiff—but he also had to sit in said suit for what seemed like hours while the preacher waxed poetic about everlasting love and commitment, the married women crying sentimental tears and single misses plotting how to land a groom of their very own.

For the life of him, he could not imagine himself up there, standing in front of God and the townsfolk, and pledging to honor and cherish his chosen bride. Those rogue thoughts he'd had at Sophie's must have been the result of blood loss.

Today he'd made an exception to his no-wedding rule. Sophie was here somewhere and, despite his warnings, he wasn't convinced she'd stay away from Landon.

Propped against the base of an elm, arms folded and one foot hooked over the other, he scanned the milling crowd. The reception for newlyweds Dan and Louise Kyker was in full swing. Guests chatted together in groups, eating wedding cake and sipping lemonade, the younger couples dancing to lively fiddle music while the older generation reclined on chairs set up on the lawn. Kids darted around, a few trying to sneak second helpings of cake.

April and her friends strolled past. When she spotted him in the shade, she waved, her smile both saucy and provocative. He nodded a response but didn't return her smile, hoping it would deter her. He wasn't in the mood for her games. Thankfully, she moved on.

Surveying the crowd again, he became impatient when he didn't see Sophie. Where was she? He pushed away from the tree. Looked as though he was going to have to join the merriment if he wanted to find her.

"Nathan!"

A small, warm female launched herself against him, arms wrapping tightly around his neck.

"I'm so happy to see you!" she exclaimed, her words muffled.

White-blond curls tickled his chin. He grinned. "Megan."

Aware now that it was his cousin accosting him, he wrapped his arms around her middle and lifted her off the ground. It had been at least six weeks since he'd seen her last. Married in July, she and her new husband had visited her eldest sister, Juliana, in Cades Cove before traveling down to New Orleans to spend time in Lucian's home-town. Relieved she was finally home, safe and sound, he set her down and away from him to get a good look at her.

Aside from the new, stylish clothes and added sparkle in her baby blues, she looked pretty much the same. He tugged on a curl. "How is married life treatin' ya, Goldilocks?"

Glancing over her shoulder at Lucian, who was deep in conversation with Aunt Alice and the twins, she turned back and flashed him a smile that hinted of secrets. "Fantastic. You should really consider trying it out for yourself."

He ran a finger beneath his collar. The late-afternoon

heat lingered in the air. "I told you before, I'm not in the market for a wife."

"Someday the right girl will come along and change your mind." Megan sounded confident. She squinted at the dancers. "Am I seeing things? That can't be Sophie Tanner. Does she have a cousin we didn't know about?"

Nathan followed her line of sight to where the musicians played beside the barn. There, standing apart from the dancers, was Sophie—breathtaking in a scoop-necked, two-piece lacy creation of pastel pink, cream and light blue. Frank was right beside her. Nathan had to admit they looked good together, Frank's dark coloring complementing Sophie's fair beauty.

"No cousin. Sophie, uh, underwent a transformation a few weeks back. Your sister is the one responsible."

One pale brow winged up. "Nicole? Why would she—" She tapped her mouth. "Oh. Of course. It all comes back to her determination to get out of town. She's quite put out with me that I didn't take her with us to New Orleans." She studied Frank and Sophie. "While I wouldn't have paired them together, I must admit they make a handsome couple. Perhaps theirs will be the next wedding we attend."

His heart squeezed uncomfortably. "Perhaps."

Her smile faltered. "You don't look happy. Why—"

She broke off, squealing as Lucian snuck up behind her and slid his arms around her waist. "You shouldn't sneak up on me," she chided playfully.

Shooting a grin at Nathan, Lucian bent his head and whispered in her ear. Something that made her blush.

Feeling like an intruder, Nathan averted his gaze, automatically seeking out Sophie. The sun's rays shimmered in her upswept hair, the slight breeze teasing stray tendrils that framed her face. She looked as though she really wanted to dance.

"Hi, Nathan." Pauline strolled in his direction, her brother Dex with her.

"Afternoon, O'Malley."

"Dex." He shook the other man's hand. Pauline hung back, her smile a touch uncertain. Nathan nodded and smiled encouragingly. Apparently he'd wrongly attributed her with a practical outlook. Guessing from her manner, she must have construed his prior invitation to mean more than it had. He hated that he'd raised false hopes. "You're looking well, Pauline."

Dumb thing to say, O'Malley.

Her dark eyes sparkled anew. "Would you care to dance?" she asked hopefully.

Sensing Dex's steady stare, Nathan extended his arm. "I'd love to."

Joining the other dancers midsong, he spotted his cousin Jane dancing with Tom Leighton. The barbershop owner appeared to be cajoling her out of a bad mood. Unusual for sweet-tempered Jane. He hoped she kept Tom too busy to notice Megan and Lucian's arrival. Seeing the happy couple would surely be hard on the rejected suitor.

Pauline squeezed his hand, pulling his attention back to her. "Megan is practically glowing with happiness. Married life suits her."

He smiled. "I wasn't confident in her choice at first, but I've since realized Lucian is the right man for her."

Executing a turn, his gaze connected with Sophie's. The haunting sadness in her eyes socked him in the gut. What could have caused such wrenching emotion? Quickly, she averted her face to address Frank.

His partner followed his line of sight. "I heard about Sophie's husband hunt."

"Who hasn't?" he grunted, still staring at the couple.

"Who do you think she'll end up with?" she persisted.

Shrugging, he looked at her with what he hoped was a bland expression. "That's anybody's guess."

Pauline tilted her head to the side, regarding him with frank appraisal. "Some people think you might volunteer for the job."

"Me?" He accidentally stomped on her toe. "Isn't it obvious the two of us wouldn't suit? Besides, I'm not interested in marriage right now. From what I've seen, falling in love is a painful, angst-ridden process that doesn't always end well."

"It doesn't have to be that way." She stared at him in consternation.

"Even so, I'm not interested," he said firmly. "Not now. Maybe not ever."

The music died away and he couldn't be more grateful. She'd bristled, her manner suggesting he'd announced his disgust for small children and pets.

Preston came to his rescue, tapping his shoulder and inviting her to dance the next song, oblivious to her clear upset.

Clearing the group, he saw that his path would take him past Sophie and Frank. Recalling her earlier expression of longing, he couldn't deny her a chance to dance at least once this day.

"Would you like to dance?"

Her eyes widened at his abrupt request. With a quick glance at Frank, she nodded and accepted his outstretched hand. The music segued into a slow, pensive number and she faltered. "I'm not good at this."

Settling an arm around her waist, he pulled her as close as he dared. "Let me lead you."

Lost in her trusting eyes, reveling in the feel of her small hand upon his shoulder, Nathan guided them both in a simple dance. Their first. For the entirety of the song, he would forget about the rumors going 'round about them, forget about everything except chasing away her sadness.

"How is it that you and I have never danced together?"

"I—I don't know." Her fingers tightened on his sleeve. She sounded slightly breathless. From the dance? Or something else entirely?

"Well—" he grinned as he maneuvered her in a tight circle that made her lips part in surprise "—you're a great partner."

"Thank you, Nathan," she said quietly, looking as though he'd handed her the moon with that one compliment.

That's because she's used to lectures from you, not praise.

He frowned.

"Is something wrong?" she asked. "Did I crush your toes?"

He pulled her closer, a move that earned him a raised eyebrow from the older gentleman sweeping past with his wife. Ignoring him, Nathan gazed down at her. "No. You did nothing wrong. My mind wandered, is all."

"How's your finger?"

He unconsciously flexed it, the bandage straining. "Still a little sore but healing nicely thanks to you."

She smiled. "I'm glad I could help."

For the remainder of the song, he focused on the moment, the surprisingly pleasant way she fit against him. When it ended, he found himself foolishly wishing for more time. "Can I get you a glass of lemonade?"

"I'd like that."

But when they separated themselves from the dancers, Frank was there with two drinks in his hand. He offered one to Sophie. With an apologetic look at Nathan, she accepted it and thanked her date. Her *date*. Right. The two of them were here together, which meant it was his cue to get lost.

At least he could boast success in one area—she looked happier than she had a few minutes ago.

"Well, I guess I'll see you both later. Thanks for the dance, Soph."

And he walked away, leaving her to her hunt.

Sophie longed to call him back. To dance with him again. Held in Nathan's strong, warm embrace, she'd felt as though she were floating in the clouds, a peaceful place far removed from her tumultuous world. His molten silver gaze had thrilled her. Made her believe, for the space of a song, that she was special to him. More than a friend.

But that was wishful thinking. And so far from reality as to be laughable.

Willing her gaze away from his retreating back, Sophie turned to Frank. "I don't see your mother anywhere. Did she stay home?"

"She's sitting over there."

Sophie glimpsed Bonnie's short brown curls. Craning her neck, she was able to get a fuller view of the woman seated alone. "She doesn't look like she's having much fun."

Frank sighed. "Ma doesn't like crowds."

"Or music."

He gave a wry smile. "Or much of anything, to be honest. She's the exact opposite of my pa. I'm not sure how they ever ended up together."

She sipped the tart drink. "She's missing out, especially with regard to your playing. Will and I enjoyed it immensely."

He flushed, clearly unused to praise. "I had a good time the other night."

"So did I," she said, meaning it. Frank was quickly becoming a friend.

She nodded her head to indicate the musicians. "You should be up there playing."

"I don't think so."

When she laid a hand on his arm, his dark brows lifted an inch. "Don't let your ma hold you back, Frank. Do what makes you happy. Life is short."

Her granddad's face flashed in her mind, and she blinked back moisture. She missed him every moment of every day. Sometimes she'd curl up on his bed simply to try to feel closer to him, dreading the day his familiar scent faded from his pillow.

"I think I'll go and get a piece of cake."

"I can get it for you—" Frank offered.

"That's all right." She waved him off. "I'll be back in a moment."

Heart hurting, Sophie weaved through the throng to the refreshment table. This wasn't the time or place to give in to her grief. Not truly hungry, she chose a plate with the smallest piece, not noticing the female trio standing nearby.

"Aw, isn't it sweet, girls?" April drawled. "Sophie's trying to imitate a lady."

She bit the inside of her cheek to keep from retorting.

"I—I think you look beautiful, Sophie," Lila offered softly.

Turning to face them, she managed a tight smile for the younger girl. "Thanks, Lila."

April rolled her eyes. "Beautiful? She looks like a little girl trying to pull off her mother's clothing. Oh, wait. Your ma isn't around anymore. Neither is your low-life pa."

Lila gasped. "April!"

Her sister, Norma Jean, looked uncomfortable, her gaze volleying between them.

Sophie's temper flared. Setting her plate down, she turned to leave before things got ugly.

But April wasn't finished. "My ma says your brother will turn out exactly like Lester—a lying, cheating, amoral philanderer."

"Leave my brother out of this," she said through clenched teeth, fingers tightening on the glass in her hand. "Say all you like about me. I'm a big girl. I can handle it. But Will hasn't done a thing to deserve your insults. He's innocent."

"I can say whatever I like. Don't think that because you've put on a dress and changed your hair and turned all the men's heads that you're better than me. Inside, you're still a dumb, dirty hick," she jeered. "And your brother is Tanner filth."

Cold fury swept through Sophie, too fast to stop her reaction. Lifting her glass, she dumped the contents over April's head.

The dark-headed girl sputtered and wailed.

Sophie was only vaguely aware of the gathering circle of spectators, her sole focus on shutting April up.

"How dare you!" April raged. Her hand shot out and grabbed a glass, then tossed the liquid on Sophie's bodice.

The sticky wetness seeped through the material. Oooh! Grabbing a fistful of cake, she smashed it in April's snooty face. "Now that's an improvement," she murmured.

Sophie's satisfaction was short-lived. A hand clamped down on her arm. "That's quite enough."

Glancing up into Nathan's stern face, her stomach plummeted. Her anger evaporated. Humiliation burned in her cheeks.

He ushered her away from the murmuring crowd, waiting until they were hidden behind a copse of trees to drop her arm as if it burned him. "How could you, Sophie?"

The disappointment in his eyes, which only moments

ago had been friendly and full of caring, made her want to disappear. He wore a path in the grass, frustration oozing from his stiff frame.

"I'm sorry."

He stopped short and tossed her a look of exasperation. "It's not me you should be apologizing to. Did you see Louise's face? This is her wedding day, possibly the biggest day of her life, and you made a mockery of it."

She bit her lip, willing herself to hold it together until he'd gone. "You're right," she rasped. "I'll get cleaned up and apologize."

"I think you've done enough for one day," he said without emotion, unwilling at that point to even look at her.

Her shoulders drooped. He was right. She'd acted like a child, causing a scene at such an important event. She deserved his censure.

"I'll just go, then."

"Soph?"

"Yes?"

Emotion burned in his eyes. "Promise me you'll try and curb your impulsive streak. After you're married, I won't be around to bail you out of trouble. To be honest, that worries me."

"After I'm married, I won't be your responsibility anymore," she choked out, then spun and fled, hot tears dripping down her cheeks.

A vortex of emotions swirling out of control in his chest, Nathan stalked to Josh's side. He felt like punching something. Beside the table, Georgette Littleton attempted to console her daughter as she wiped frosting from her forehead. People cast curious glances his way, as if he could explain what had happened.

"Is it time to leave yet?" he growled, silently vowing

to make his excuses the next time a wedding invitation arrived.

Concern wreathed Josh's face. "You gave her a hard time, didn't you?"

Guilt penetrated his ire and pricked his conscience. "She deserved it."

"Are you sure about that?"

"What did you expect me to do?" he snapped. "Applaud her creativity? 'Gee, Sophie, the cake was a nice touch. Good aim.'"

"You aren't her judge and jury, Nathan." His older brother's piercing glower could still make him squirm even after all these years. "I made that same mistake with Kate and almost lost her. You know, you two have been at daggers drawn ever since we were kids. I don't think Sophie instigated it, either. She was merely reacting to your condescending behavior. You're the only one who had a problem with her. Have you ever stopped to wonder why that is?"

"I don't have to wonder," he snapped, beginning to feel like a parrot. "Sophie and I are as different as night and day, that's why."

Josh cocked a sardonic brow. "You have love of God and family in common. You're both hard workers. Both love the outdoors."

"So what? There are a lot of people with those same values. Doesn't really make things easier between us." When he made to leave, his brother clamped a hand on his shoulder.

"I heard the entire exchange. April said some rather cruel things about Lester and Will."

His gaze locked with Josh's. The grim truth in the blue depths soured his stomach. When it came to her little brother, Sophie was as protective as a momma bear with her cub, a trait he'd always admired.

With a frustrated groan, he dragged a hand down his face. "I've been a real idiot, haven't I?"

Josh winked. "Nothing a little groveling won't cure."

Chapter Seventeen

Nathan hated that he'd jumped to conclusions. Hated that he'd hurt her.

You're not her judge and jury, Nathan. Josh's statement continued to cut at him. His brother was right. Who did he think he was? And why had he erected barriers between them all those years ago? Continually searched for reasons to push her away?

Too much of a coward to delve too deeply for answers to those questions, relief swept through him when he entered the meadow near her cabin and saw her boots dangling from her favorite tree.

When a stick snapped beneath his boot, she didn't turn her head to look at him. She sat very still, spine straight and hands braced against the thick branch supporting her, floral-print skirts billowed around her with a hint of ruffled pantaloons beneath the hem.

He halted at the tree base. "I need to talk to you. Will you come down?"

"No."

"Please?"

"I can't," she breathed. "I'm stuck."

Huh? "What do you mean?"

"My hair's caught in the branches," she confessed, frowning. "I wasn't paying attention and sat farther out than I normally do."

Shrugging out of his suit jacket, he draped it over a low-lying limb. "I'm coming up."

She was quiet as he climbed and, maneuvering himself onto the branch, scooted close, her frothy skirts overlapping his black trousers. "Good thing this is sturdy." He patted the rough wood that barely gave beneath his added weight.

"I'm glad you came," she said somberly, "otherwise, I might've been here awhile. I've tried to untangle it but ended up making it worse."

At the sight of the tear tracks on her cheeks, the dewy moisture clinging to her eyelashes, he cringed. He was an ogre. Heaving a sigh, he leaned slightly back to inspect the problem. There were a number of branches snagged in the hair loops and pink ribbons.

"It doesn't look bad. I'll be as gentle as I can."

She nodded, then winced.

"Careful, now." Angling closer, he worked to disengage the ribbons first, then her hair, which was like fine silk whispering through his fingertips. Being this near to her, inhaling her scent and registering the changes in her breathing, heightened his senses. Awareness turned his blood to sludge and his thoughts had trouble connecting. He risked a glance at her profile. Where her cheeks had been colorless before, they were now flushed a soft pink. Her pulse beat frantically in the dip of her throat.

Focus, O'Malley.

Fingers fumbling, he somehow managed to free her. "There." His voice croaked. "All finished."

Sophie lifted a hand to her hair, grateful to be free. "Thank you."

She started when Nathan laid his palm gently against

her cheek, his thumb brushing the wetness away. Remorse darkened his eyes.

"I'm sorry I scolded you," he whispered. "I'm a terrible friend. Please forgive me?"

Leaning into his hand, she whispered back, "You were right to lecture me."

His brows pulled together. "I should've asked what happened before reading you the riot act. I was wrong."

"I should've kept my temper in check."

His expression turned fiercely tender. "You have a right to defend yourself and your family. I would've done the same in your situation."

Obviously he'd found out what April had said. "I can't see you dumping lemonade on anyone."

Lifting a shoulder, his mouth softened. "Maybe not. I can think of a few people who deserve cake in the face, though."

"You wouldn't do any of those things. You have heaps more self-control than I have."

His hand slipped to her nape, a warm, wonderful weight, the work-roughened skin sending delightful shivers along her shoulders. Her scalp tingled.

His face hovered near hers, their noses nearly touching. "I've given you a hard time all these years, not once telling you how much I actually like you." His husky drawl enveloped her, cutting off the birds and squirrels, buzzing insects and trickling water. All that existed was this man. "You possess many fine qualities, Soph. I admire your fire and determination. Your courage. The way you put others' needs before your own." His beautiful eyes shimmered, inviting her in for the first time.

Sophie's heart whirled and dipped in a dizzying dance. "You do? L-like me, I mean?"

"I do." His gaze dropped to her mouth. "Very much."

He was going to kiss her. Not because of some silly game. Because he wanted to.

His fingers tightened a fraction. *"Soph."*

Dipping his head, his lips brushed hers, gentle and warm and soft. Exploring. Caressing.

Feeling bold, Sophie delved a hand into his hair and poured all her pent-up emotions into her response. Surely he could sense the depth of her feelings for him!

When he framed her face with his other hand, together their balance shifted and Sophie experienced a falling sensation. Nathan broke off their kiss and, chuckling low, grasped her waist with one hand and an overhead branch with the other.

His lazy smile made her heart sing. "I guess I forgot where we were there for a minute."

"Me, too," she said, suddenly shy. What did this mean?

"Sophie?"

At the sound of Will's voice, Nathan's gaze shifted to the ground and his expression shuttered closed. There, a few steps behind her brother, was Josh, watching them with keen interest. And Frank.

She'd forgotten all about him! Had he witnessed their embrace?

No matter what, you could never, ever, forget Nathan.

"I'll go first," Nathan said stiffly, "then I'll help you down."

Her joy deflated, she accepted his help. Was he regretting his actions? Once on the ground, she attempted to smooth her disheveled coiffure.

"Why did you leave early, Sophie?" Will asked, brow crinkled. "Frank was looking all over for you."

Dare she hope her brother hadn't heard of her lapse in judgment and, more importantly, the slurs April had cast on their family? "I, uh, needed some time to myself."

"I was worried." Frank approached, shooting a curious

glance at a frowning Nathan, who didn't budge from her side. "I saw what happened with April."

His utter lack of condemnation didn't surprise her. He'd inherited his generous spirit from his father.

"I apologize for abandoning you."

"What matters is that you're all right."

Sophie couldn't think of a single thing to say. Oh, what an awkward coil this was! Frank was utterly clueless about what had just transpired between her and Nathan. And Nathan—what must he be thinking? She couldn't bring herself to look at him.

"Thank you for bringing him home," she finally managed to say. "You, too, Josh."

"No problem." When his lips twitched in amusement, indicating he was aware of her predicament, her cheeks flamed in mortification. This was worse than any food fight.

Hands deep in his pockets, Will rubbed at the ground with his shoe. "I told Josh I'm old enough to see myself home, but he insisted."

Josh laughed. Sophie grimaced. "He did that as a favor to me. Please use your manners and thank him."

"Thank you," he murmured. "Can I go change now?"

"Yes, you may. And don't forget to hang your clothes up," she called after him.

He didn't look back, just waved a hand over his head.

Risking a glance at Nathan, she caught him shaking his head at his brother, who was wearing a knowing smirk. What was that all about?

"I've got to get back to Kate," Josh told her. "Are you coming, Nathan?"

Please stay, she silently pleaded. *Stay and explain what that kiss meant to you. Tell me I can call off this ridiculous scheme because* you *want to marry me.*

But that wasn't possible with her date looking on, was it?

"Yeah, I'm coming." Looking grim, he retrieved his suit jacket and slung it over his shoulder. When he'd joined his brother and the duo turned to leave, she raised a hand.

"Nathan, wait."

He halted and looked over his shoulder at her, grim and closed off.

"Frank, would you mind waiting for me at the cabin?"

"Sure."

Josh tugged on his hat brim. "See you later, Sophie."

"I'll catch up with you in a minute," Nathan called after him, facing her with trepidation.

That didn't bode well.

Summoning her courage, she went to him, stared deep into the silver recesses of his eyes and came away frustrated by the lack of answers. "What just happened here?"

"I lost my head," he said woodenly. "I apologize."

An apology wasn't going to cut it. "This wasn't a forfeit," she told him. "There was no one around to see. Why'd you do it?"

Nostrils flaring, he buried his fingers in his hair. "What are you angling for? A proposal? It was just a kiss, Sophie. It meant nothing."

She fell back a step. Nothing? "That didn't feel like nothing." Not to her. To her, it had meant *everything*.

"Look, you're all grown up now, and you're—" he waved a hand up and down "—you're wearing dresses and fixing your hair differently. It was bound to happen sooner or later. Attraction. That's all this is. Plain and simple attraction. Now that we've got it out of our systems, things can go back to normal."

"Attraction." She nodded, her throat knotting with unshed tears. "Sounds reasonable."

Only, what she felt for him was far from reasonable. And it wasn't simple at all.

"Yeah, well…" He angled his thumb over his shoulder. "I should go. Frank is waiting for you."

"I don't want to keep him waiting." Her voice sounded completely calm. Surprising, considering her insides were quivering with suppressed emotion.

This is it, Sophia Lorraine. It's time to give up this childhood dream. Time to move past your feelings and plan for a different future. One without Nathan O'Malley. Because loving him will get you nothing but heartache.

Following the Sunday meal, Nathan escaped to his sanctuary. Normally he enjoyed the conversation and camaraderie of his extended family, but not today. Not after yesterday's fight with Sophie. That kiss. And their less-than-ideal parting.

He was a total wreck. He'd lashed out at her in anger. Only, she wasn't the one he was mad at. He was angry at himself, for being weak and careless, for acting on impulse—the very thing he disliked in her.

Pulling on a pair of deerskin gloves to protect his injured finger, he found the pitchfork in the corner and began the tedious task of ridding the straw of rubbish. The physical exertion did little to clear his mind.

"Here you are." Caleb waltzed in through the double doors standing ajar, the habitual scowl curling his mouth. "We need to talk."

Nathan forked a pile of straw. "I'm busy."

Resting an arm on the stall's edge, Caleb challenged him with a glare. "Too busy to tell me what Sophie's doing with Landon Greene?"

He straightened, hand tightening on the handle. "Did you see them together?"

"After services. As soon as Will left with Cordelia, Sophie and Landon rode off."

"Maybe she was going to the Greenes' for dinner." Icy dread pulsed through his veins.

Caleb shook his head. "Uh-uh. They were headed in the opposite direction." Brown eyes impaled his. "Why didn't you warn her?"

"I did," he snapped, despising the sense of helplessness coursing through him. If Sophie was in trouble, there'd be nothing he could do about it. "She wouldn't listen."

Caleb pushed off from the stall, jammed his hands into his pockets. "Have you told her everything?"

"No."

"I think you should."

"You're right." Propping the pitchfork against the wall, he snagged his hat. "I just hope it's not too late."

Striding into the aisle, he fetched Chance's saddle.

"Where are you going?"

"To her place to wait. If she isn't back by nightfall, I'll head over to the Greenes'. Find out where they went."

"Want me to come with you?"

Smoothing the blanket over his horse's back, Nathan tossed him a grateful look. "Thanks for the offer, but I've got to handle this on my own."

"Sophie's family." Caleb stroked Chance's neck while Nathan worked to saddle him. "If he lays so much as a finger on her, he'll have the wrath of the O'Malley clan raining down on him."

Vaulting into the saddle, Nathan smiled grimly down at his younger brother. "I'm glad you're here."

His resulting expression warned him it wasn't for long. As soon as Nathan said the word, Caleb would be gone again.

"Be safe" was his response.

As Chance picked his way along the familiar forest

trail toward the Tanner homestead, Nathan prayed. For Sophie's safety. For his peace of mind. And for forgiveness. For if not for his pride, she wouldn't be courting the enemy right about now.

"I could never tire of this view," Sophie sighed. A break in the trees allowed them a glimpse of mountain ridges stretching into the far distance. The air was fresh and slightly cooler at this elevation. Behind them, their horses grazed. "It's stunning. A true testament to God's glory."

Landon, shoulder pressed against hers, turned his head to regard her with blatant appreciation. "I could never tire of it, either," he said softly, clearly referring to her, not the mountains.

She chose to ignore the insinuation. Up until this point, Landon had been his entertaining self, and the afternoon had passed rather pleasantly. When he'd approached her after church and asked if she'd like to accompany him on another picnic, she'd hesitated. Nathan didn't like the man. Nor did he trust him. Sophie's curiosity had prompted her to agree. She was dying to learn what had transpired between the two men.

"Tell me something…" He ran a finger down her cheek. "Where is my name on your list? I hope I'm near the top."

Sophie's jaw dropped. "How do you know about that?"

"Gossip is kind of like poison ivy. One slipup and it spreads without you even realizing it. Until the itchin' sets in, that is." His grin seemed a touch mean-spirited.

Head spinning with the revelation, she smacked at a mosquito humming near her neck. "Who was it? Nicole?" she demanded with rising irritation. The younger girl had vowed to keep her secret, and Sophie had trusted her. Wasn't it enough that folks knew about her need to marry without them knowing about her suitable husband list?

"Patrick heard it from his sister, Carrie, who helps out

the Lamberts. She overheard your aunt telling Mrs. Lambert."

Aunt Cordelia! "I don't understand. Why would she do that?"

"That's beside the point." He waved away her concerns with an arrogant smirk. "Let's talk about the list some more. So, am I number one?"

"I'm not discussing this with you."

"Give me a name, then. A man needs to know who he's up against."

"Nathan."

Beneath his hat brim, his face hardened, eyes glittering with dislike. She'd tossed out the name to irk him, and perhaps to goad him into revealing something of the past.

"Is that right?" Velvet voice cloaked in menace, he edged closer, his hulking body looming over her. "I've been wondering something. What is the exact nature of your and O'Malley's relationship?"

Though adrenaline raced through her body, priming her for flight, Sophie held her ground. "What do you mean?"

"I know you two are friends, but it seems to me he's awfully protective of you. Some would even say possessive." His gaze raked her with awful suggestion. "Are you lovers?"

She gaped at him. "How dare you! Nathan and I have done nothing to be ashamed of."

His large hands snapped around her rib cage. "You've gone beyond the bounds of friendship, though. I can see the truth in your eyes."

Their complete and utter isolation hit her then, stole the air from her lungs. Maybe this outing hadn't been her smartest move, after all.

Alarmed now, she braced her hands on his biceps. "He warned me about you."

Thrown off guard, one blond brow quirked. "Did he, now? What did he accuse me of?"

"Nothing specific." She met his gaze unflinchingly, unwilling to let him see her fear. "I inferred that you used to be friends. Nathan isn't a vindictive person, nor is he so shallow as to sever a friendship over a minor dispute. Whatever you did must've been pretty bad."

"We were never friends. I tolerated him." His lip curled. "The reason he hates me is because I know he's a fraud. A weak excuse of a man."

Outrage seared her insides. "You're the fraud, Landon. You pretend to be the perfect gentleman when deep down you're really a conniving snake." Pushing against him with all her might, she demanded, "Let me go."

He was bigger and stronger than her, and her attempt to break free failed miserably.

Landon sighed long-sufferingly. "There's no one around to hear if you protest, *sweet* Sophie. Don't fret, all I want is a kiss. You need to see for yourself what a real man is like."

His mouth came down hard on hers. Sophie froze. He was really doing this. *Forcing* himself on her. Taking her lack of resistance as compliance, Landon crushed her to his chest and tilted her head back at an awkward angle.

Defiance bubbled up, bursting forth in a cry of protest. Her heel came down hard on his toe. He ripped his mouth away. Muttered a stinging oath. Her knee contacted high on his inner thigh, and his hold slackened.

But before she could scramble out of his reach, his fingers fisted on her dress. She reared back. The sound of material ripping frightened her as nothing ever had before. Drawing on strength she hadn't known she possessed, she elbowed him in the nose. A cracking noise met her ears. Blood gushed down his face, a face she'd once thought of as boyishly good-looking. Now that she was privy to his true nature, he just looked ugly.

"I'll make you pay for this!" he growled.

Hurrying toward her horse, she mounted clumsily, urging him to flee while she was still half in the saddle. He obeyed. The shakes overtook her halfway down the mountain, but there were no tears, only anger. At Landon for his boorish behavior. And at herself, for not heeding Nathan's warnings.

Chapter Eighteen

When she rode into the yard, Nathan was sitting on her front stoop looking mad enough to spit nails.

She wasn't prepared to face him. Not when she was so very vulnerable and desperate for his arms around her, for his reassurances that everything was going to be all right.

Dismounting on wobbly legs, she paused to bury her forehead in her horse's flank and to pray for strength. *Baby steps, Sophie. Letting go of him is going to take time. Lots of it.*

"I suppose you're here to check up on me," she muttered without glancing his way, taking the reins and starting past the cabin in the direction of the barn. Her unbound hair acted as a curtain, masking his view. "Who told you?"

"My brother." His boots scuffed the grass as he strode after her.

Inside the barn, he intercepted her efforts to heft the saddle off, gently nudging her aside. Sophie kept her head bent, taking her time locating the brush amid the assorted tools and tack in an effort to delay the confrontation.

"Look, I didn't come here to argue with you." Lowering the saddle to the ground, he spoke to her back. "I wanted to make sure you're okay."

"I'm fine." Picking up the brush, she gripped it tightly. *Please leave before I throw myself in your arms.*

"Funny. You don't sound fine." He stepped closer, his nearness welcome and unthreatening. Not like Landon's. "Are you sure everything's okay?"

How was it that Nathan was perceptive of her moods and yet blind to her feelings for him? She sighed. No sense hiding this. She was fairly certain she'd broken Landon's nose. News like that would travel fast.

Slowly, she faced him. The concern wreathing his handsome features dropped away the instant he spotted her ripped sleeve. Horror widened his eyes. "What happened? What did he do to you?"

"Nathan—"

Looking ill, he skimmed his thumb across her lower lip. She jerked. "Your lip is bleeding."

She touched her mouth, only now aware of the dull soreness. Landon must have inadvertently bit her when she'd stomped on his foot. She shuddered. "You were right. He's not a nice man."

"Tell me what happened, Sophie," he urged, panic edging his voice.

"He kissed me. That's all."

It was just a kiss, Sophie. Nathan's harsh words taunted her. *It meant nothing.* Funny, his rejection had wounded her more deeply than Landon's attack.

"He hurt you." A terrible anger turned his face to cold marble, frightening her. "He's going to pay for that."

Nathan wasn't a violent man, but threaten someone close to him and he became the noble avenger. What if he confronted Landon and got himself into trouble? What if he got hurt?

She pressed a hand against his hard stomach, determined to calm him. "I'm perfectly fine, Nathan. Honest."

She scraped up a shaky smile. "I didn't need a rescuer this time. I rescued myself. Aren't you proud of me?"

She'd meant it as a joke. He stared at her, more somber than the day his favorite bloodhound died. "I'm very proud of you, Soph. Fighting back took a lot of courage."

He carefully skimmed her hair behind her shoulders, his tenderness inviting her to lay her head on his capable chest and cry it out. But she couldn't. Not if she was to extinguish the love burning like the North Star in her heart and soul.

"It's my actions I'm ashamed of. I should've told you everything from the beginning." Pivoting, he sank onto the wooden chest shoved up against the wall and buried his face in his hands. "If not for my pride, you wouldn't have been in harm's way."

Setting the brush on the shelf, she went to sit beside him. "What happened today was not your fault. By ignoring your warnings, I put myself into an unpredictable situation. Fortunately, nothing serious happened."

Shifting so that the barn wall supported him, hands resting on his thighs, he shot her a look filled with regret. "He hurt you."

"He hurt you, too, didn't he?" she countered softly. "What exactly did Landon do? I want to know."

A muscle jumped in his tight jaw. "You may find this hard to believe, but he and I were once friends."

Gatlinburg's most popular and quiet, shy Nathan? Yeah, it was a stretch.

"Imagine my surprise when he started paying attention to me. Here was this kid who had everything going for him—a nice, well-established family, good marks in school and more friends than he knew what to do with—and he wanted to hang out with *me*. I thought maybe, by associating with him, some of his good traits would rub off on me." He scowled in self-recrimination. "I quickly learned Landon was a fake. His ego demanded constant feeding and, more than anything, he needed to be in control. He must've seen me as a weak mark."

"Don't say that. There's nothing weak about you, Nathan O'Malley."

Nathan surged to his feet and commenced pacing, his towering presence shrinking the small structure.

"At first, we did normal things. Fishing. Swimming. Then one day, we were up in the barn loft playing with his new kittens, and he dared me to throw one over the side."

Sophie gasped, dreading his next words. That poor, helpless animal.

"I refused, of course, but he grabbed the one from my lap and tossed it over, laughing hysterically as I cried over its limp body."

Knowing Nathan's depth of respect for animals, she could only imagine his anguish. "That must've been a nightmare."

Still pacing, he ruffled his already tousled hair.

"I was so upset I didn't speak to him for days. You can imagine how well that went over. At first, he was livid. Then he changed tactics, apologizing and promising never to do it again."

"And you believed him."

"I did. The cycle kept repeating itself. Stretched on for months. The final straw came in late July, a few days before my eleventh birthday. Landon and I were out at old man Miller's swimming hole, horsing around, when he lured me up into a tree. He dared me to jump off into the water. It was high, and I didn't want to do it. When I tried to get down, he pushed me." Grimacing, he held up his right hand. "Broke two fingers. One of the bones pierced the skin. Now you know why I can't stand the sight of blood. It was a gruesome injury. Doc had to perform surgery. Ma was beside herself with worry."

Nauseous, Sophie forced herself to stay seated instead of going to him. "I recall asking you about the scars. You were evasive."

"I didn't share what happened with anyone outside my immediate family. I swore my brothers to secrecy."

"Josh didn't want to pound Landon?"

"Oh, yeah, he did, but Pa warned him against it."

"Surely other people have discovered his true nature," she said, amazed she hadn't seen through Landon's act before now.

"He has countless acquaintances and no true friends. He doesn't let anyone close. Control is his obsession. He's been very careful not to reveal himself. That's why he can't stand me, because I know who he really is." His expression turned stormy. "Your connection to me is the reason I think he lost it today."

Sophie nodded, her hair swinging forward. "He questioned my relationship with you." She clamped her hands tightly together. "H-he accused us of…"

He muttered something unintelligible. "I'm going over there."

"No!" She whipped her head up. "There's no need. He won't be bothering me again…. I broke his nose."

His brows collided with his hairline as his jaw dropped. "I can't believe you did that." Dismay flitted across his face, followed by grudging admiration. "Wait. Yes, I can. You're the gutsiest girl I know."

She deflected the praise, intentionally dredging up his flippant disregard of what had been the sweetest moments of her life. *Just a kiss, Sophie. Attraction. That's all this is.* During the long, arduous ride down the mountain, she'd had ample time to think. To stew over her problems. And she'd had a revelation. If she were to have any chance at all of moving forward, of having a fulfilled and content life, she had to oust him from her heart. The easiest way to do that? Embrace a different future than the one she'd envisioned. Embark on a new life with a new husband. She'd create a new and different family for her and Will.

"I've made a decision."

"A decision about what?" Distracted, he was still thinking of Landon, of the attack.

"My hunt is over. I've decided to marry Frank," she said with as much dignity as she could considering she was sitting there with her dress ripped and hair falling down around her face. "If he'll have me."

He went very still. "This is awful sudden, isn't it?"

"As you are aware, time is not on my side."

Looking pained, he slipped his hands into his pockets. "Are you certain?"

Pushing to her feet, she stepped around him. Pressed her hands to her chest where, beneath flesh and bone, her heart cracked and bled drops of regret. "He'll make a fine husband. We've become friends." Through the opening, a cloud passed over the sun, blocking its radiance.

Tension-filled silence stretched between them. "If you're sure that's what you want, I'll support your decision."

"Thank you. I appreciate that." Why did this have to hurt so much? "Now, if you don't mind, I need to go inside and change before I pick up Will from the Lamberts'."

"Of course. I'll go." In the doorway, he turned back and propped a hand against the frame. "But first I want to apologize for my hasty words yesterday. I was harsh. That was uncalled for. I was angry at myself, not you. I'm the one who instigated the kiss—"

"Stop." Holding up a hand, she struggled to maintain her composure. "There's no need to rehash the details. I'm hoping to become engaged very soon and once that happens, I won't spare another thought on what was an unfortunate mistake."

Liar, an inner voice accused. *You'll never, ever, forget it.*

Nathan flinched a little, then nodded. "Right. Well, that's my signal to leave. Bye, Sophie."

Watching him stride away, she felt utterly bereft and, as usual, alone.

Her parting words, stinging like a thousand fire ant bites, stayed with him all the way home.

What did you expect after your sorry behavior? You deserved worse and you know it.

Sophie had made her choice, had she? He tried to be happy for her and felt petty when he couldn't. Her and Frank? He found it difficult to believe they'd be happy together. Frank was too passive. And everyone knew he didn't take a single step without his mother's permission.

Beneath the dissatisfaction burned a desire to exact retribution on that scum Landon Greene. Something had to be done. Look at what had happened because of his continued silence.

Reining in Chance at the barn entrance, Nathan hollered for Caleb. His brother appeared after a minute—sweaty, bits of straw sticking to his pant legs, hands propped on his hips, impatience marking his expression. One look at Nathan and he started forward. "What happened?"

"Sophie finally showed up at her place with a busted lip and her dress ripped." At the alarm skittering through Caleb's brown eyes, Nathan held up a hand. "She's fine. She handled Landon."

Caleb's mouth firmed. "Now it's our turn," he said, pivoting on his heel. "I'll just be a minute."

Nathan foolishly allowed his mind to wander to Sophie's encounter, imagining Landon's hands on her, forcing himself on her, and the real possibility that things could have gotten much, much worse. If not for her bravery and quick thinking...

White-hot rage simmered in his veins. His horse shifted nervously beneath him, no doubt detecting Nathan's wrath, and he smoothed a hand along his powerful neck. "It's okay, boy."

As he waited for Caleb to saddle Rebel, he prayed and asked God for guidance, wisdom and self-control. As much as he longed to plant his fist in Landon's face, it wouldn't accomplish a thing, would only spur the bully to further action.

His brother led his horse out of the barn and mounted up. As they were about to ride out, Josh emerged from the orchard and waved them down, insisting on joining them when he heard what they were planning.

The ride out to the Greenes' place was accomplished in tense silence. Nathan was glad of his brothers' support—this confrontation had been brewing for years—however, the last thing he wanted was for one of them to suffer injury. While neither of them went out seeking violence, the pistols in their holsters said they meant business.

It being Sunday afternoon, a time most families in these parts spent relaxing and visiting with neighbors, they found Jedediah Greene rocking on his porch. At the sight of them entering his yard, he lowered his pipe and came to the top of the steps.

"Howdy, gentlemen." Scanning their serious expressions, his bushy brows met over his nose. "What can I do for you?"

"We need to talk to you and your son," Nathan said. Jedediah was a reasonable man. Maybe exposing Landon's true nature to his family would be the wisest course.

He waved the still-smoking pipe. "Come on in. I think he's in his bedroom."

Dismounting, they left their mounts in the yard and

preceded the short, balding man inside. Wanda Greene, who'd been reading at the table, quickly masked her surprise at the sight of three armed men entering her home. Glancing at her husband, she hurriedly stood and offered them coffee, which they refused.

"Landon," Jedediah called, "you've got company." As he chose a chair beside the fireplace, he indicated the leather sofa. "Please, have a seat." He watched them with open curiosity. It wasn't every day the O'Malley brothers paid a formal visit.

Nathan hadn't been here since he was a kid. It was still neat and tidy, the furnishings plain yet sturdily built, pictures on the walls. A home to be proud of.

Landon strolled into the living area, stopping short at the sight of them, immediately on the defensive. "What do you want?" Hands fisting, he glared at his father. "What's going on here?"

"Calm down, son," Jedediah ordered, clearly confused and embarrassed. "Why would you have a problem with the O'Malleys paying us a visit?"

Lips thinning, he didn't answer. At the sight of the bandage covering his nose, the bruising beneath his eyes, Nathan battled the urge to do further damage.

"You'll have to excuse his bad mood." The older man shifted uncomfortably in his seat. "He's in a lot of pain because of his broken nose."

"Did he mention how that happened?" Nathan queried, leveling a challenging look at Landon.

Sensing an undercurrent of antagonism, Jedediah's gaze bounced between the two men. "Ah, yes…he wasn't watching where he was going and ran smack into a tree."

"And you believe that pitiful story?" Caleb snorted.

Nathan nudged his knee against Caleb's. With a quelling look, Josh spoke with quiet authority.

"That's not how it happened."

Having recovered from his initial shock, Landon regained control of himself. "How dare you come into my home and accuse me of being a liar. Father, I won't stand for this. They're here simply to stir up trouble. I want all of you out. Now." His voice radiated insult and disbelief. What a performance.

"I've known these men all my life. Why would they want to cause trouble for you?"

Startled at not having his father's immediate support, he affected an affronted scowl. "They're jealous of my popularity. My success."

Jedediah's dawning disappointment permeated the room. "How did you break your nose, Landon?" he demanded. "The truth, this time."

"I told you the truth."

Impatient, Nathan surged to his feet. "Earlier today, Landon led Sophie Tanner to an isolated place and accosted her. She resisted and, in doing so, injured him."

Hovering near the pie safe, Wanda's hand flew to her mouth, eyes wide with horror. "My baby wouldn't do such a despicable thing!"

Jedediah's complexion darkened, a muscle jumping in his cheek as he shoved out of the chair. "Sit down, son."

"You believe him over me?"

"I can have the young lady in question brought over here to clear up the matter, if you'd like."

His eyes narrowed. "I'm not a kid anymore. I don't have to listen to this."

Jedediah halted his retreat with a rebuke. "As long as you live under my roof, you'll respect your mother and me. Sit down."

Tossing Nathan a look of pure hatred, Landon did as he was told. As the details unfolded, and Nathan proceeded to relate all that had transpired years earlier, Landon schooled his features to careless impassivity. He wasn't the least bit sorry. And that niggled at Nathan.

Would he leave them alone? Or would he bide his time, waiting for a chance to get even?

Resting his hand on the Colt .45 at his waist, he leaned in, hovering over his enemy. "If you value your life, you'll stay away from Sophie. Don't approach her. Don't look at her. Don't even say her name." The sight of her torn dress flashed through his mind, and his fingers tightened on the gun handle. "Erase her from your mind."

Caleb edged to his side. "If you don't heed Nathan's warning, you won't have just one O'Malley to worry about. Got it?"

Landon looked first at Josh, whose forbidding expression eliminated the need for words, then at Caleb and Nathan. His lip curled. "You think I care about that—"

"Be very careful, Greene," Nathan growled. "My restraint has its limits."

Jedediah scooted closer. "I think you've made your point, gentlemen."

Silence, thick with tension, stretched through the room. Josh made the first move. Nodding, he touched Nathan's arm. "Time to take our leave."

Caleb pointed a finger at Landon. "I'll be watching you."

Outside, Nathan and his brothers mounted up.

Josh stroked his goatee. "That needed to be done. However, I'm not sure we didn't throw grease on the fire."

Caleb's gloves tightened on the reins. "He's a slick one. I say we warn Sophie to be on her guard." He looked at Nathan. "He despises you. And since you and she are close..."

His gut clenched with dread. "Yeah, I already put two and two together. I'll talk to her." *And pray she'll listen.*

Chapter Nineteen

A quarter of a mile past Main Street, Wayne and Amelia Lambert resided in a plain but roomy white clapboard house situated on a lovely plot of land dotted with weeping willows and crepe myrtles. When their youngest child had married and relocated to Maryville five years ago, the couple decided to open their home to paying visitors.

So far, Cordelia hadn't voiced any complaints about her accommodations. On the contrary, she'd praised Amelia's cooking—simple though it was—as well as her proficient management of her household. And though Amelia was about ten years older than Cordelia, the two women appeared to be striking up a friendship, a development that surprised Sophie. Her aunt's prickly demeanor made it difficult for people to get close.

Walking down the worn path, Sophie spotted the two women on the wide, welcoming front porch, leisurely sipping tea on the porch swing. When they noticed her, Amelia waved. Cordelia didn't smile, exactly, but her expression bordered on pleasant. That is, until Sophie came near enough for her to see her damaged lip.

"Amelia," her aunt began, "I believe my niece and I

have some things to discuss. Would you mind giving us a moment?"

Leave it to Cordelia to boss someone in their own house. Amelia didn't seem to mind, however. A smile creasing her plump face, silver hair swept back in a simple bun, she came and patted Sophie's hand. "Will is inside playing checkers with Wayne. As soon as you're finished, come inside and have a drink and a snack."

"I will. Thank you, Mrs. Lambert."

When she had disappeared through the glass-paned door, Cordelia indicated the empty space beside her with an incline of her head. "Come and sit, Sophia." Bare-headed and dressed in a casual gray skirt and white blouse, she didn't cut quite as imposing a figure as usual.

Sophie sank onto the swing, setting it to rocking, exhaustion seeping into her bones. She hadn't slept well the night before—tossing and turning amid disturbing dreams of losing Will—and after the trying meal at the Dennisons', the altercation with Landon and the horrible scene with Nathan, she was drained. Depleted of energy. Defeat sat like a heavy railroad tie across her shoulders, and hope for a brighter future was nothing more than a distant memory.

Balancing her glass on the white porch railing, Cordelia angled slightly to study her. "Do you care to tell me how you acquired that busted lip, young lady?"

Sophie ran a finger along the crease in her blue pants. After Nathan had left, she'd changed into her most comfortable pair, and brushing out her hair, plaited it as she used to. Just for today, she'd needed to feel like her old self.

"Do you know who Landon Greene is?"

One brow arched. "He's the young upstart who blathered on and on the day you bowled everyone over with your new look."

"That's him." Gaze lowered to her lap, Sophie related the afternoon's events.

"He should be whipped!" Cordelia exclaimed with more emotion than she'd hitherto displayed, furiously fanning herself, bright flags of color in her cheeks. "However, I will say that you handled yourself quite well. Your unconventional upbringing aided you in this instance. A broken nose is the least he deserves."

Having expected a dressing-down for her unladylike actions, Sophie could only stare at the rare praise. "I thought you'd be angry."

"For defending yourself? No." Her pearl-handled fan paused midair. "In the city, you would've had a chaperone, of course." She sighed. "As for that dreadful scene at the wedding last evening, I hear you were defending your brother's honor. While I don't condone your actions, I at least understand the reasons behind them." Her lips turned down. "Growing up, I sometimes liked to pretend that Lester wasn't my brother. In my daydreams, I imagined a very different sibling, someone who would protect me and play with me." She shook away the thoughts. "But dreaming didn't get me anywhere. It took leaving this place to change my situation."

This was the first time her aunt had willingly opened up about her childhood. "I suppose him taking off was actually a good thing for Will and me."

Cordelia relaxed back against the bench and lowered the fan to her lap. "Yes, I believe it was. In the short time I've been here, I've seen how much you care for Will."

A lump formed in her throat. "I love him very much. Sometimes I feel more like his mother than his sister." When her aunt remained silent, Sophie cautiously ventured, "Are you certain you won't change your mind about my need to marry? Now that you've seen the depth of my devotion?"

Her chin set at a stubborn angle. "Since you refuse to come and live with me, I want to see you settled before I leave. It's what your granddad would've wanted."

"What about love?" Sophie countered hotly, resentment knotting in her chest. Not that she'd ever find love—her heart would forever belong to Nathan. Her aunt shouldn't have any say whatsoever in where or how Sophie lived, but the prospect of having to fight for custody choked off further argument.

Please, God, help me not to harbor anger toward this woman who's more like a stranger than family.

"Love?" Cordelia huffed a dry laugh. "Love is a foolish emotion, my dear. I'm certain your poor ma fancied herself in love with Lester when she married him, and where did that get her?

"Lawrence and I married because of the many advantages we each brought to the union. We coexisted quite peacefully for twenty-five years without the burden of romantic entanglements."

She patted Sophie's knee. "Forget romance, my dear. Find yourself a sensible man, someone you respect and trust. That's far more important."

Sophie watched a blue jay flit to the railing and perch there for a time as she admired its brilliant color and interesting face. Clouds had rolled in during her walk over, and now thunder sounded in the distance even as raindrops splattered on the steps.

Cordelia rescued her glass from the sudden onslaught and stood. "It looks like you and Will will be joining us for supper."

Sophie stopped at the steps and peeked up at the blackening sky. "I didn't think to bring an umbrella."

"Come on, Amelia always makes extra food."

Cordelia held the door open, waiting to be obeyed, as usual.

Sophie preceded her inside the house, spirits turbulent and gloomy like the storm whipping up outside. Tomorrow she would go and see Frank. She would make the sensible choice.

The rain didn't let up until the following morning. Thick, white mist clung to the treetops, an incessant drip-drip-drip echoing through the understory. Beyond their front stoop, puddles filled the yard.

Sophie didn't relish the prospect of venturing out—a minute or two in that and they'd be a muddy mess—but something told her that if she didn't pay Frank a visit today, she would chicken out.

Will gave her an earful of complaints. "Why can't we wait until tomorrow?" he grumbled for the third time as he stuffed his head through the slicker. "What's so important?"

Umbrella held aloft, Sophie's boot tapped the floor impatiently. "As I've already told you, Frank and I have important business to discuss." Fingers on the latch, she swung the door wide. Her hand flew to her throat.

"Nathan!" Clad in a drenched slicker, black hat tugged so low it nearly obscured his eyes, his hand was lifted to knock.

With a little squeal, Will fisted Nathan's sleeve. "Can you stay with me?" he pleaded. "I don't wanna go to Frank's. I wanna stay here."

Shifting the basket to his other arm, Nathan's guarded gaze shot to hers. "I didn't realize you were going out. Ma asked me to deliver a couple of loaves of sourdough bread and some cheese."

"That's very kind of her," she managed to say, stepping back to make room for him to enter. Conscious of the water sluicing onto her floor, he didn't venture far into the room, staying near the row of hooks holding their coats, scarves and hats. If he noticed her braided hair and the pants peeking out from beneath her slicker, he didn't let on. A girl should be dressed up when she went fishing for a marriage proposal, but the weather combined with her mood had eclipsed that notion.

Feeling sorry for ourselves, are we, Sophie?

Accepting the cloth-covered bundle, she carried it to the table, oblivious to the mouth-watering aromas wafting upward.

"Can't you stay and play checkers with me while Sophie conducts business with Frank? I promise to let you win at least once," Will wheedled. "Please?"

Her back to the room, Sophie winced. Business with Frank. That sounded so…so impersonal.

"I don't know," Nathan hedged. "Your sister may want you to accompany her."

Sadness washed over her. After her marriage, both her and Will's relationship with Nathan would change. He wouldn't be dropping in whenever the mood hit, wouldn't be delivering food or lending a helping hand around the farm or taking Will fishing. If he agreed to marry her, Frank would be assuming the role of both husband and father.

Spinning around, she forced a too-bright smile. "Actually, Nathan, I'd appreciate it if you could hang around. I'm certain I won't be gone long, and Will would love to spend time with you. That is, if you don't have pressing matters to attend to."

His gaze narrowed and she feared he could see through to her soul. He gave a curt nod in her direction before aiming a tight smile at his buddy.

"I'd like that."

"Terrific!"

As Will shrugged out of his rain gear and tugged off his boots, Sophie hurried to the door, anxious to make her escape. But she paused in the doorway, arrested by Nathan's sober expression, watching as he hung his hat up and, retrieving his handkerchief, mopped the rainwater from his neck. What she wouldn't give to rewind time, to go back to when life was simple.

"I'd like a word with you before you leave."

Avoiding his gaze, she picked up her umbrella. "What about?"

"Not here." Moving close enough for her to catch a whiff of his spicy aftershave, he reached around her to tug open the door. His rock-hard chest bumped her shoulder. "Sorry." To Will, he said, "I'll be outside with your sister for a few minutes."

"Okay. I'll set up the checkers."

The stoop wasn't large. Huddled beneath the overhang with him, the rain boxing them in lent the situation disturbing intimacy. Her obvious reasons for going to see Frank hung in the air, an invisible yet tangible barrier.

Water droplets clung to his sleek hair, sparkling in the light penetrating the window glass. "After leaving here yesterday, my brothers and I paid Landon and his family a visit."

"You did what?" She raked his person for obvious signs of injury. Seeing none, she threw up her hands. "Why? I thought you weren't going to confront him."

"I never said that. You *assumed*." Folding his arms, he raised a mocking brow, a silent reminder of their argument over her first outing with Landon.

"What happened?"

Anger darkened his eyes to smoky gray, a reflection of the dreary day. "He denied everything, of course."

"And his parents? Did they believe you?"

"Jedediah accepted our account of what happened more easily than I'd anticipated. I think he's seen signs along the way that all wasn't right with Landon. Wanda had a harder time coming to terms with it."

Sophie thought of April. "I think it's easy for some parents to blind themselves to their children's faults to the point of it being unhealthy."

"Sophie, we think he still may be a threat to you. I want you to promise me you'll stay alert to your surroundings. Don't go anywhere near him."

"Why would he bother me again? Especially after what I did to him. He knows I can take care of myself."

Genuine concern passed over his features. "Exposing him was the right thing to do, but you didn't see his utter lack of remorse. He simply doesn't care if he hurts others, including his own family. The outright hatred in his eyes when he looked at me... I'm afraid he'll try to exact revenge by targeting you."

Wrapping her arms around her waist, she suppressed a shiver. What Landon couldn't know was that she really wasn't all that important to Nathan. He'd incorrectly assigned a relationship that simply didn't exist.

"Promise me, Soph," he said quietly, rigid steel punctuating his words.

"I promise."

When he continued to stare at her, she rolled her eyes. "I have absolutely zero desire to be around that man. You have no reason to worry." She opened her umbrella. "Look, I have to go. Thanks for watching Will for me."

Looking unconvinced, he merely nodded.

What more could she say? She left him standing there, acutely aware that she was headed for a future she hadn't asked for and certainly didn't want.

The journey to the Walters' place wasn't nearly long enough. The modest spread a mile east of town was smaller even than hers. Neat as a pin, the dogtrot-style cabin tucked into a narrow cove. Riding into the yard, Sophie dismounted next to the two-pen barn. Faint music filtered from the right side of the structure.

Frank.

Praying for courage, she eased open the door and entered the cozy lamp-lit space, the smell of damp hay and livestock heavy in the air. Against the opposite wall, Frank sat on a low stool usually reserved for milking, strumming his banjo. The lively tune defied the dreary weather outside.

Catching movement, he lifted his head and his fingers stilled on the strings. "Hi, Sophie." Standing, he rested his instrument on the stool and gave her a smile riddled with questions. "You caught me playing hooky."

Sweeping off her hat, she glanced around to avoid looking him in the eyes. "Not much you can do with all this rain." She gestured to the banjo. "That was a pretty song. What is it?"

He tugged on his earlobe, hesitating to answer. "It's, uh, one I made up."

Sophie looked at him then. "You're very talented, Frank. You should share that gift with others."

Color darkened his cheeks, but his brown eyes held hers. "Thank you, Sophie. Your encouragement means a lot. To be honest, I composed it with you in mind."

Surprise flashed through her. "Really? I don't know what to say." Shifting her weight from one foot to the other, nervous energy had her slapping her hat against her leg, spattering raindrops everywhere. "I...I'm flattered. No one's ever written a song about me."

His gaze following her jerky movements, he held out his hand. "Want me to take your hat and coat? Mother's taking a nap. Her arthritis always flares up with the rain. We can visit in here for a while, though."

"No, thank you. I have to get back to Will."

He dropped his hand, clearly disappointed.

Get it over with, Sophie. Either he'll have you or he won't.

"You are aware of my need to marry?"

Frank's brows inched up at her bluntness. "I heard your aunt mention it, yes." A calico cat emerged from the shadowed corner and wound its way between his boots, long tail curling around his calf. "Hey, Pumpkin," he greeted softly, bending to pick it up and hold it against his chest. Stroking the sleek fur, he said, "I suppose you've come to tell me you've chosen Landon. I don't blame you. I understand that our association will have to end, but I admit I'll miss our conversations. If it weren't for you, my banjo would still be in the cabinet collecting dust."

So not all news got around. No doubt Landon wouldn't want folks to know the real cause for his broken nose and had fabricated a story.

Reaching out to pet the purring cat, their fingers collided. "I'm not marrying Landon."

"You're not?" Confusion, then hope, swirled in the brown depths of his eyes. "I thought… Well, the assumption was—" He broke off with a grimace. "I'm glad you're not marrying him. There's something about him I don't trust."

"I feel the same way."

Purpose stole over his features. Setting Pumpkin on the floor, he grasped Sophie's hands, his pleasant face arranged in serious lines.

"Sophie, I know our friendship is still new, and I'm probably not who you envisioned for a husband, but would you consider marrying me? In the short time we've spent together, I've come to care for you. What do you say?"

"Yes." Her acceptance whooshed out. Bittersweet tears glittered in her eyes. *At least you didn't have to do the proposing,* she consoled herself.

"Yes?" he repeated incredulously. "You'll marry me?"

Unable to speak, she nodded. With a blinding grin, Frank bussed her cheek. "Come on, let's go tell Mother." He tugged her toward the doors. "This is news worth waking her up for."

Chapter Twenty

Whether Bonnie Walters was irritated because of her abbreviated nap or because of Frank's announcement, Sophie couldn't tell. Brown curls askew, mouth pinched in annoyance, she perched stiffly on the edge of her straight-backed chair situated beside the fireplace.

"I was afraid of this." She threw an accusing glare at her son. "Are you sure about her, Frankie?"

Seated next to Sophie on the ancient golden-hued sofa, his arm stretched out behind her, his jaw firmed. "I wouldn't have asked her if I wasn't certain, Mother."

"Humph." Bonnie's brown gaze snapped to her. "If you plan to join this family, I expect you to act and dress like a young lady at all times. Hoydenish behavior will not be tolerated."

Sophie squeezed her hands tightly together. *Father, help me to be polite to this woman, my future mother-in-law.* Too many decisions had been taken out of her hands. She wasn't going to bend on this matter.

"With all due respect, Mrs. Walters, it's my choice how I dress. While I intend to wear dresses for church and other outings, I will wear pants for everyday chores."

"Frankie?" Her irate tone silently induced him to do something.

"Sophie is entirely capable of making her own decisions, Mother." He flashed Sophie a shy smile. "She can wear whatever she wants."

Her respect for him went up a notch. The fact that he'd stood up for her on this small issue gave her hope he'd do the same on more important ones.

"You and your brother will live here, of course," Bonnie announced matter-of-factly. "I need Frankie. I can't keep up the farm at my advanced age."

Whoa. Live here? With Bonnie? She turned to Frank. "What about my place?"

He smoothed a hand over his jaw. "Is it important that you keep it? There's always the option of selling it."

"I don't want to sell it. It's been in my family for generations."

He looked stumped. "I suppose we could bring the livestock over here. I'd need to build an addition to the barn, though."

Sophie battled rising panic. Leave her childhood home? The memories, both faint and fresh, that bound her to her lost loved ones?

"What about my furniture? All our things?" This cabin had only two rooms. "Where will my brother sleep?"

"Don't be materialistic, girl," Bonnie chided. "What we can't use, we can sell or donate."

Removing his arm from the sofa back, Frank shifted uncomfortably. "Mother, do you think you can be a little less harsh? Sophie's things are important to her."

Getting to her feet, Bonnie threw her hands up. "Is this how it's gonna be? Now that you've got yourself a bride, you're gonna talk to me as if I'm a child? Boss me in my own home?"

With a sigh, Frank stood and went to her. "Mother,

please…let's not argue. I realize you've been given a shock, but we're going to have to make some compromises. Sophie and Will are going to be family. This is a good thing."

A marriage announcement wasn't supposed to come as a shock, but a pleasant surprise. Sophie stared at a portrait of the mountains, heart heavy for Frank. He clearly loved his mother, difficult though she was, and did his utmost to please her. Trouble was, Bonnie wasn't inclined to be appeased. Today or any other day.

What kind of life could they have here?

The older woman shrugged him off and, making a beeline for the stove, began banging pots around.

Frank motioned for Sophie to join him on the small covered porch. The rain was starting up again, this time a light drizzle.

"I'm sorry about that. Mother doesn't like change."

Strolling to the far railing, she peered out at the wet grass, watching as a greenish-brown frog hopped along the cabin's foundation. "Are you sure us moving here is going to work, Frank? You never did say where Will would sleep. And my things…where will we put them?"

"We have time to figure it all out. I'll build an extra shed if I have to." He stopped beside her. "And don't worry about Mother. It'll just take some time for her to get used to the idea."

She glanced at his somber, studious profile, the dark hair brushing his forehead, and wondered if she'd ever grow to love him. Would he ever grow to love her? Or would his mother's negativity poison their relationship before it even had a chance?

At least you and Will will be together.

"My aunt is impatient to see me settled," she said, forcing the words through wooden lips. "She would like for me to wed before she returns to Knoxville."

"Oh? When is that?"

"Two weeks."

"Oh." He digested that information. "That moves things up a bit. I don't need an elaborate ceremony, though. Do you?"

This wasn't the wedding of her dreams, so... "No."

"How about next Saturday?"

"Fine."

If he noticed her lack of excitement, he didn't comment. "We don't have to sort all the details out yet. Plenty of time for that. I'll go talk to the preacher right now." He gave her an awkward hug. "In less than two weeks' time, we'll be husband and wife. How about that?"

"Yes." She faltered, patting his back. "How about that?"

Her future yawned in front of her, as bleak and lonely as the gray, cloudy day pressing upon them.

Dawn chased the clouds from the sky Wednesday morning as the sun peeped over the mountain peaks, showering buttery rays onto the valley floor. At last, a clear day. Nathan had had enough of foul weather.

Because of his sizable deliveries, Caleb had agreed to ride along. He sat wordlessly on the bouncing seat, soberly taking in the passing scenery, scowl deepening the closer they got to town. Nathan knew his younger brother was getting antsy, that he yearned to retreat to the high country and his precious solitude.

If Sophie's business with Frank had been successful, Caleb would soon get his wish. When she'd returned to her cabin Monday afternoon, she'd been close-lipped. He hadn't had the nerve to force the issue.

He guided the team across the still-damp bridge leading into town. This early in the morning, Main Street was quiet, a couple of horses tied to hitching posts on either side and the boardwalks empty. At the last store, Nathan urged the team left, circling around to the back of the buildings so that he and Caleb could make use of the mercantile's rear entrance.

Another wagon waited there. Nathan eased his team to a stop behind it, set the brake and climbed down, slimy mud squishing beneath his boots. He and Caleb had their arms full of crocks and were ascending the stairs when the mercantile's wooden door swung open and out stepped a pretty, dark-haired girl whose clothing had obviously seen better days. Her gaze collided with Nathan's, then careened to Caleb's. Her nostrils flared in dislike.

"Good morning, Rebecca," Nathan greeted with a friendly smile. *Please let her keep her peace, Lord. There's no chance my brother will stick around for long if he can't escape the past.*

Rebecca and Caleb used to be friends. Before the accident that had left Adam, her former beau and Caleb's best friend, in a wheelchair.

With a scowl that matched Caleb's in ferocity, she nudged the sagging bill of her faded bonnet out of her eyes. "It was a good morning until *he* came along and ruined it."

Behind him, Caleb's hiss stirred the air. As they reached the landing, Rebecca scooted away as if to avoid sharing the same space, clutching an empty chicken cage to her chest. Despite her poor attitude and his plentiful flock, Nathan resolved to purchase a chicken or two of hers. With both parents recently deceased and a younger sister to care for, Rebecca Thurston needed all the assistance she could get.

Maybe he'd give the animals to Sophie.

Dismissing the thought, he toed open the door and held it ajar with his shoulder. But Caleb had stopped to address the girl.

"How've you been, Becca?" he asked quietly.

"Don't pretend to care, Caleb O'Malley." Glaring, she

jerked her chin up and edged around him to the top stair. "I don't buy it, and neither does anyone else in this town."

Caleb's jaw tightened, but he didn't defend himself. He wouldn't. Not when he placed the blame for what happened squarely upon himself. "H-have you heard from Adam?" He practically scraped the words out. "Do you know how he's doing?"

She sucked in an audible breath. "That's none of your business."

When she turned to go, Caleb reached out and touched her sleeve. "Please, Becca," he softly intoned, "I need to know."

Head bent, her jaw worked. "I haven't heard from him since he left town over a year ago." Bitterness laced her words. "My letters went unanswered."

Nathan's heart went out to her. Adam's decision to break off their engagement had spread like wildfire through the town, stunning everyone. Adam and Rebecca had been childhood sweethearts, and after his accident, she'd remained faithfully by his side. His leaving must have felt like a betrayal.

"I'm sorry." Caleb's face turned to stone.

"Right," she huffed in disbelief. "Like I believe that. Why don't you do the rest of us a favor and stay away?" Whirling, she hurried down to her wagon, threadbare skirts swirling an inch above the muddy ground.

"Don't listen to her," Nathan urged. "She's just upset."

Anguish, quickly extinguished, sparked in his brown eyes as he passed by. "I don't wanna discuss it."

"Not talking about it for two years hasn't helped matters," Nathan pointed out as the door thudded closed behind them.

No response. Typical. Like the rest of their family members, Caleb had inherited the O'Malley stubborn streak.

Passing the private quarters and the floor-to-ceiling

shelves of supplies, they entered the store, pausing at the long counter where Emmett Moore assisted a customer.

The store owner stood at the scale weighing out sugar, curly hair sticking out in tufts. Nodding a greeting, he said, "Set those down on the counter, boys. David will be in shortly. The rest I'd like stored in the springhouse. The cheese, too. Ruthanne will get you the key."

"I'll get it," Caleb offered, slipping away.

Wandering over to the jewelry case, Nathan's gaze immediately homed in on the sparkling sapphire ring amid the brooches and earbobs. It was the same brilliant hue as Sophie's eyes. The simple setting, a classic circular design in white gold, would suit her perfectly.

Somehow he doubted Frank was the type of man to buy a woman a ring like that. Pity.

The bell above the door jangled. April Littleton's mother, Georgette, walked in with list in hand. Striding to the counter, her warm welcome did not include him. Apparently she held him personally responsible for Sophie's "attack" on her dear daughter.

Her fingers clutched the paper, wrinkling it beyond repair. "I hear your little friend snagged herself a fiancé." Her eyes flared with annoyance.

"Who's engaged?" Emmett's ears perked up.

Ruthanne zipped out of the office behind them, spectacles perched on the end of her nose. "Someone's getting married?" She gazed expectantly at Georgette.

"Sophie Tanner, that's who." She sniffed.

Nathan gripped the counter's edge, tuning out the resulting conversation.

She'd really done it. She'd gone and engaged herself to Frank.

The questions pelting Georgette sounded fuzzy to his ears, the words distorted.

A hand seized his elbow. "Come on, brother." Caleb

propelled him back the way they'd come. "Let's go fin-ish unloading."

Out in the fresh air and sunlight, Caleb released him. "What's with you, Nate?" He squinted at him. "I thought you were gonna pass out or something."

He forced himself to focus on the here and now. "I'm fine."

Descending the stairs, he hefted a crate of cheese from the wagon bed. Caleb went ahead to the springhouse, lo-cated beside the river at the base of a slight embankment, and bent to unlock it. Over his shoulder, he called, "It has something to do with Sophie, doesn't it? I always wondered about you two. After all, they say where there's smoke, there's fire. And there's a ton of smoke, not to mention sparks, when you and she get together. Always has been."

Nathan gritted his teeth. "Let's just get this stuff put up and go home. I've got a list of chores a mile long wait-ing on me."

Straightening, Caleb reached for the crate with a know-ing smirk. "Now who doesn't wanna talk about it?"

Ignoring him, Nathan trudged up the slippery incline. Not even the sun warming his back and drying out the earth was enough to cheer him. The image of that ring refused to let go.

They worked in silence until all the crocks were stored and the key returned to Ruthanne. When Caleb met him at the foot of the stairs, he crossed his arms and looked him straight in the eyes. "Once Sophie weds, am I free to leave?"

He'd known this was coming. He just hadn't expected it so soon. "That's your choice," he snapped, brushing past him to climb into the wagon.

Heaving a sigh, Caleb walked around to his side and dropped down onto the seat. Swaying with the forward motion of the team, he tugged his hat brim low, a habit he'd formed after the accident. "If you still need me, I'll stick around awhile longer."

Pulling around the buildings, Nathan scanned the street and, seeing nothing, edged onto Main Street. Customers were beginning to fill the boardwalks. Spying Josh unlocking the furniture store, he lifted a hand in greeting.

"Having you around these past few weeks has been great. Not only is my workload lighter, but I can see the difference your continued presence has made in Ma and Pa."

"Thanks for the guilt trip," Caleb muttered, hands fisting on his thighs.

The horses' hooves clattered over the bridge. Nathan shot him a sideways glance. "I'm not going to sugarcoat the facts, Caleb. You're a part of this family, and we need you."

Caleb kept his silence, turning his head to scan the forest on his side.

As much as they needed him, Nathan understood what drove him. Seeing Rebecca again couldn't have been easy.

"Look, we can manage without you," he conceded, relenting. "We've done it before, and we can do it again. But I'd like you to promise me something."

He twisted his head to look at him. "What's that?"

"Promise me you'll deal with this. After all, you can't run forever."

Exiting the church, Nathan waited near the stairs, determined to speak with Sophie. He hadn't seen her all week. Although he'd toyed with the notion of going to see her, he'd ultimately decided against it, surmising she was probably busy planning her wedding. Watching her during the service today, however, sandwiched between Frank and his domineering mother, he couldn't deny she looked miserable. As miserable as he felt.

Those in attendance now making their way to their wagons tossed him curious glances. Moving deeper into the shadows cast by a live oak planted at the building's corner, he attempted to uncoil his taut upper back muscles, to relax his shoulders. He didn't want to argue with her. This would be a pleasant how-are-you-doing conversation.

Gaze on the doorway, he saw Cordelia and Sophie emerge first, followed by Will, Frank and Bonnie. At the top of the stairs, Sophie happened to glance his way, full lips parting in surprise. Dressed in a butter-yellow creation that highlighted the blond streaks in her hair, she was a vision of loveliness.

When their party reached the ground, he lifted his hand and called to her. With a quick word to Cordelia, she separated herself and joined him beneath the tree. Frank tipped his hat before moving on. Bonnie looked disapproving. He ignored them, training his focus on Sophie.

The scent of dandelions filled his nostrils, and he breathed deeply, wanting to contain the delicate fragrance for future reference. He pressed damp palms against his trousers. "Hello."

"Hi." Fidgeting with the pearl buttons on her bodice, she exuded a guardedness that irked him. His childhood friend was one of the most open, transparent women he knew. Was this what he could expect from now on?

"Do you want to come over for lunch?" he blurted, hoping for some time alone with her. He missed his friend. "Ma baked peach pie."

"I can't." Her face was a blank mask. "Will and I are having lunch at the Lamberts'."

"Oh." Frustration speared him. "Have you been spending more time with your aunt, then?"

"Yes." Her gaze moved to some distant point beyond his shoulder. "I've come to realize she's not a mean-spirited person. Just incredibly lonely with a penchant for boss-ing people around. I believe she's learning that in order to have friends, she has to first be a friend."

Nathan wanted to shake her. "I find it difficult to fathom how easily you've accepted her role in your current situation."

Mr. and Mrs. Conner strolled past, openly gawking.

Taking hold of her hand, he tugged her around the corner, away from prying eyes.

"She's my aunt," she stated defensively. "She's the only family we have left. I can hardly cut her out of my life."

Folding his arms across his chest, he demanded, "When were you planning on telling me of your engagement?"

A storm surged in her eyes, unnamed emotions swirl-ing, clashing with his. "I told you of my plans that night in the barn."

At last, proof she was alive inside that indifferent shell. Softening his tone, he touched her sleeve. "You don't look happy about it. Is Frank's ma treating you fairly?"

She tried to shrug off the question. "Bonnie's in shock right now. I'm sure she'll eventually grow accustomed to the fact she has to share her only son."

Nathan could see the hurt simmering beneath the sur-face, the unhappiness she was trying so desperately to hide from him. This wasn't a future worthy of her. He couldn't stand by and do nothing. He had to fix this.

"Marry me," he blurted.

Sophie's head snapped up. The color leached from her face. Groping for the wall behind her, she sagged against it. "W-what did you just say?"

He wasn't at all sure where that proposal had come from, but an odd sense of rightness swept away the shock reverberating through him. They were friends. He could do this for her. "Think about it, Soph. You're already an unofficial member of our family. If you marry me, you won't have to worry about a thing."

Wary, disbelieving, she studied his face. "I thought you said we wouldn't suit."

"We've managed to stay friends all these years," he pointed out. "I think we could make it work, don't you?" Intent on helping her, he took her hands in his. "When I found out you were with Landon, and I couldn't get to you, didn't know whether or not you were okay, the fear and worry nearly crushed me. As my wife, you'll be safe. Protected."

Wincing, she tugged her hands free. "That's just it, Nathan, I don't need protecting. As much as you refuse to see it, I can take care of myself. I appreciate the offer, but I can't marry you."

Why was she being so stubborn? Couldn't she see she'd be miserable with Frank? "Maybe you should take some time to think about it."

Pushing away from the wall, she set her shoulders and looked him square in the eyes. "I won't allow you to sacrifice your happiness. Not for my sake."

"My happiness isn't at issue here. Since I've never been keen on the idea of marriage, it doesn't really matter who—" He clamped his lips tight at the dawning horror on her face.

"Go on, finish it. It doesn't matter who you marry."

"That didn't come out right," he mumbled. *Way to go, O'Malley.*

"No, I think your meaning is crystal clear."

When she turned to go, he clutched her wrist. "Wait, Sophie—"

"You know what your problem is?" She pivoted back, eyes glittering. "When it comes to me, you have this warped sense of duty. You've made it your life's mission to protect me, Nathan, if not from others then from myself."

"What's wrong with that?"

Her mouth fell open. "What's wrong with that? If I married you, you'd quickly grow to resent me! I'd become a burden."

Sophie? A burden? "No. That's impossible."

Her mouth pursed in disagreement.

"Besides, how are Frank's reasons for marrying you any better than mine?"

Her luminous gaze speared his. "Frank admires me. He wants to marry me because he believes I'll be a good wife to him. Can you say the same?"

The direct question leveled him. Worry and an over-abundance of protective instinct where she was concerned had prompted his spontaneous proposal. Not attraction, despite the fact Sophie had but to look at him to heat his blood to dangerous levels. Not admiration, although he couldn't deny she possessed many admirable traits. Certainly not love...

"Is there any other reason you'd want to marry me, Nathan?" she softly prompted, her vulnerable expression a dagger in the heart, especially considering what he was about to do.

"I—" Regret weighing him down, he gave a slow shake of his head. "No. There isn't."

Her face crumpled. "Then there's nothing left to say."

"I'm sorry—"

"Please." She held out a hand to ward him off. "I can't—"

"Sophie?" Frank appeared around the corner, brow furrowing in concern when he spotted her. His gaze volleyed back and forth. "Sorry to interrupt, but your aunt sent me to tell you she's impatient for her lunch."

"T-thank you, Frank." Indifferent acceptance wreathed her pale features. However, twin flags of bright color in her cheeks revealed her disquiet. "I'll walk with you."

Without a single glance Nathan's way, she went to join her intended.

Watching Frank take her arm in quiet consideration, Nathan felt as if something precious was slipping through his fingers. And he had no one to blame but himself.

Chapter Twenty-One

So she'd rejected his proposal. It wasn't as if she'd broken his heart or anything. There were no feelings involved here. He'd offered to help based on their long-standing friendship. Turned out she hadn't wanted his help.

So why was he so disappointed?

Shaking off the traitorous thought, he rounded the bend leading to Megan's house. Needing to clear his head, he'd excused himself immediately after lunch and gone for a walk. And here he was on his cousin's doorstep. May as well announce his presence. He could do with a distraction. Besides, he hadn't seen much of the newlyweds since their return.

Madge Calhoun answered the doorbell's summons. "Come on in." She waved him inside the spacious entryway and offered to take his hat. "They're in the garden parlor. Go on back and I'll bring you some coffee."

She bustled in the opposite direction before he could thank her. Glancing in the oval mirror above the hall table, he attempted to smooth his hair that, come to think of it, was in desperate need of a trim. He shook his head at his reflection. Normally he kept on top of these things. That's what happened when a man allowed himself to become preoccupied by a woman and her problems.

With a sigh, he made his way past the gleaming stairway swirling toward the lofty ceiling and along a floral-papered hall to the back of the house. "The garden parlor," she'd called it. A person had too many rooms when they took to naming them, he thought wryly.

He was happy for Megan, though. If anyone deserved love and happily-ever-after, it was his big-hearted cousin. Nathan had had his doubts about the wealthy New Orleans gentleman at first, but he'd seen with his own eyes how much Lucian treasured her.

Stepping over the threshold, boots sinking into the plush sage-and-cream rug, his gaze landed on Megan, seated together with her husband on the sofa, a pile of cloth napkins in her lap. Momentarily forgotten, from the looks of it. Lucian cradled her close to his chest, gazing deeply into her eyes, mirroring sappy expressions on their faces.

He should go. The floorboard creaked as he took a retreating step, preventing his escape.

Megan's blond head and Lucian's dark brown one snapped up.

"Nathan!" Her face lit with pleasure. Setting the napkins aside, she navigated around the mahogany coffee table and approached with hands outstretched. "I'm so glad you're here."

In her flowing pink dress, curls held back with a matching ribbon, she looked beautiful and refreshed, her eyes shining with contentment.

Lucian stood. To his credit, he didn't appear perturbed at the interruption. Reaching his wife's side, he shook Nathan's hand. Grinned wryly. "We're supposed to be decorating for this afternoon's bridal shower, but I'm afraid we got sidetracked."

His breath hitched. "Bridal shower?"

"For Sophie." She smiled happily, white-blond curls quivering. "Maybe you can help us," she suggested, waving a hand around the airy, botanical-inspired room. "We'll need chairs brought in from the library, and of course, Fred will need help carrying in the flower vases. I've got to finish folding these napkins—"

Mrs. Calhoun arrived then with cups of steaming coffee spread out on a large tray. "I've brought cream and sugar," she said, sliding it onto the low table. Smoothing her apron, she addressed Megan. "Would you like cookies or slices of apple pie to go with it?"

"Oh, no, thank you. We'll be indulging in plenty of sweets when our guests arrive."

With a nod, the older woman left.

"Come sit down, Nathan." Resuming her seat, Megan motioned for him to take the chair closest to her. "Have some coffee while you tell me everything that's been going on with you these past weeks."

Reluctantly he lowered himself into the sumptuously cushioned chair and took the cup and saucer she held out. He sipped the slightly spicy brew.

"Do you like it?" She watched him expectantly. "It contains chicory. We brought a barrel of it from New Orleans."

Leaning back against the cushions, Lucian smiled indulgently at her, then tossed Nathan a lifeline. "It's not for everyone. If you don't like it, we can get you the regular stuff."

He lowered the cup to his lap. "It has an interesting flavor."

"It took me a while to get used to," she admitted, "but now I prefer it."

"Good thing we can order a supply whenever you wish, *mon chou*," Lucian murmured.

"Now if we could only teach Mrs. Calhoun how to make

beignets." She sighed wistfully. "You would adore them, Nathan. Little fried bits of doughy heaven."

Recognizing an opportunity to forestall further questions about himself, he suggested, "Tell me about your trip. What did you like most about Lucian's home?"

The ploy worked. Megan answered his questions in full detail, and when she'd exhausted that subject, Nathan inquired after her older sister, Juliana.

Immediately following their July nuptials, Lucian and Megan had traveled to Cades Cove to see Juliana, Evan and their new baby before making their way down to Louisiana. Watching Megan's excitement as she described the infant, Nathan could see how eager she was to start her own family.

When the mantel clock chimed the three o'clock hour, Megan's hand flew to her mouth. "I lost all track of time! We only have an hour before the guests arrive."

"There's plenty of time." Lucian began clearing the cups. "I'll go and get the chairs while you finish those napkins."

"I'll help you," Nathan told him, pushing to his feet. Since he was responsible for Megan's distraction, he would do his part, making certain he left before the bride-to-be arrived.

That's how he must think of her. The bride-to-be. Frank's fiancée.

Not Sophie or Soph. Not the girl next door. Not his lifelong friend.

Just a girl who was about to walk the aisle to marry someone else.

This was proving to be the longest day of her life.

What should have been a fun-filled afternoon with friends and family, eating too-sweet cake and opening gifts, was turning out to be a sore test of Sophie's acting abilities. Seated in the middle of Megan's lovely parlor, all the prettily dressed ladies circled around oohing and aahing over each and every gift, her smile was pasted on, her enthusiasm forced. She was playing the part of the enthusiastic bride, and, from the looks of things, was executing her part rather well.

Her aunt, however, was not fooled. Sophie sensed it in the way the older woman watched her, a subtle knowing in her astute gaze. Spending time with Cordelia this past week had wrought a change in Sophie's heart, a softening toward the other woman, a deep well of compassion that could have only been accomplished by God. Knowing the resentment and anger she'd harbored didn't please Him, she'd asked Him to alter her attitude, and He had.

Cordelia was abrasive at times, and irritatingly demanding, but she'd suffered a lot of heartache in her life, much of it at the hands of Sophie's pa. Unable to have children, all she'd had was her husband. And now that he was gone, she was all alone. Sophie was certain loneliness had prompted her ultimatum. Cordelia had no doubt assumed Sophie and Will would choose to live with her, and when they didn't, pride prevented her from backing down. Pride and old-fashioned thinking. Her aunt just couldn't accept that Sophie could hack it on her own.

Focus on the positive, Sophia Lorraine. You get to keep Will. You get to stay here, in the mountains you adore and the town that knows you.

Positive. Right. If only Nathan hadn't proposed. If only she hadn't glimpsed, for sweet, precious seconds, a lifetime with her one true love. Those seconds were enough to bring her to her knees. How perilously close she'd come to accepting. The only thing capable of stopping her was the utter lack of true emotion on his face. If she'd seen even a glimmer of longing or affection or admiration, she'd have done it. Instead he'd been logical and calm and perfectly reasonable. This was Nathan assuming his knight-on-a-white-horse persona. This was him helping out a friend in need without a thought to what price he'd be paying.

She'd have made him miserable. Maybe not in a week or a month or even a year. But eventually, he'd have regretted marrying her. And that would've killed her.

Jane had been tasked with handing out the gifts, while Jessica kept a list for thank-you notes. Auburn ponytail swinging, Jane placed a present, a square box tied up with wide yellow ribbon, on her lap. "This is the last one." She winked. "It's from your aunt."

A hushed silence settled over the room as she untied the ribbon and lifted the lid. Staring down at the snowy-white, ribbon-and-lace-adorned nightgown and housecoat, Sophie's heart pounded with dread. Her cheeks flamed. Wedding night attire.

"What is it, Sophie?" someone asked after a minute.

"Uh..." With trembling fingers, she lifted the garments, holding them up for everyone to see.

"How beautiful!" Ruthanne Moore breathed, hands pressed to her thick throat.

Beside Cordelia, Bonnie's face turned a horrific puce color. "Scandalous," she whispered.

Adrift in her misery, Sophie didn't register the male voices entering the room until it was too late.

"Lucian," Megan scolded teasingly from her place near the table, "no males allowed in here."

Sophie didn't hear his response. Heartbeat thundering in her ears, all she could see was Nathan. Still dressed in his church clothes, charcoal-gray suit pants, black vest and white button-down shirt that enhanced his tanned good looks, he stood rooted to the spot inside the doorway, his gaze on the nightgown in her hands. Hastily, she lowered it back into the box and handed it off to Jane.

His features hardened into a frozen, forbidding mask,

his mouth a hard slash of discontentment. Without a word, he pivoted out of the room.

Icy pain burst inside her chest, unfurling outward like ripples on a lake's surface, scalding every nerve, sinew and muscle and bone tissue it came in contact with. She was dying, wasn't she? Every part of her screamed for relief. *I can't do this.*

"P-please, e-excuse me," she stammered, rushing from the room. Let them say what they wanted. Escape was her only focus.

Locating the door that led to the gardens behind the house, she burst through it, stumbled down the steps and half ran for the trees. The stone paths wound along riotous, rainbow-hued flower gardens. Hidden beneath a rose arbor was a stone bench. Shudders racked her body as she collapsed onto it, but no tears came.

How she wished her ma was here to hold her. Or Granddad. Someone to lean on, someone to comfort her but also to remind her of what was at stake if she didn't follow through with this wedding. Circumstances had forced her to be strong all her life. She couldn't afford for weakness to triumph now.

After a while, the sun's warmth chased away her inward chill, and she sat there limp and defeated, unmindful of the beauty surrounding her.

"Here you are, Sophia dear." Cordelia appeared in front of her, her towering height blocking the sun's rays. "Are you all right?"

"I apologize for running out on everyone, but I couldn't stay." Gaze downcast, she plucked at the ruffles marching across her skirt.

"Do you mind if I join you?"

Sophie scooted over to make room. *Please, Lord, I can't take a lecture right now.*

Cordelia sat and meticulously arranged her lavender

skirts before folding her white-gloved hands primly in her lap. "What a lovely garden," she observed with approval. "Not as expansive or elaborate as my own, but still quite nice."

Raising her head, Sophie cast a sidelong look at her aunt. She didn't appear perturbed in the slightest.

"You must come and visit sometime," she continued, still glancing around in interest. "There's one room in particular I think you'd fancy. The rose room, all done up in soft mauves and pinks and greens with an enormous canopy overtop the bed. It has one of the finest views of the property."

"It sounds beautiful." For the first time, a visit to Knoxville appealed to her. A visit on *her* terms.

"It's yours whenever and however long you'd like." To her surprise, Cordelia smiled. It sat a bit awkwardly on her face, as if the muscles weren't accustomed to such an action.

"Thank you, Aunt. Perhaps after the wedding…"

The smile faded and was replaced with a concerned pucker. She tipped her head, pastel feathers bobbing wildly. "I gather your current mood has something to do with Nathan, since it was his untimely arrival that drove you from the party. Have you and he had a spat?"

"Not exactly." Bowing her head, she recalled that agonizing interlude outside the church hours earlier, the hurt he'd inflicted with his brutal honesty. "He asked me to marry him," she moaned.

"Did he now? You regret refusing him, I take it," her aunt observed dryly.

"I had to. He was doing what he does best—rescuing me." She gave a vehement head shake. "I couldn't let him do it."

"Is that what you told him?"

"Yes."

"You love him."

Sophie met her aunt's direct gaze. "Yes."

"Hmm." Her expression turned thoughtful. "What about Frank? What do you feel for him?"

Guilt made her wince. How could she honor Frank when her heart belonged to Nathan? "He's a sweet man. I care for him as a friend."

"I see." Her pencil-thin brows met in the middle. "I confess to never having been in love. I admired and respected my husband. He was intelligent. Kind. We shared many similar opinions. We had a good life together."

Covering Cordelia's clasped hands with one of her own, Sophie said, "After what you went through with Pa, it must've been extremely difficult to trust. To open up your heart and let someone in."

Her steel-blue eyes widened and, for a moment, Sophie braced herself for a sharp rebuff. Then she nodded resignedly. "You're right. I'm not like you, Sophia. As much as Lester's abandonment must have confused and hurt you, I'm glad he left. You and Will were better off without him."

Sorrow pierced her heart. "I miss my ma. My memories of her have faded over the years…. I had so little time with her. As for Granddad, I feel his absence every moment of the day."

Lifting a finger to wipe a tear from her cheek, Cordelia said, "Don't fret, my dear. You don't want to return to your guests looking like a drowned cat." Then she tacked on an admission with an expression bordering on tender. "My time here hasn't been as horrible as I'd feared it would be. Spending time with you, especially, has made it all worthwhile. I'm proud of you, Sophia."

The unexpected praise brought forth more tears. Fishing a handkerchief out of her reticule, Cordelia awkwardly patted her knee. "Come now, let's stroll for a few minutes and let the fresh air calm you."

"What excuse will I give for my disappearing act?" Sophie sniffed.

Cordelia shrugged. "Let them assume it was pre-wedding jitters."

"Bonnie will be livid."

Strolling side by side along the path, Cordelia said archly, "That woman is a menace. I believe I gave you the wrong gift, my dear. I should've purchased your future mother-in-law an extended vacation in the Orient."

He couldn't sleep. Every time he closed his eyes, the image of Sophie displaying that feminine garment—a personal gift he'd had no business seeing—mocked him.

He was glad the day was over. It had been a rotten one. First, the disturbing sight of Landon with his parents in the service, smoldering with antagonism and making no attempt to preserve his happy-go-lucky facade. Then afterward, that heart-wrenching scene with Sophie. And finally, the intrusion on her bridal shower.

If only his mind would settle and let him slip into slumber's blessed oblivion. The desk clock ticking, the occasional creak and groan of the cabin and Caleb's soft snoring across the hall were magnified in his ears.

After a couple of hours of tossing and turning and fluffing his pillow in the futile hope it would get softer, Nathan gave up.

Lighting the bedside lamp, he scooted up in bed and spent the next hour reading his Bible. He checked the clock again. It was four in the morning, an hour and a half earlier than his usual wake-up time, and pitch black outside. But he was wide awake. May as well go ahead and get a head start on the day.

Dressing as quietly as possible, he carried his lamp downstairs and, instead of making coffee, made do with a sip of water from the ladle. He wasn't hungry, anyway.

Ma would be up shortly to make biscuits and fry up ham and eggs. He'd wait until then.

Outside, the tranquil night wrapped around him, the air cool against his skin, the stars in the sky above winking like diamonds in a black-velvet skirt. Kerosene lamp dangling from his fingers, he leisurely traversed the dark yard toward the barn, where his cows were likely stirring from their straw beds. He'd need to change out their water and check the bedding to see if it needed more materials. Pulling open one of the heavy doors, he thought he heard Rusty, their new puppy, whine.

"Rusty?" The door scraped along the ground as he pulled it closed. "Come here, boy."

Striding down the aisle, he glanced into the doorless stalls on either side, surprised all the animals were up and alert. He looped the lamp on a nail.

Bracing his hands on his hips, he shook his head. "Couldn't sleep, either, I take it."

A soft thump, like a rock hitting the far wall, had him swerving around. His pulse spiked. Adrenaline surged. Something wasn't right. He could feel it in his bones.

Creeping toward the last stall, footfalls absorbed by the straw-covered earth, his gaze swept from left to right. He wasn't armed, so he kept his hands free and ready to defend.

When he reached his destination, Nathan surged around the waist-high wall, half expecting to be tackled. But it was empty. No intruder here.

A horse blanket in the corner rustled, and a rust-colored head popped out. He sighed. "There you are, you little scamp."

Starting forward, he picked up the shivering dog and huddled him close to his chest. "Next time, don't scare me like that."

"I'm afraid there won't be a next time."

Before Nathan could make a move, what felt like a shovel collided with his head and blackness engulfed him.

Chapter Twenty-Two

Nathan stirred to the sounds of coursing water and birds far above whistling to each other. His head ached something fierce, and his ribs and stomach were sore. Why—

The awful memories rushed in. Landon. The barn. The shovel.

Opening his eyes, he squinted in the unrelenting sunlight, the heat and humidity already oppressive. How long had he been out? Struggling against the metal restraints binding his wrists behind his back and the thick ropes securing him to the tree trunk, he cast around the surrounding forest for his enemy. Landon's horse munched on the grassy bank.

"Finally, you're awake." Landon entered his field of vision, brandishing a pocketknife. "I thought I was going to have to upend a bucket of water over your head."

Nathan fought the dread and panic threatening to take hold. *Think, O'Malley. There has to be a way out of this.*

His mouth felt stuffed with cotton. The remembrance of that single sip of water hours earlier tormented him. "What do you think you're doing?"

Squatting in front of him, Landon thumbed up his hat brim, an ugly scowl marring his features. "Do you know what I've been forced to endure these past days? Because of you, Ma bursts into tears every time I walk into the room, and Pa treats me as if I'm some sort of circus freak." The blade glinted in the light. "No longer am I their beloved only son, capable of no wrong. Instead of looking on me with pride, they look at me with a mixture of pity and revulsion. All because of you and your interference."

"You've brought me here why?" He kept his gaze straight ahead and not on that knife. "To teach me a lesson?"

"No." Pushing to a standing position, Landon snapped closed the knife and stuffed it in his pocket. His cold gaze bore into Nathan's, the complete lack of emotion worrying. "I see this more as an act of revenge. You see, I'm gonna ride outta here in a few minutes, leaving you to the mercy of the elements and nature. If the heat doesn't get you, perhaps a mountain lion or bear will happen along." A sick smile curling his lips, he gestured to the stream. "That serves two purposes. Not only will it draw animals, I like to think how seeing and hearing the water will torment you as the sun gets hotter and you get thirstier. So close, yet so far away...."

Seizing the pail behind him, he dumped a heap of gutted fish at Nathan's feet. To lure wild animals?

Bile burned his throat. The man was more depraved than he'd realized. "There's no way you'll get away with this, Landon. There are too many people who can link my disappearance to you."

A fire ant crawled beneath his trousers. He shook his leg to dislodge it before it could bite him. He scoured the ground, wincing when he noticed the ant mound near his boot. Landon laughed at his predicament.

"I don't care if they do. You see, I'm leaving town. It's time for a fresh start, compliments of my folks." He patted a bulge in his left pocket.

"You stole from your own parents? They're good people. They don't deserve that." A fiery sting near his ankle meant he hadn't been successful. He pulled his knees up to his chest.

"I figure they deserve it for believing a stranger over their own flesh and blood." Sauntering over to his horse, he grabbed hold of the reins and led the large animal closer. "I'm ready for some fresh faces. A new crop, if you know what I mean." He wiggled his brows. "Ya know something though, I think before I leave town I should pay sweet Sophie a visit. She and I have some unfinished business."

Growling, Nathan strained against the ropes, ignoring how they dug into his flesh. "Don't you dare go near her," he snarled through clenched teeth.

"You'll never know if I did or didn't, will you? I kind of hope the animals stay away. It'll give you more time to worry over her possible fate."

When he vaulted into the saddle, Nathan struggled harder, but the ropes wouldn't budge. He let his head fall back against the trunk, gasping as sharp pain vibrated through his skull. "If you touch her, Greene, my brothers will never stop looking for you." He'd growled out the warning, hating the helplessness spreading through his chest.

I'm begging You, God, please protect Sophie. It's out of my hands. I was fooling myself to think I could control what happens to those I care about. I've been no better than Caleb in that area. You are the one who holds ultimate control, as it should be.

"I welcome the challenge." He nudged his mount into motion. "Good riddance, O'Malley."

After Landon left, the solitude of the forest, the feeling of utter isolation, closed in. And just as his enemy had predicted, the unknown haunted him.

* * *

Sophie was at the laundry line beating dust and dirt from a rug when the sound of an approaching rider rolled through the meadows. Propping the cane carpet beater against the post, she walked toward the lane, smoothing stray wisps from her damp forehead. Whoever was paying her a visit, they sure were in a hurry.

When she recognized Caleb's mount, her heart skipped a beat. The youngest O'Malley rarely darkened her doorstep anymore.

He reined in Rebel, his dark gaze scanning the farm. From the saddle, he said, "Is Nathan here?"

"I haven't seen him since yesterday." Not since that unfortunate moment at her bridal shower. "Why?"

His lips thinned. "He didn't come down for breakfast, so I went looking for him. None of the horses or wagons are missing, and he didn't milk the cows. Something's happened. He wouldn't have gone off without tending to them first."

Stark fear slithered through Sophie. "You don't think—"

"I'm headed over to the Greenes' now. Josh is on his way to the sheriff's."

She worried her lip. "We were so sure he'd target me." *Oh, Father, please watch over him. Keep him safe. Help us find him.* "I'm going with you."

"No." Rebel shifted beneath him, and his gloves tightened on the reins. "It's not safe. Take Will over to our place. Josh and I will report back there in half an hour."

"But—"

"Putting yourself in harm's way won't help bring him back, Sophie."

She stifled a groan of frustration. The adrenaline pumping through her body demanded action. "Fine." She clipped the word out. "But if you don't find him right away, I'm joining the search party. Don't try to talk me out of it."

"Understood." Wheeling his horse around, he bolted away.

Hands shaky and knees like jelly, she ran to the barn hollering for Will. He dashed outside and skidded to a stop, eyes as big as marbles.

"We're going over to Sam and Mary's for a little while," she breathlessly explained, making a beeline for her horse.

Will dogged her steps as she struggled to lift the saddle, her limbs devoid of strength. Images of Nathan, of his possible condition, scrolled through her mind. Landon was a ruthless man. He wouldn't blink twice at harming another human being.

"Why are you so upset?"

She strove to keep the fear from her face, but it proved a difficult task. "I'm concerned about Nathan. His brothers can't find him."

"You mean, he's missing?" His voice rose. "Where could he be? What if he's hurt?"

Turning from her task, Sophie placed her hands on his shoulders. "We need to pray for his safety, Will. Remember that verse we learned? 'So do not fear, for I am with you. Do not be dismayed, for I am your God. I will strengthen you and help you. I will uphold you with my righteous right hand.'"

"I remember."

"God isn't going to abandon Nathan. Nor will He abandon us. We have to trust Him, okay?"

He nodded solemnly. "Okay."

"Okay." *Lord, help me be strong for him.* "Let's go. We'll ride together."

The ride over seemed to take longer than usual. Sophie was on edge, jerking at every sound, her gaze scanning the forest in the foolish hope Nathan would come waltzing through the trees, oblivious to everyone's alarm.

That didn't happen, of course.

At the house, Mary and Kate wore matching expressions of unease. Sam was searching the property on the off chance Nathan had gone for an early morning walk and, as Will had suggested, gotten hurt and needed assistance. Ever the hostess, Mary doled out cookies and milk for Will, cake and coffee for the adults. Sophie couldn't eat. She stalked from window to window, restless for answers, until Kate came and linked arms with her, guiding her back to the table.

"You should drink your coffee. Or would you prefer tea? I can brew you some."

"No, thank you, I—"

She broke off as male voices filtered through the glass. Rushing out the door, she saw Josh, Sheriff Timmons and Sam conversing at the corner of the cabin.

"Any news?" She hurried over, spirits sagging at the sight of their hangdog faces.

Sam shoved his spectacles farther up his nose. "I didn't see anything out of the ordinary. I called for him, but got no response."

Sheriff Timmons looked around. "You're sure all the horses are accounted for? No wagons are missing?"

Josh stroked his goatee. "Nothing. Nathan wouldn't have willingly gone anywhere without first milking those cows."

"What if there was an emergency?" the sheriff suggested. "A friend who urgently needed help?"

"I know my son," Sam quietly asserted. "If that were the case, he would've let one of us know."

"So no one in the house heard any commotion this morning?"

"No."

Josh held up a hand. "Wait a minute, Caleb said Nathan's bedside lamp was gone. Maybe he got up early, went to the barn to start on chores and was jumped."

Sophie ground her back teeth. The endless posturing spiked her aggravation. It was clear who did this. Enough talking, already. They needed to go searching for Nathan. Now. Before it was too late....

Caleb rode into the yard then, and the men turned as one to wait. He dismounted while Rebel was still in motion, boots slamming to the ground.

"Landon's skipped town," he declared, thumping his hat against his thigh in frustration. "Most of his things are cleared out. Jedediah's coin stash is gone, too."

"Do they have any idea which way he was headed?" Sophie asked.

"None. I say we round up a search party and spread out across the area."

The sheriff headed for his horse. "I'll gather the men. We'll need a day or two's worth of supplies."

"My wife and daughter-in-law can help with that." Sam pivoted and made for the door.

"Meet me at my office in an hour."

Another hour of waiting and agonizing. With a frustrated groan, Sophie stalked over to Caleb, who was riffling through his saddlebag. "I'm going with you."

Beneath the low brim of his hat, brown eyes touched hers. "I know."

Having expected a battle, she fell back a step. "You aren't going to try and talk me out of it?"

"If you were any other female in this town, I would. But you're capable, an excellent shot and a so-so cook. I can live with that."

Nodding gratefully, she lowered her suddenly watery gaze to the ground. Caleb placed a finger beneath her chin and lifted her face. "Hey, we will find him. I won't accept any other outcome, and I know you won't, either." His gaze probed hers, making her feel exposed. "He's lucky to have someone who cares about him as much as you do."

She didn't deny it. What would be the point?

"I'm gonna run to the mercantile for a new canteen," she said. "I'll meet you at the sheriff's."

"All right."

On the ride into town, Sophie's mind wandered to Landon and their many encounters, the subtle signs she'd stubbornly ignored. Forcing a kiss was nothing compared to kidnapping. She'd never dreamed the seemingly charming young man would be capable of such evil....

Straightening in the saddle, she thought of their last outing and the remote location he'd led her to. "What if?"

Crossing the bridge at a fast clip, she slowed her horse when she caught sight of the young Thompson brothers playing marbles beside the barbershop. They looked up at her approach.

"Davey. Grant." She leaned over the saddle horn. "I need you to do me a huge favor."

Grant, the older brother, scrambled up. "Certainly, ma'am."

"Go to the O'Malley's and find Caleb. Tell him I'm headed up to Lookout Point. If you do this, I'll personally take you to the café and you can choose any dessert you want."

Davey's eyes rounded. "Truly?"

Nodding, she urged, "But you have to hurry, okay?"

"Yes, ma'am!" Holding their caps, they ran off.

Please, Lord, don't let this be a huge waste of time.

Her gut told her this was right. She had to pursue it. She just hoped her impulsiveness didn't cost Nathan his life.

Chapter Twenty-Three

Nathan smelled the bear before he saw him.

Resting his head against the tree—gently this time—he squinted against the early evening sunlight slanting across the forest. The scene was a peaceful one. Trees all around, a sloping mountain stream gurgling over moss-covered rocks, white and yellow flowers bobbing in the thick grass carpet. No clear sign of danger, but he knew it was there. Somewhere.

It didn't matter if he sat motionless. The predator would catch a whiff of his scent, the sweat drenching his shirt and the blood from the head wound matted in his hair. And the fish. Black bears weren't all that aggressive, but with a ready meal available, who knew what the outcome might be.

He prayed harder than he'd ever done before.

When he opened his eyes, his heart jumped into his throat. There, on the opposite bank, stood a massive animal. This was no youngster. This was a full-grown adult, his black eyes shiny, his nose bouncing as he sniffed the air.

Although it was a futile act, Nathan tugged again on the metal restraints around his wrists, wincing at the sting of skin rubbed raw. Even if he could get them off, he doubted he'd be able to free himself from the ropes securing him to the tree.

Sophie's beautiful face drifted through his mind again, and he felt the sharp pang of regret. He prayed she was safe. That Landon's threats had been empty, intended only to torment him.

Nathan must've blacked out, for the next thing he knew the beast's rancid breath blasted his head. Looking up, he willed himself to stay absolutely still.

"Nathan!"

He jerked. Was he hallucinating?

"It's going to be okay." Sophie's voice rang with promise.

There. To the left. He glimpsed her dear, sweet face, the pucker of determination on her forehead, the glint of the battered Winchester in her steady hands.

The bear shifted closer, his plate-size paws with razor-sharp claws about a foot from his feet. The metallic taste of fear entered his mouth.

"Uh, Sophie…" She loved bears. She wouldn't—

Three quick reports of the rifle blasted through the forest. Again, Nathan jerked. The beast weaved on his feet before falling to the earth with a shudder. Nathan stared. It had been a clean shot, the second and third shots unnecessary. Guess she wanted to make certain…

Then she was there beside him, kneeling in the dirt, hands running over his arms and legs, checking for breaks. Blue eyes large and beseeching, she smoothed his hair, his cheeks. Her face lacked all color. Where she'd been cool and steady in the face of danger, she was now shaking like a leaf.

"No need to look at me like I'm going to disappear before your eyes," he rasped, relief swamping him at the sight of her safe and sound. *Thank You, God.*

"I'll be right back."

He got a little nervous when she disappeared into the woods. But she returned a minute later, leading her horse, canteen in hand. *Water.* Kneeling again, she lifted the canteen to his lips and helped him drink.

"Slow down," she murmured. "A little at a time."

Taking it away before he'd gotten his fill, she pulled out a knife and, going around to the other side of the tree, worked to free him.

"I'm sorry about the bear," he said, knowing her actions would bother her later.

The tension around his shoulders and chest went slack as she cut through the last rope. He scooted upright. Coming around, she studied the fallen animal with a frown. "It was either him or you. Besides, it won't go to waste. The meat and hide will go to a deserving family. You can help me decide who in town needs it most."

Crouching behind him, her fingers skimmed his hair. When they encountered the knot, he sucked in a breath.

"What did Landon do to you?" Outrage and horror marked her words.

"Not as much as he could have." Twisting, he studied her. "You haven't seen him today, have you?"

Her brows winged up. "No. Why?"

He shook his head. "Never mind."

Frown deepening, she bent to study his bound hands. "I can't get these handcuffs open," she lamented.

Nathan stiffened. "Did you hear that?"

"What?" Scrambling up, she skirted the bear and grabbed her rifle.

"Sounds like we might have company."

Sophie helped him stand, then aimed her weapon in the direction he indicated, prepped for danger. When his brother rounded the bend, they both sagged with relief.

"Caleb!" Sophie lowered the rifle. "I didn't know how long it'd take you to get here."

Assessing gaze taking in the scene, Caleb dismounted and strode over. "You okay, Nate?"

"I'm fine, thanks to Sophie's quick thinking."

Caleb looked at the bear, then transferred his gaze to her. "How did you know to look here?"

"Because this is where Landon brought me that day."

Remembering, Nathan felt fury burn in his gut. "We have to find him."

Caleb grunted. "That 'we' doesn't include you. You, dear brother, are going home and going to bed. As soon as we cut those handcuffs off."

"I'm fine," he protested.

Faced with their disbelieving stares, he insisted, "I'm just a little worn out, is all. And in need of a bath. After I get a fresh change of clothes and a bite to eat, I'll be as good as new."

His brother shook his head and strode to dig in his saddlebag for a pair of pincers. While he worked to cut him free, Caleb addressed Sophie. "Take him home. After I take care of this bear, I'll meet up with Timmons and the men." He clapped Nathan on the shoulder. "Don't worry, we'll find the louse and bring him to justice. We'll make sure he doesn't hurt anyone else again."

Sophie caught his wince. "Doc Owens is going to be paying you a house call."

"I don't recall agreeing to this."

They ignored him. And he wasn't really in a condition to fight the issue. He was weaker than he'd first realized. Leaving Caleb behind, he and Sophie set off.

Halfway down the mountain, as dusk descended, he remarked, "You do realize you saved my life back there."

The smile that had been absent too long transformed her face. "I guess."

"I suppose it was your turn to be the hero, huh?"

"Me? A hero?" She laughed it off, carelessly shoving her ponytail behind her shoulder. "I don't think so."

"Oh, yes, you are. Your quick thinking, your skill and bravery, saved me. You are very much a hero in my eyes, Soph."

She ducked her head, but not before he glimpsed her look of pleasure. "I couldn't have done any of that without God's help."

He smiled at her humility and firm faith. If anyone had a reason to doubt, it was her. She was one amazing woman. Why had he waited too late to see it?

Sophie waited until Doc left to go upstairs to Nathan's room.

"Your mom sent up another bowl of soup for you." She hesitated beside the bed. "Do you want it now or should I put it on the table?"

Shifting beneath the blue-and-white quilt, he eyed the steam rising from the bowl. "I'll wait for a bit."

Upon their arrival two hours ago, he'd eaten two full bowls along with three biscuits slathered in butter and honey. His mother must be trying to make up for the meals he'd missed.

Sinking into the hard-backed chair that had been scooted close to the bed, Sophie folded her hands in her lap, unable to keep from examining him with her gaze. His hair and skin gleamed from a recent washing. Scruff yet darkened his jaw. The only visible signs of his ordeal were the bandages encircling his wrists.

"I'm fine." His lips lifted in a smile meant to dispel her serious mood. "The only reason I'm in this bed is to avoid a fuss from you and Ma."

"Just reassuring myself," she quipped, grateful the sick, terrifying feeling was gone. *He was safe.*

Josh appeared in the doorway. "I have news."

"Spill it." Nathan scooted up and settled against the headboard.

"I've just come from town, where they received a telegram from Sheriff Timmons. He has Landon in custody."

Sophie squeezed her eyes tight. There'd be no more looking over her shoulder, no more worrying he'd return someday to wreak further havoc in their lives.

A warm hand covered hers. Looking up into Nathan's familiar gaze, he gave her an encouraging nod. To Josh, he said, "Where did they catch him?"

"The outskirts of Sevierville."

"I assumed he would've headed for North Carolina."

"He may have needed supplies first."

Mary's voice drifted down the hall. Stepping inside the room, she smiled and smoothed her apron over her hips. "You have a visitor. Come on in." She motioned.

Hat in his hands, Frank moved into their line of vision. Sophie froze. Could it be possible she hadn't given a single thought to her fiancé in more than twenty-four hours? Reality came crashing in like a rogue wave, her brief happiness and relief slipping away.

His gaze fell on her and Nathan's joined hands. "I, uh, heard about your ordeal, Nathan, and Sophie's role in rescuing you. She's something, isn't she?"

Nathan's expression closing, he smoothly removed his hand. "Yes, she certainly is."

"I'm glad to see you're both all right." He smiled nervously at Sophie. "Mother doesn't care that your actions were honorable. She doesn't think you should've involved yourself in what was a man's responsibility. However, I think she'll cool off by Saturday."

Sophie couldn't think of a single response. Saturday. Only four days away.

"Bonnie is a fool." Nathan's demeanor turned frosty.

"And so are you, Frank Walters, if you allow her to soil your relationship with Sophie. This young woman is a treasure. You ought to treat her as such."

Sophie gaped. Josh cleared his throat, suppressing a smile. Mary shifted from one foot to the other. And Frank? Not surprisingly, he didn't take offense.

"You're absolutely right." Coming forward, he settled a hand on Sophie's shoulder. "I'm very fortunate she agreed to be my wife. I'll do my utmost to be a good and faithful husband."

She had to get out of there. Before she shook off his too-familiar touch and announced she didn't want to marry him. That Nathan was the only man for her.

Bolting to her feet, she edged toward the door. "I, um, have to get going. Will is no doubt tired and ready to return home."

"I'll escort you." Frank took a single step.

She put up a hand. "No, thank you. I'm tired, too. I need to go home and clean up." Avoiding looking at Nathan, she said, "Goodbye, everybody."

And then she fled, desperate for solitude.

Sophie was getting married tomorrow.

The fact dominated his every waking moment, weighing him down, making him feel like a man condemned.

Lugging a crate full of crocks to be washed, he turned the corner and smashed into Caleb. The crate slipped from his hands and crashed to the barn floor.

"Why don't you watch where you're going?" he demanded, crouching to inspect the damage. He lifted a jagged piece. "See what you made me do?" he huffed, hurling it down, impatience humming through him.

Caleb thumbed his hat brim up. "What *I* made you do? I was minding my own business when you came out of nowhere."

Pushing upright, Nathan's fists clenched. "You could've warned me you were there."

Caleb's eyes narrowed to slits. "You're being unreasonable. What's with you? I know you had a terrible ordeal, but these past few days you've been a bear. Even Ma doesn't wanna be around you, and that's sayin' something."

Nathan grimaced as shame swept through him. Caleb was right. He'd been grumpy and short with anyone and everyone who'd crossed his path. "I'm sorry. I shouldn't have taken my foul mood out on you."

Righting the crate, he began to gather the pieces strewed across the straw.

Caleb bent to help. "You didn't answer my question. What's bothering you? I've never seen you this unsettled."

That's because he'd never had his world upended before.

"Is it what happened with Landon? He's in jail awaiting trial. He's never coming back."

"No, not that. It's this whole wedding fiasco. Sophie shouldn't have to marry if she doesn't want to."

Caleb frowned. "I agree. But what can we do?"

With the crate in his arms, Nathan walked back to the counter and plunked it down. "I did the only thing I could think of—I offered to marry her myself. She chose Frank instead."

Caleb rocked back on his heels. "*You* proposed to Sophie?"

"Yeah."

"I can't believe it." He huffed out a rusty laugh. "You're in love with her."

Nathan, hand poised to toss a shard into the waste bin, stilled. Stared at his brother. "No, I am not."

"Oh, yeah." Caleb nodded, grinning infuriatingly. "You most definitely are."

Laying the shard on the counter, Nathan jammed his

fists on his hips. "Just because Sophie's happiness is important to me doesn't mean I love her."

"Her happiness is just as important to me, brother, but that doesn't mean I'm prepared to make her my wife."

"You're wrong." Seizing his hat from the counter, he smashed it on his head. "I'm going out for a while. Not sure what time I'll be back."

Caleb kept right on grinning. "Tell Sophie I said hi."

Chapter Twenty-Four

"I don't wanna move to Frank's." Will slumped onto the bed stripped of linens, his narrow face sullen and wan, blue eyes brimming with accusation. Watching his home being dismantled was upsetting him as much as it was her.

Sophie wished she could make this transition easier. Carefully placing Granddad's folded quilt into the shallow trunk at her feet, she went to sit beside him. "I know you don't, but Frank's mother can't take care of their farm all by herself. It makes more sense for us to live with them. Eventually our animals and things will be moved over there."

Sam O'Malley had promised to care for her animals until Frank finished the barn addition.

The pitiful way Will looked at her, like an abandoned puppy, broke her heart. "Do you have to marry him?"

"We've been over this already," she reminded him gently, looping her arm around his shoulders. "It will take a little time, but we will adjust. We'll learn to make the best of the situation." They had no other choice.

He scuffed the floor with his shoe. "I guess it beats leaving Gatlinburg. I'll still have my friends."

"That's true. You'll go to the same church. The same school." She hugged him close. "I like Frank. Don't you?"

Will scratched his head. "He's okay, I guess, but his ma's an ole sourpuss."

Sophie stifled a startled laugh. "You mustn't call her that." She searched for the right words. "Some people are hard to get to know at first."

"Like Aunt Cordelia? She used to make me uncomfortable, but now I sort of like her."

Sophie glanced through the open bedroom door, unable to see Cordelia or the Lamberts as they packed up their belongings. Hopefully they hadn't overheard that last bit.

"Yes, like that," she murmured. Although she suspected the outcome wouldn't be the same with Bonnie, she had to encourage Will to treat her with respect. Their lives would proceed more smoothly if they all got along. "You never know what's going on in a person's life to make them the way they are. We'll have to pray and ask God to help us be patient and kind."

"I suppose."

A heavy footstep on the stoop alerted her to a visitor. "I'll go see who that is."

Cordelia, who'd been stacking pots in a crate, reached the door first. "Nathan." Over her shoulder, she shot Sophie a significant look. "Come in."

Hat in his hands, he hesitated just inside the door. Sophie drank in the sight of him. His brown hair was a little on the shaggy side, and he hadn't shaved in a day or two, if the dark stubble on his jaws and chin was anything to go by. The fact that he looked a bit of a mess, and a whole lot distracted, made him that much more appealing to her.

Foolish girl. He doesn't want you. He told you so to your face. His near-death experience hasn't changed a thing.

Poised beside the cold fireplace, Sophie twisted her

hands, hating that, despite everything, she still longed to throw her arms around his waist and hug him tight.

"You'll have to excuse the disorder," Cordelia said into the strained silence. "We're helping Sophie ready her things for the move to Frank's."

She winced. Did her aunt have to phrase it that way?

His molten gaze burned into Sophie's. "I stopped by to see if Will might like to come fishing with me."

Will shot out of the bedroom. "Of course I wanna go. Do you mind, Sophie?"

"Not at all."

She recognized this for what it was—a sort of farewell outing. While their move would take them across town, their relationship with the O'Malleys, Nathan in particular, wouldn't be the same.

Selfishly, she wished she could go along. That she could have one more carefree afternoon with him.

Nathan greeted Will with his usual smile, yet there was a sadness in his eyes he couldn't hide. He silently waited as her brother located his shoes and hat.

Cordelia resumed her place in the kitchen.

"I packed snacks in case he gets hungry," he told her. "We may be gone a couple of hours."

Like a moth drawn to a flame, Sophie drifted closer. "Take all the time you need."

"I'm ready." Grinning with anticipation, Will plopped his hat onto his head and swung open the door. "Let's go."

With a halfhearted wave, Nathan turned and left, closing the door softly behind him. Sophie moved to the window and watched them go. Walking side by side, Nathan's hand resting protectively on Will's shoulder, her heart stuck in her throat. The pair could almost pass as father and son. At the very least, brothers.

Tomorrow would mark the beginning of a new life for

her and Will. Mindful of everything she was turning her back on, she wondered if she was making the biggest mistake of her life.

Their outing proved to be a bittersweet experience. For the sake of the boy, Nathan put on a brave face, teasing and joking as he had in the past, chatting about nothing of consequence as they waited for the fish to bite. Inside, he was wondering how his and Sophie's lives might have turned out if Tobias hadn't died. If Cordelia hadn't interfered.

He wasn't naive enough to believe Sophie would have remained single forever. She was too sweet, too incredible, for the men in this town not to have noticed, given enough time. But they were out of time, weren't they? After tomorrow, she'd be Mrs. Frank Walters.

A strange sense of impending disaster spiraled through him, leaving him with the impression that if she went through with this wedding, his chance at happiness was lost forever.

Fanciful thinking again, O'Malley? You told her you didn't care who you married.

He glanced across at Will lounging on the opposite bank, hair in his eyes and looking content for a change. Poor kid. He'd faced a lot of uncertainty and upheaval lately.

Frank better treat him right, or he'll answer to me, he silently vowed.

"It's time for us to head back, buddy."

Will's brows snapped together. "Already?"

"Your sister will be wanting you home for supper." Reluctantly, he gathered his pail and pole. "I didn't have much success today." He showed Will the three small fish he'd caught. "How about you?"

"Me, either." He lifted his bucket.

"Just one, huh? At least it isn't scrawny like mine."

Will peered up at him with wide, somber eyes so much like Sophie's it made his chest hurt. "Will you still wanna spend time with me after Sophie marries Frank?"

Nathan stopped in his tracks. Bent to his level. "We're friends, right?"

He slowly nodded.

"Just because you're moving to a new house doesn't mean we can't hang out. I still need a fishing buddy."

An uncertain smile lifted his lips.

"And you know you're welcome at our house anytime. Ma is continually baking up batches of sweets. Caleb and Pa and I need someone to help us eat it all so we don't get fat." He patted his stomach.

Will's eyes lit with appreciation. "Miss Mary is the best cook around."

"Listen, I want you to remember that you can talk to me about anything. Anytime you need to get something off your chest, come and see me. That's another thing friends do. They help each other."

"Okay." Will appeared to be satisfied with Nathan's answer.

"Good." He straightened, taking note of the sun's lowered position in the sky beyond the trees. "We'd better make tracks."

When they approached the cabin, Nathan noticed the Lamberts' wagon was gone and his cousin's horse was in the yard. What was Nicole doing here?

As they stowed their gear in the barn, he hated to think of the Tanner homestead empty and abandoned, the buildings crumbling from neglect. Tobias and Sophie had worked tirelessly to keep the place up and running. It must be killing her to leave it.

Reaching the door a second before him, Will shoved it open and went inside to hang up his hat and wash his hands. Nathan followed closely behind. The girlish chatter ceased at once, calling his attention to the far corner of the room. He halted abruptly, jaw going slack at the sight that greeted him.

Framed by the window, the gentle light setting her hair to shimmering like burnished gold, Sophie stood modeling her bridal gown. His gaze skimmed over the details, soaking in the overall impression of pure, natural beauty. This wasn't a fussy dress. Simple yet elegant, like the woman wearing it. The soft white material clung lovingly to her curves, the sweeping neckline affording him a generous glimpse of gently sloping shoulders and creamy skin, the short puffed sleeves revealing smooth, tanned arms, dainty wrists and graceful hands.

In a word, she was stunning.

Sophie should be my bride, not Frank's. He doesn't love her like I do.

Nathan's heart knocked wildly against his rib cage.

What a crazy thought. This was Soph. His *friend*.

The friend you've fallen in love with.

Sophie was watching him intently, head tilted to one side as if trying to decipher his reaction.

"You shouldn't be seeing her like this," Cordelia chided, arching that imperious brow of hers at him, intimidating despite her casual dress and lack of feathered creation atop her head.

Crouched at the hem, Nicole gave a dismissive wave. "It doesn't matter if Nathan sees her dress. He's not the groom."

He's not the groom. The words struck him with the force of a horse's hoof to the head.

The intensity of his feelings was wholly alien to him. Like a turbulent, roaring river overflowing its banks, it ripped away his reserve, those previously held notions that love and romance were for everyone else but him, that he would be perfectly content on his own, that he and his childhood friend would never, ever, suit.

Lies. All of them.

He. Loved. Sophie. Laughing or arguing, he loved her. Happy or sad, dusty overalls or pristine skirts, he loved her.

"I want Sophie for myself," he whispered the words out loud.

Strange, the sun didn't fall from the sky. The buildings around him didn't collapse into piles of dust. The ground didn't open up and swallow him whole.

"What was that?" Cordelia asked. "Nicole was speaking. We couldn't hear you."

His fingers tightened on his hat, unknowingly crumpling it. "Nothing."

So the world hadn't stopped turning. There was just one problem—he'd come to the realization too late. She'd made her choice. Hadn't he caused her enough trouble for one lifetime? Loving her meant he had to respect her decision. Loving her meant he had to do the right thing and let her go.

No matter how much it killed him to do so, he'd wish her well. And plead with God to help him get over her.

Nathan looked as if he'd been conked on the head with a milk pail. Not exactly a reaction to inspire a girl's confidence.

Admit it, an inner voice accused, *you harbored the hope that one look at you in this amazing dress and he'd fall at your feet and declare his undying devotion.*

That hope died a swift death.

She fidgeted, earning a warning glance from his cousin, who was attempting to shorten the dress's hem. "Stand still. I don't want to accidentally poke you."

"I need to talk to Sophie," Nathan stated, serious and determined.

What now? she wondered frantically. Another argument? More hurtful truths?

"Go ahead," Nicole murmured, black head bent to her task, "don't let us stop you."

Advancing into the room, Nathan set his hat on the sofa and slipped his hands into his pockets. "Alone." His tone brooked no argument.

"We don't have time for this—"

"I'm sure we could afford to give them five minutes of privacy," Cordelia spoke up, surprising the other women. To Nicole, she suggested, "Why don't we take a short stroll? I'm sure you could do with a bit of fresh air after the long hours you've put in. Besides, I've heard rumors of a boutique, and I'd like to hear your plans."

"Oh." Her violet eyes sparked with anticipation. Wedging the pin into the material, she stood and wagged a finger at Sophie. "Don't move from this spot. Got it?"

"Got it."

"Come along, Will," her aunt called to the bedroom, "we're going outside for a bit."

When the trio had left them alone, the cabin walls seemed to close in on her, an undercurrent of urgency vibrating the air between them.

"How are you feeling?" she asked.

"My head's a bit tender, but other than that, I'm as good as new."

Nathan approached with measured steps. Coming very near, careful not to let his boots soil her dress, his hungry gaze roamed her face. "You look like a dream."

Sophie commanded her heart to slow down.

Her disobedient hand lifted, lightly caressed the side of his head, his brown hair tickling her skin. "You've let your hair grow out."

His mouth quirked even as he grasped her hand and, lowering it, held on tight. "I look like a shaggy mutt."

With his warm, capable fingers clinging to hers, time slowed, her breathing slowed, her blood turned to sludge in her veins. His beautiful mouth was near enough to kiss.

"No, it suits you." Her voice came out scratchy. "I like the stubble, too."

He looked approachable, easy this way. Less forbidding. *You're getting married tomorrow. Or have you forgotten?*

Nathan gingerly tucked a curl behind her ear, silver eyes bright like the midnight stars. "All I've ever wanted was for you to be happy." A frown tugged at his lips. Releasing her hand, he stuffed his deep into his pockets. "I wanted to tell you that no matter what happens in the future, I'll always be here for you. We've been friends for as long as I can remember, and that's not going away. Not ever."

Her heart broke a little. What had she expected? Pressing her hands against her middle, she nodded, willed away the what-ifs, the broken dreams. "I know."

"Don't forget it," he said with a fierce smile. "Promise."

"I promise." *Please, please go now. I'm not as strong as you think.*

"Good." With a slow pivot, he walked to the sofa and retrieved his hat. At the door, he stopped and looked back. "I'll see you tomorrow."

Then he left her. And she feared the words they'd just exchanged were nothing more than optimistic lies.

Chapter Twenty-Five

"I'm getting married today." On her knees in the dewy grass, Sophie splayed a hand atop the stone marker flush with the ground. She'd placed a hastily assembled bouquet of wildflowers, mostly daisies, along the top edge. "I think you'd like the idea of Frank as a grandson-in-law, Granddad. I wish you could be here to walk me down the aisle. I wish Ma could be here, too."

So many impossible wishes.

Twisting, she sat and pulled her knees up to her chest, surveying the scene sprawled out in front of her. Situated on a hill, the cemetery overlooked the quaint, one-room church and this end of Main Street, tranquil and quiet due to the early hour. Dawn was just breaking, the sun barely gracing the mountaintops ringing the valley.

Unable to sleep, she'd quickly dressed in her favorite pants and shirt and left the cabin, drawn to this last place of connection with Tobias and her ma. Will wasn't home. He'd spent the night with a friend; a good thing because she'd needed to be alone this morning.

Sophie's gaze settled on the church, the short, fat bell tower silhouetted by the pale pink horizon, the recently repainted white clapboards gleaming. Later that day, in front of the entire town, she'd walk the aisle. She'd pledge to honor and cherish and obey Frank Walters. She would bury her dream of a life with Nathan.

She forced her mind to her groom. She wouldn't allow herself to be bogged down with sorrow—it wouldn't be fair to Frank. She wondered about his mind-set this morning. Was he nervous? Excited? Having second thoughts?

Thursday evening, when he'd joined her and Will for supper, he'd seemed as steady as always. Sensitive to her feelings about the move, Frank had been especially attentive, intent on pleasing her and her brother. He hadn't mentioned the scene in Nathan's bedroom, and neither had she.

"Lord, I need Your help." She pushed her loose hair away from her face. "Frank deserves my utmost respect and devotion. Please help me to honor him with my thoughts, words and deeds."

Help me forget the love of my life.

Tracing her granddad's name carved into the stone, she murmured, "It's time for me to go now, Granddad. Lots to do today."

Pushing to her feet, she tilted her face toward the lightening expanse above. *I don't know if it's possible, Lord, but I'd really appreciate it if You would tell him hello for me.*

When Nathan descended the stairs at a quarter until three, he found his parents in the living room already dressed for the wedding. Pa looked up from his task of clasping Ma's necklace, spectacles reflecting the afternoon light. Deep wrinkles appeared in his forehead when he took in Nathan's casual clothes. Ma, whose back was to him, didn't notice.

Josh, wearing head-to-toe black, emerged from the dining room, Kate following closely behind, glowing and vibrant in an emerald-green frock that matched her eyes.

"Why aren't you dressed?" Josh demanded, tugging on his suit sleeves.

Pausing on the bottom step, he saw Ma twist around. "Nathan, you're going to be late if you don't hurry. Why, you haven't even shaved!"

Josh sauntered over, speculation ripe in his expression. "Those clothes look like you slept in them." He ruffled Nathan's hair. "And when was the last time you visited the barbershop?"

Flicking away his brother's annoying hand, Nathan edged sideways. "I'm not going."

"What?" Ma gasped. Pa and Kate looked concerned.

"Why not?" Josh demanded.

His mind raced. What reasonable excuse could he give for not attending? While everyone was aware of his general distaste for weddings, this was different. This was *Sophie's* special day.

Up until that morning, he'd fully intended on going. However, faced with the prospect of sitting idly by and watching the woman he loved marry another man, he found he just couldn't do it. Not for his family. Not even for her.

When he said nothing, Ma came over, covered his hand gripping the banister. "Sophie is practically family. Your father is giving her away. How will she feel if you don't come?"

He was certain that his absence would be best for everyone.

"Have you had another argument?" she ventured, clearly upset. "After you've made up, you'll regret not going."

"I can't explain right now." His voice was gruff. "Please, just accept my decision."

Pa squeezed her shoulder, urging her to leave him be. "We need to get going, Mary. The reverend wants me there a little early." Wise eyes brimming with sympathy, he patted Nathan's hand. "Let me know if you need to talk later."

Emotion welled up. "Thanks, Pa."

For too long, he'd convinced himself he was content with his single state, determined to avoid messy, unpredictable relationships he couldn't control, that wouldn't fit into his neat, tidy world. Too late, he realized his world was awfully lonely without Sophie in it. Staid. Boring. Colorless.

He wouldn't have a marriage like his parents'. Wouldn't be blessed with a loving wife and children like his brother.

You have no one to blame but yourself, O'Malley.

Josh and Kate lingered after their parents left.

"Sophie won't understand." His brother studied him intently.

Above him, a door closed. Footsteps echoed along the hallway and Caleb appeared at the top of the stairs sporting his Sunday best, a deep brown suit that hadn't gotten much wear in the past years. He'd even shaved and slicked his midnight-black hair away from his face. His dark brown gaze rested on Nathan, his knowing smirk flashing.

Descending the stairs, he announced nonchalantly, "He's not going because he's in love with Sophie."

Nathan winced, anticipating Josh's reaction. "Thanks, Caleb."

"No problem." He passed by and, circumventing the couple, went to retrieve his hat.

But his older brother didn't laugh or act surprised. "I was wondering if you'd ever get around to admitting it to yourself."

Kate's eyes grew round. "You knew and didn't tell me?" she addressed her husband.

Pulling her arm through his, he said, "I wasn't certain, but I've long suspected. He and Sophie have a long, turbulent history. There was too much friction for there not to be something below the surface."

"That's what I told him." Caleb leaned against the door and folded his arms, observing the fallout of his treachery with open interest. "Opposites attract, I've often heard."

Nathan held up his hands in surrender. "I admit it, I love her. That doesn't change anything."

Caleb consulted his pocket watch. "She's not shackled yet."

"If you love her," Kate earnestly urged, "you have to tell her. Give her the chance to make an informed decision."

"It's too late. Everyone's expecting her to marry Frank. Guests are probably arriving as we speak." He couldn't stop what was already set in motion.

"You mean to tell me you're going to sit around and sulk while the woman you love marries another man? Don't make the same mistake I did." Josh glanced at his wife with reverence and love that mirrored what Nathan felt for Sophie. "I let my foolish pride almost rob me of the most precious gift God has ever bestowed upon me."

His sister-in-law's lips trembled and moisture glistened in her eyes. Sophie would never look at him that way. He'd blown it too many times. "You're forgetting something. I asked her to marry me once already, and she turned me down." Scrubbing a weary hand down his face, he stepped down and moved to the window, pushing the curtains aside. "I somehow doubt that after the countless lectures and set-downs I've subjected her to she'd harbor any tender feelings toward me."

"You won't know until you try," Josh prompted. "Isn't she worth the effort?"

Nathan's father was waiting for Sophie on the church steps. He smiled when he saw her and came to help her alight the buggy. "You make a beautiful bride, my dear." He reached to take her hand.

Sam was like a favorite uncle, a man of integrity who'd

raised his sons to love and serve God and to respect others. He was the perfect choice to give her away. If only...
But no, she couldn't allow regrets to distract her from her course.

"Hold on a second, Uncle Sam." Clutching Sophie's bouquet, Nicole descended and hurried around to her side. "I'll hold up her skirts so they don't get dirty. Can you take the flowers, Sophie?"

Wagons lined the parking area. Horses belonging to single riders shifted in the shade provided by the copse of trees surrounding the building. Had all the Gatlinburg residents turned out for her wedding?

With each step, panic built in her chest. While her hands and feet were blocks of ice, perspiration dampened her nape and forehead.

Think of Will, she repeated again and again.

Sam swung open the heavy oak door. They entered the alcove and Nicole rearranged Sophie's skirts. Straightening, she smiled with satisfaction. "You look stunning, if I do say so myself."

Sophie focused on the young woman who'd freely given of her time and talent. Her raven hair had been swept up in an intricate French twist, random glossy curls left to sweep over her shoulders. The elegant lavender outfit enhanced Nicole's pale, creamy skin, the perfect foil for her wide violet eyes.

She clasped her hand and squeezed. "I can't thank you enough for all you've done, Nicole. If it weren't for you, I'd still be sporting a braid and overalls."

Color blossomed in her cheeks. "It's been a pleasure dressing you."

Hushed conversations died down when the piano music began. Sam extended his arm. "It's time." A hint of apology behind his spectacles put her on guard.

Nicole went ahead of them to find a seat. Sam paused

in the entryway. When she caught sight of the guests packing the pews—far more than attended Sunday services—her throat closed up. Her fingers clutched his suit sleeve.

Reverend Munroe was there conversing with Frank.

Instead of observing her groom, Sophie's errant gaze swept the crowd for a dear, familiar face. The O'Malley clan occupied the first two pews. Josh and Kate, Caleb and Mary were seated together. Alice, Nicole and the twins shared space with Megan and Lucian. Nathan wasn't there. Her stomach burned with disappointment.

She glanced up at Sam. "Nathan isn't coming, is he?"

He frowned. "I'm afraid not."

"Perhaps it's for the best," she murmured, earning her a curious look. He didn't question her, however. There wasn't time. The music swelled, cuing the start of the ceremony. When the reverend and Frank left off speaking to focus on her, the guests turned as one to get a glimpse of the bride.

Sophie felt light-headed. Focusing on her little brother, handsome and grown-up-looking in his very first suit—a gift from Cordelia—and seated in the front row beside their aunt, she forced her feet to move.

I'm doing this for him. For our future.

She willed her gaze to Frank. He was smiling, a serene smile, his brown eyes full of admiration. *Frank's a good man. No...he's a great man.*

But you don't love him, her heart accused. *You love Nathan. Always will.*

By the time they reached the altar, her throat was so dry she wondered if she'd be able to recite the vows. Sam handed her off to Frank, who held both her hands. If he noticed their dampness, he didn't let it show.

"Ladies and gentlemen, we are gathered here today—"

The rear doors banging open startled the reverend, and nearly everyone in attendance jerked in their seats. Boots thundered on the floorboards. A disheveled man rounded the corner, a man whose face was set in determined don't-mess-with-me lines.

"Nathan," she whispered, heart leaping at the sight of him.

What was he doing here? What on earth could have possibly possessed him to disrupt her wedding?

Chapter Twenty-Six

Nathan shrugged off the weight of all those stares, his sole focus the beautiful bride at the altar. He strode toward her, rumblings forming in his wake.

"What's he doing?" A little girl's voice carried.

"Is that Nathan O'Malley?" Another man peered after him. "I thought he was the shy one."

Frowning deeply, Frank dropped Sophie's hands. Bonnie popped up from her seat, waving her handkerchief like a white flag. "What's the meaning of this? Aren't you going to do something, Reverend?"

Nathan ignored them all. This was *his* Sophie. *His* friend. *His* girl. He didn't know if she could ever love him, ever want him, but he couldn't let her go without trying to find out.

When he reached her, she stared at him as if he'd dropped down from another planet. "Nathan?"

Without a word, he bent and tossed her over his shoulder. What they had to discuss couldn't be done in front of the entire town. Sophie's outraged gasp was punctuated by a few of the spectators'.

He leveled a challenging gaze at Frank, who stood

watching in wide-eyed shock. "I'm sorry, but I can't let you marry her."

Swinging around, he winked at Will, who responded with a huge grin. Cordelia looked like the cat that had caught the canary.

"There won't be a wedding here today, folks. You may as well head on home." Tuning out the resulting uproar, Nathan strode for the exit with his precious cargo.

Outside, Sophie's fists pounded his back. "Put me down this instant, Nathaniel James O'Malley!"

"Your wish is my command." Reaching a nearby tree, he set her sideways on his horse and vaulted up behind her.

Sapphire eyes as wide as saucers, she sputtered, "Wh-what do you think you're doing?"

Nudging Chance into a trot, he grinned like a fool. "Rescuing you, what else?"

Her mouth fell open. Although he had his arms securely around her waist, she gripped the saddle horn with one hand and his forearm with the other. Wisps of honeyed hair danced around her forehead and temples. The scent of spring meadows enveloped him.

"Who are you?" she demanded, eyes narrowing. "Did you fall and hit your head? Stay outside in the sun too long without a hat?"

"Nope. I'm thinking more clearly than I have my entire life."

She studied the passing landscape. "If you don't stop this horse right this minute and tell me what's going on, I'm going to jump off."

There was just enough heat behind the words to make him slow Chance. They'd ridden north of town toward the river and adjacent fields where his family often picnicked and had the whole countryside to themselves. Safe enough, he surmised, given the likely chance she'd give him an earful once they dismounted.

She didn't prove him wrong. The instant her white kid boots hit the ground, she rounded on him, frothy skirts billowing around her like a bell, and shoved his chest. "What's gotten into you? How dare you humiliate me like that, tossing me over your shoulder like a sack of sugar! I'll never hear the end of it!" She shoved him again, forcing him back a couple of steps. Red seared her cheekbones. "And what about Will? Do you want me to lose him? Is that what you want?"

Capturing her wrists, Nathan circled them behind her back, a move that brought her flush against his chest. She was a radiant vision of loveliness—her skin flushed with exertion, eyes brilliant fire, fine eyebrows arched in defiance.

"Are you finished?" he intoned, face angled downward.

Tears glistened. "I was prepared to give you up." Her voice quivered. "How am I supposed to do that now?"

The abject misery in her pale countenance made his heart ache. His stubbornness and pride had caused her this anguish.

"I don't ever want you to do that," he whispered softly. "Not ever."

Overcome with emotion, he lowered his mouth to hers.

This was all a wonderful dream. A delicious, lovely dream. It had to be. Dreams didn't come true in her world.

When she wiggled her wrists, he instantly let go, instead settling his hands around her waist in a possessive move that thrilled her. His lips were sure and firm against hers, seeking reassurance, giving love. Going up on her tiptoes, she framed his face and tugged him closer, the light stubble on his lean jaw prickly on her palms. A low moan slipped past his lips.

Easing back, he rested his forehead on hers. "I'm sorry

I embarrassed you. I couldn't let you marry Frank, not without telling you how I feel."

Sophie's heart flip-flopped. Could this be real? Could Nathan truly want her?

Caressing her cheek, he smiled tenderly, beautiful eyes bright with a fierce, blazing love that literally took her breath away.

"For the longest time, I couldn't see past our friendship, our history, such as it is. When you blossomed into this amazing, lovely young woman before my very eyes, I was blown away by the strength of my attraction. To say that I was confused is an understatement. Here you were, my neighbor and friend, younger than me by several years and someone I felt extremely protective toward. I wasn't supposed to think of you in a romantic way. It felt wrong. I fought it with everything in me."

The insight thrilled her. He'd been as drawn to her as she'd been to him. Assuming he was referring to her transformation, she said, "Nicole is gifted at what she does."

"No, Soph—" his gaze grew intense "—I'm talking about before the dresses and sophisticated hairstyles. It started months ago, way back in early spring. To me, it doesn't matter what you wear or how you style your hair. You could wear a flour sack, and you'd still be the most beautiful girl I've ever seen."

Her lips parted. "You're serious?"

"Very much so." He nodded gravely. "Remember the night we played Blind Man's Bluff?"

How could she forget? She'd been humiliated, thinking he'd kissed her out of pity.

"I desperately wanted to kiss you for real, but I was afraid of my own reaction. That's why, at the last minute, I settled for a chaste one on the cheek."

"Then the comments started and you gave in because you felt sorry for me."

"Pity had nothing to do with it." He laughed suddenly, shaking his head. "That embrace rocked me to the core. I knew then that I was in big trouble."

Growing serious once more, he skimmed her satiny sleeve. "The moment I saw you in this dress, the truth of how I felt about you hit me like a ton of bricks. There was no more denying it. I love you, Soph."

She could hardly process the words she'd never imagined she'd hear. "That was days ago. Why didn't you say something?"

A grimace twisted his lips. "I didn't think I had a chance with you. Not after the way I've acted…like an overbearing big brother more than a friend."

No chance with her? "Nathan, I've loved you since I was fourteen years old. No amount of lectures or disagreements could've changed the way I felt about you. You'll always have my heart, my love and affection, my respect."

Eyes sparkling with happiness, he released her and, digging in his pants' pocket, produced a sapphire ring that flashed and shimmered in the sunlight. When he dropped to one knee and took her left hand in his, Sophie's heart began to pound.

"We've known each other all of our lives. There are no surprises and, after today, no secrets between us. We've seen the good and the not so good in each other, we've hurt each other, too, and yet our bond has remained unbreakable. You are vital to my happiness, Sophia Lorraine Tanner. Will you marry me? My best friend and my dear, sweet love?"

"I want that more than anything in the world." Smiling down at him, she lovingly cradled his cheek, heart bursting with a joy she couldn't contain. Nathan wanted her for his wife!

Grinning, he stood and pulled her close. "You've made me the happiest of men."

Hands curled around his neck, she stroked his hair. "I'll always have a tendency to act impulsively."

"And I'll probably always be tempted to scold you when you do." He smiled ruefully.

"We will have differences of opinion," she warned. "We'll argue."

"I figure that's standard for most couples." Arms looped around her waist, he held her snugly against him. "The fun part is making up." He waggled his eyebrows before brushing a soft, all-too-brief kiss on her mouth.

"Nathan, what about all those people? They bought gifts. They came expecting to see a wedding. And poor Frank? Here I am rejoicing over my happiness while he's left to face the crowd alone. I feel awful about that."

A line appeared between his brows. "Since I'm the one who kidnapped the bride, I'll go back to the church and explain everything to the crowd. Unfortunately, there's nothing I can do to help Frank. He'll have to come to terms with the fact that I love you, and I'm not willing to give you up."

Sliding her hands to his chest, she smoothed his shirt collar. "He's not suffering from a broken heart, I'm sure. However, he must certainly be feeling humiliated at being abandoned at the altar."

"I'll pay him for the supplies he used to add on to his barn."

"And I'll return the gifts."

"You may want to hold off on that." He smiled. "I want to make you my bride as soon as possible. *After* I've had a chance to court you properly."

"Oh? What do you have in mind, Mr. O'Malley?" she prompted, the church guests already forgotten. The prospect of being courted by him intrigued her.

"Hmm…let me see. I'm thinking picnics by the river. Chess games if you agree to allow me to win sometimes."

He winked. "Flowers. I'll shower you with flowers and baked goods."

"Sounds lovely." She laughed, giddy with excitement. "This courtship, how long do you see it lasting?"

"I predict it will be a brief one."

Epilogue

Three months later

"Will, hurry up and put your coat on," Sophie called up to the loft. "We don't want to keep everyone waiting."

His face appeared at the top of the ladder. "One minute, okay? I'm almost finished with my list."

"All right. Make it a fast minute." She smiled, thinking of the O'Malleys' Thanksgiving dinner tradition. After the meal, everyone around the table took turns sharing what they were thankful for. Unlike her brother, she didn't have to pen hers on paper. Her many blessings were written upon her heart, and she considered them daily, thanking God for His goodness and grace.

Humming to herself, she retrieved the basket containing two apple pies from the counter and went outside into the crisp fall day. Above her, thick, white clouds floated in a cerulean sky. The meadows and forests bore witness to the changing seasons, the trees resplendent in hues of scarlet, orange and gold. A container of mums and daisies added a splash of much needed color to their front stoop.

"I'll take that, Mrs. O'Malley." Nathan took the basket and captured her hand, weaving his fingers securely through hers.

Her husband of two months flashed her a devastating smile, one that hinted of intimacies shared, of enduring love intertwining their hearts and souls into one. Since their wedding day—a small family affair performed on his parents' property—he'd grown more precious to her than ever before, so much so she had to sometimes combat the fear of losing him and trust God to guide their steps.

Over the course of the past months, losing Tobias and coming very close to losing Nathan, she'd learned that while she may not always understand God's ways, His plans were best. "And we know that in all things God works for the good of those who love Him, who have been called according to His purpose."

"Quoting Romans this morning?"

She wasn't surprised he recognized it. Every evening after supper, Nathan read from the Bible and, together, the three of them prayed, a most special time that brought them closer as a family.

"Just reminding myself of God's provision."

His gaze warmed, and she reveled in the affection she witnessed there. Handsome and fit in a hunter-green shirt that molded to his chest and brown trousers encasing his lean, muscular legs, he wore his brown hair a tad longer than he used to, and he'd gone to shaving every other day now, lending him a more relaxed, approachable air.

He indicated the pies. "These smell delicious."

"I hope they taste as good as they smell." Shortly after their engagement, she'd enlisted Mary to help her learn to bake. Not only did she make bread on a daily basis now, she sometimes tried her hand at desserts.

"If they taste anything like the rhubarb pies you made last month, I'll have to fight my brothers for a piece."

The door shut behind them and Will bolted past in a blur

of green and brown. "Come on, you guys," he teased over his shoulder, dark hair flopping on his forehead. "What's the holdup? We don't want to be late!"

He shot off into the woods, no doubt as eager for the companionship as he was for the food. Will loved that he was now officially part of the O'Malley family. He'd taken to calling Nathan's parents Aunt Mary and Uncle Sam, titles that greatly pleased the older couple.

Following at a more sedate pace, they entered the woods that separated the properties, quiet for a moment as they absorbed the beauty of the forest spread out in all directions.

"I forgot to tell you. I received a letter from Cordelia yesterday."

"Really? How is she doing?" He guided her around a fallen moss-encased log.

"She wrote that she's glad to be home, but it sounds to me like she's lonely."

"Admit it, you miss her," he said good-naturedly, "bossiness and all."

"You know, I do. I got used to having her around." Cordelia had stayed on another week after their wedding, keeping Will with her at the Lamberts' so that she and Nathan could have time to themselves. "She invited us for a visit sometime before Christmas. Before the weather turns bad."

His silver gaze cut to her, dark brows raised in question. "Would you like to go?"

"I've never been to Knoxville," she mused. "I'd like to see her home and visit her church. Perhaps you and I could do some sightseeing while Will visits with Cordelia."

Downcast gaze on the lookout for exposed roots, he considered her words. "I like that idea. It's a short day trip. Why don't we go next week? We can ask Will's teacher to send his lessons along so he won't get too far behind."

"That would be wonderful." She smiled over at him, grateful beyond words. "Thank you, Nathan."

Casting around the forest and seeing no one, Nathan stopped and set the basket on the leaf-littered ground. Hands on her shoulders, he pulled her close.

"What are you doing?" She laughed, completely at ease with him.

"When you look at me like that, Soph," he breathed, "it makes me want to forget about my family, toss you over my shoulder and carry you back home." His earnest bordering-on-vulnerable expression triggered longing of her own.

Lifting her face to his, she kissed him, a toe-curling experience that made the day at his folks' seem very long indeed.

"You know you want to spend time with Juliana and Evan," she reminded him after a while. "They're only here for a week."

Smoothing her hair behind her ear, he nodded regretfully. "You're right."

"And—" she ducked beneath his arm and away "—think of all that delicious food you'd miss out on. Turkey and dressing, pumpkin pie, collard greens, warm, gooey yeast rolls." She ticked them off one by one, squealing when he picked her up and whirled her around.

"Nathan!"

Chuckling, he lowered her to her feet. "Okay, okay, you've convinced me, woman. Let's go before I change my mind."

Both of them grinning ear to ear, they hurried on their way.

His parents' house was, of course, chaotic. Laughter spilled in from the living room, and in the kitchen, bustling activity abounded as his ma and Aunt Alice plied Jessica and Jane with heaping platters to carry to the dining room table. Rich aromas wrapped around him, making his mouth water and his empty stomach growl.

When he reached out to snag a green bean from a nearby bowl, his ma playfully swatted his hand. "No filching. If I let all of you men do that, there'd be nothing left. Sophie, dear, how are you? Happy Thanksgiving." Ma greeted his wife as if she hadn't seen her the day before, pulling her into a warm hug.

His wife. The term still startled and pleased him in due measure.

His thumb grazed the gold ring on his fourth finger, reassuring himself it was still there. That this was real. Sophie was well and truly his, a fact that filled him with gratitude and a humbling understanding of God's goodness, the blessing she and Will were to him.

Gazing at her now, cheeks rosy from the cool air and quite possibly from their interlude in the forest, big blue eyes alight with contentment, his chest expanded with love and pride. She was truly lovely, inside and out.

Together, they drifted into the living room. Amid greetings and hugs and the shaking of hands, Nathan took note of the new additions to the O'Malley clan this year. Lucian lounged on the sofa, relaxed and content with Megan tucked close to his side. While he hadn't lost his formal manners altogether, he wasn't above joking and teasing along with the rest of them.

On the other end of the sofa was perhaps the most popular addition, six-month-old James. At present, he was being bounced on his father's knee. With his fine jet-black hair and blue eyes, the baby bore a striking resemblance to Evan, whose look of paternal pride was unmistakable.

And then there was Will and Sophie. *His* new family.

Pushing to her feet, Juliana hurried over, flame-colored hair swept up in a dignified bun. "Welcome to the family, Sophie. I was ecstatic when I heard the news."

"She's not exaggerating." Evan grinned, holding the baby steady with a large hand on his tummy. "I came in from feeding the animals one afternoon and she was jumping up and down, waving the letter around and basically scaring poor Jamey here."

Juliana didn't deny it, just laughed.

Nathan was next in line for a hug.

"Congratulations, Nate." Pulling back, her forest-green eyes communicated her delight. "I wish we could've been here for the wedding. I hear it was a touching ceremony."

It had been a perfect day. Sensitive to Frank's feelings— they'd planned to marry only three weeks after that first interrupted ceremony—they'd decided against a church wedding. And so here on his family's land, beneath a bright blue sky and with a handful of family and friends in attendance, he and Sophie had exchanged heartfelt vows.

"We understand how difficult travel must be with an infant."

"Would you like to hold him?"

"If you're sure I won't break him." He winked, waiting as she transferred her son to him. Cradled against his chest, the baby was small and warm and smelled like fresh flowers and milk, a curious combination. "Hey there, little guy," he murmured, aware of Sophie's keen interest.

Holding out a finger, she allowed James to wrap his fist around it, her eyes going soft when he smiled at her. "He's beautiful," she said wonderingly.

Juliana beamed her thanks. "Someday you and Nathan will have a baby of your very own."

Sophie's widened gaze collided with his, and they shared a smile. A baby. With Sophie. A thrill shot through him at the prospect. She'd make a wonderful mother.

"Time to eat," Mary called from the dining room, and everyone began filing around the table. It was cramped, but no one cared. They were just happy to be together.

The meal was delicious. Afterward, the sharing of everyone's lists evoked both tears and laughter, especially Will's. He was over-the-moon excited to have Nathan as a brother-in-law and was hoping for a niece or nephew very soon.

All in all, it was a great day, but as the sun sank lower in the sky, Nathan became impatient to escort his bride home. As she was packing up leftovers, he caught sight of Caleb slipping out the kitchen door and followed him.

"Hey." Nathan closed the door behind him. "Where are you sneaking off to?"

Caleb pivoted back, shrugging up a shoulder. "Just going to check on the cows."

"Too much togetherness for one day?" Nathan stepped off the porch and joined him, sensing the nervous energy his brother radiated. Sorrow overtook him as the truth sank in. Caleb was leaving.

"You could say that," he hedged, his restless gaze scanning the horizon.

"When are you leaving?"

His brows shot up. "How did you know?"

Nathan settled a hand on his shoulder. "Wasn't that hard to figure out. I'm surprised you've stuck around as long as you have."

"Figured I'd ease the workload for a while after your wedding." A ghost of a smile crossed his lips. "Give you and Sophie time to adjust to married life."

Nathan huffed a laugh. "Thanks, Caleb. I appreciate that."

"No problem."

"Are you sure you won't stay a little longer?"

Caleb's gaze darkened. "I couldn't, even if I wanted to."

What did that mean?

Seeing the unspoken question, he continued. "My presence around town bothers Rebecca. Well, let's be honest, it bothers more folks than just her. But she's the one I'm most concerned about."

"You can't let others' opinions rule your life. If you're around more often, seeing you wouldn't come as such a shock."

Pulling away, Caleb's jaw set in a stubborn line. "I've already made my decision, Nate."

The door opened then, and Sophie joined them, linking her arm with Nathan's. "Will is staying the night with your parents again."

"Okay."

She looked from one to the other. "I'm sorry, am I interrupting something?"

Caleb shook his head. "No, not at all. I was just leaving." Pointing at Nathan, he addressed her. "You keep this one in line, you hear?"

"I—I'll try." Her frown meant she knew something was off, but she didn't comment.

As his brother took off for the barn, Nathan summoned a smile. "Ready to go?"

Indicating the basket looped around her arm, she nodded, and they headed for the woods.

"Caleb's leaving for real, isn't he?" she questioned him at the halfway point. "I thought, since he's been around for a while, that he'd decided to forego his jaunts into the high country."

"I think we all hoped for that scenario, but no. He's restless. I'm afraid he won't come around again for a long while."

"I'm sorry, Nathan," she said, her voice thick with compassion. "I know how much you miss him, how much you worry when he's away."

"Right now, the only thing we can do is pray for him."

They'd reached the cabin by now, his new home that Sophie had gone out of her way to make as cozy and comfortable as possible, and his sole wish at that moment was to focus on his wife. "Wait here."

Taking the basket from her, he placed it inside the kitchen and, rejoining her outside, led her to her favorite tree. With a playful grin, she climbed up first in a flurry of skirts, and he followed close behind. Wedging himself against the trunk, he motioned for her to scoot close and lean back against him. He anchored her with one arm around her tiny waist, thumb lazily skimming her rib cage.

He heaved a grateful sigh, a lazy smile lifting his lips. "This is more like it."

Her head beneath his chin, her soft hair tickling his neck, she held tightly to his arm, trusting him to keep her from falling. "I'm so happy I can hardly stand it," she said with a low chuckle. "You and me. Together…."

"I know." And he did. They almost hadn't made it to this place.

Twisting her head, she gazed up at him with humbling adoration. "I love you, Nathan."

"I love you, my dear, sweet Sophie." And then he kissed her to show her how much he meant it.

* * * * *

Dear Reader,

Thank you for choosing this latest installment of my Smoky Mountain Matches series. There's something fascinating about the journey from friendship to love, don't you think?

Exploring Nathan and Sophie's relationship was such fun. This was my first time writing about a couple who knew each other well, and it was nice that they each had so much insight into the other's behavior. Although keenly aware of each other's quirks and faults, they still cared deeply.

In this book, we also got to spend a little more time with Caleb O'Malley, Nathan's mysterious younger brother. Caleb's story is next in line, so I hope you enjoyed getting to know him a bit better.

If you'd like to find out more about the O'Malleys and this series, drop by my website, www.karenkirst.com. I'm also on Facebook and Goodreads. Or you can email me at karenkirst@live.com.

Best Wishes,

Karen Kirst

Discussion Questions

1. Sophie was thrust into a role of responsibility at a young age. How do you think this shaped her character and personality?

2. In your opinion, what initially prompted Cordelia's ultimatum? How did her motives and feelings change as the story progressed?

3. Sophie has suffered loss and hardship in her young life. At one point in the story, she questions God, feeling as if He's ignoring her needs. Have you ever felt that way? What Scripture verses helped you?

4. Why did Nathan resist telling Sophie about Landon's true character?

5. The O'Malleys are quick to help others. Do you think people are as generous with their time and possessions today? Why or why not?

6. Nathan and Sophie approach life situations differently. What are some advantages/disadvantages of a cautious nature? Of an impulsive one?

7. Do you think Nicole's willingness to help Sophie stems solely from selfish reasons?

8. Why is it so difficult for Nathan to admit to himself that he loves Sophie?

9. Because of his role in the accident that left him scarred and his best friend in a wheelchair, Caleb thinks his

family will be safer if he keeps his distance. What would you say to someone who felt this way? Are there any specific Bible verses you would point them to?

10. What other reasons do you think prompt Caleb to stay away?

11. Why doesn't Sophie tell Nathan how she feels about him?

12. Have you ever had a relationship you wanted to move beyond friendship? How did you handle the situation? What was the outcome?

13. Have you ever encountered someone like April? How did you handle the situation?

14. After the food fight, Josh accuses Nathan of judging Sophie. Do you agree? What do you think prompts his lectures?

15. At the end of the book, Nathan and Sophie acknowledge they will always have differences. How can differences be good for a couple?

COMING NEXT MONTH FROM
Love Inspired® Historical

Available December 3, 2013

MAIL-ORDER MISTLETOE BRIDES
by Jillian Hart & Janet Tronstad

When two brides journey to the Montana Territory, will they find a love—and family—amid the Rocky Mountains?

THE WIFE CAMPAIGN
The Master Matchmakers
by Regina Scott

The Earl of Danning is quite certain a house party is *not* the place he'll find his future bride. Especially not one arranged by his valet! But the lovely Ruby Hollingsford could change his mind....

A HERO FOR CHRISTMAS
Sanctuary Bay
by Jo Ann Brown

Amid the bustle of her sister's wedding plans, Jonathan Bradley's sense of humor is Lady Catherine Meriweather's only respite. But will secrets from Jonathan's past thwart any chance they have of a holiday happily ever after?

RETURN OF THE COWBOY DOCTOR
Wyoming Legacy
by Lacy Williams

Hattie Powell won't let anything hinder her dream of becoming a doctor—especially not the handsome new medical assistant. When an epidemic strikes, can they work together to save their small town?

LIHCNM1113

REQUEST YOUR FREE BOOKS!

2 FREE INSPIRATIONAL NOVELS
PLUS 2
FREE
MYSTERY GIFTS

Love Inspired.

HISTORIC

INSPIRATIONAL HISTORICAL ROMANCE

YES! Please send me 2 FREE Love Inspired® Historical novels and my 2 FREE mystery gifts (gifts are worth about $10). After receiving them, if I don't wish to receive any more books, I can return the shipping statement marked "cancel." If I don't cancel, I will receive 4 brand-new novels every month and be billed just $4.74 per book in the U.S. or $5.24 per book in Canada. That's a saving of at least 21% off the cover price. It's quite a bargain! Shipping and handling is just 50¢ per book in the U.S. and 75¢ per book in Canada.* I understand that accepting the 2 free books and gifts places me under no obligation to buy anything. I can always return a shipment and cancel at any time. Even if I never buy another book, the two free books and gifts are mine to keep forever.

102/302 IDN F5CN

Name	(PLEASE PRINT)	

Address		Apt. #

City	State/Prov.	Zip/Postal Code

Signature (if under 18, a parent or guardian must sign)

Mail to the Harlequin® Reader Service:
IN U.S.A.: P.O. Box 1867, Buffalo, NY 14240-1867
IN CANADA: P.O. Box 609, Fort Erie, Ontario L2A 5X3

Want to try two free books from another series?
Call 1-800-873-8635 or visit www.ReaderService.com.

* Terms and prices subject to change without notice. Prices do not include applicable taxes. Sales tax applicable in N.Y. Canadian residents will be charged applicable taxes. Offer not valid in Quebec. This offer is limited to one order per household. Not valid for current subscribers to Love Inspired Historical books. All orders subject to credit approval. Credit or debit balances in a customer's account(s) may be offset by any other outstanding balance owed by or to the customer. Please allow 4 to 6 weeks for delivery. Offer available while quantities last.

Your Privacy—The Harlequin® Reader Service is committed to protecting your privacy. Our Privacy Policy is available online at www.ReaderService.com or upon request from the Harlequin Reader Service.

We make a portion of our mailing list available to reputable third parties that offer products we believe may interest you. If you prefer that we not exchange your name with third parties, or if you wish to clarify or modify your communication preferences, please visit us at www.ReaderService.com/consumerschoice or write to us at Harlequin Reader Service Preference Service, P.O. Box 9062, Buffalo, NY 14269. Include your complete name and address.

LIH13R